# A Curious Case of
# Plagium

## HAILEY MORRISON

PERAGRATE PRESS

Library of Congress Control Number: 2024923600

ISBN: 979-8-9987830-0-5

--------------------------------------

First edition, 2025

Peragrate Press. Atlanta, GA

Visit us at www.peragratepress.com

*Dedicated to Heather.*

*Thank you for being the best audience a ~~sister~~ writer could ever ask for.*

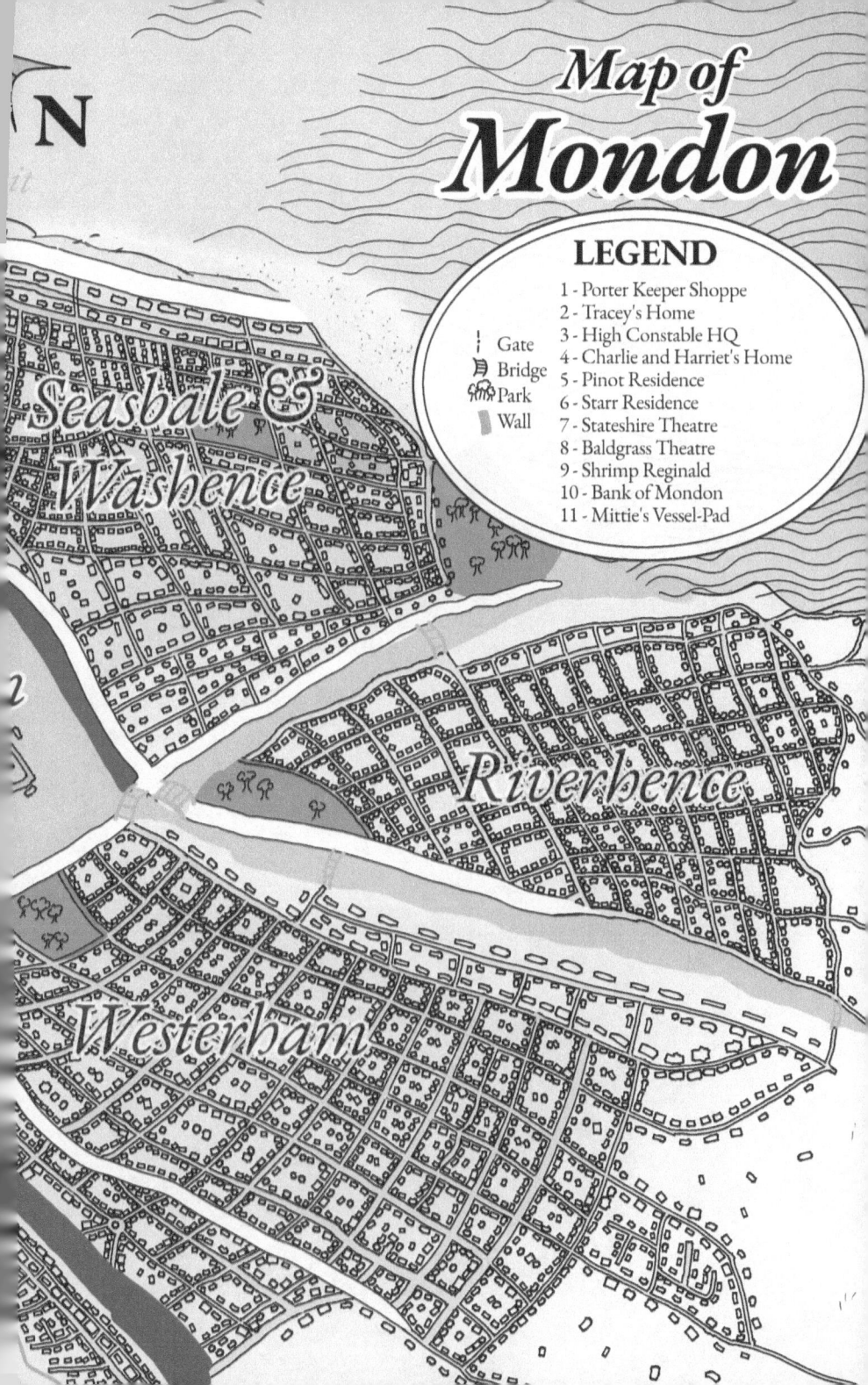

# Act I

# CHAPTER 1

# In Which Tracey Higgenbottom Encounters a Dilemma

TRACEY HIGGENBOTTOM found herself speechless.

Which, for others who knew her, was next to impossible. Speechless was not a word to describe Tracey. Tracey was a quick-witted, sharp-tongued young lady who almost always had some sort of banter or another to supply to any situation.

And yet here she was—speechless.

In front of her was the familiar shop of which she knew well. For five years, she'd been working at this shop and for almost twice as long practically lived in it. Here she would start early in the morning, opening the shutters, lighting the gas lamps, and checking the motor-mail for the daily letters.

Sitting behind his desk, Mr. Porter, her guardian and employer, would be well underway in his own morning routine. Only this morning, however, Mr. Porter wasn't there.

The lamps were already lit, much to Tracey's surprise, and the door and shutters were wide open. And yet, this was not what baffled the young lady so. As she stepped inside and cautiously looked about her, she found nothing but pure disorder. Papers were strewn across the floor, filing cabinets were half-opened, and several books' pages looked as if someone were frantically rifling through its contents. Tracey softly gasped as she took in the chaos of the room.

*A robbery?* she thought. Further inspection proved that she was alone in the room. She quickly checked the gas-powered safe and snatched up her inventory clipboard (thankfully still on its hook on the wall). A review of the room resulted in nothing—nothing was stolen.

"Well," said Tracey, the first word she uttered since arriving at the shop, "what's one supposed to do in a situation like this?"

She checked once more if she may have missed Mr. Porter. Up in the attic. Back in the delivery room. Under the desk, even.

"Hello..." Tracey muttered as the light reflected on something below the desk. She grabbed the item and lifted it into the daylight. "Mr. Porter's spectacles?"

Tracey became alarmed. He could hardly see two feet in front of himself. How did he manage to leave without them?

*Cl-clunk.* The motor-mail rolled to life. Tracey spun around. *I'd forgotten about that thing!* She watched as a solitary piece of paper drifted to the receiving port. *Strange...* Tracey cautiously took the paper. On it was a solitary message:

*Tracey: I am on vacation. I will see you tomorrow.*

Below was a rather crude signature from Mr. Porter. "No, that's not right!" Tracey exclaimed as she searched through the rubble for Mr. Porter's calendar. When she finally found it, upside down and nearly torn apart, her suspicions were confirmed—*nothing on today's date!*

"I need the constable," Tracey said, her lips tightening into a small furrow. *I don't know what's happened, but something is wrong.*

The paper in her hand heated up. "Wha—" she said.

Unfortunately, she was soon interrupted by the paper suddenly...well...going up in smoke.

Literally.

"Combustible paper?" she gasped, wrinkling her nose at the sickly-sweet smell of the fumes. "That was made illegal years ago!"

Combustible paper, dear reader, was a craze that died as quickly as it had started. A large company experimenting with ways in which they could monetize and capitalize on the new steam-powered technology soon stumbled upon a rather curious invention: paper that could vaporize at a set time. Suddenly everyone wanted their hands on combustible paper—to spring a joke on someone's day, to write a secret message, to hide incriminating evidence, and other increasingly devious reasons. Unfortunately, unsolved crimes spiked as a result. For this reason, the High Constable of Dnalgne shortly banned the use of combustible paper and imprisoned anyone in possession of it. Understandably, it quickly became one of the most unpopular products out there, to the sad demise and bankruptcy of the company responsible for its creation.

And now, poor Tracey, with the only shred of palpable evidence of a crime that she might have had gone, decided that Mr. Porter may indeed be in danger. *Well*, thought Tracey in dismay, *at least I have these spectacles. And a break-in to report.*

Tracey Higgenbottom shut off the gaslights, closed the shutters, locked the front door, and hurried down the foggy Mondon streets to the High Constable office.

# CHAPTER 2

# In Which Mr. Bentam Berkley Is Cross

"Right this way, ma'am," the receptionist in the High Constable office said as she led Tracey from the room in which she had been waiting. "He's in there," she whispered, pointing to an office toward the back. "His name is Bentam Berkley."

"Why are we whispering?" Tracey asked, glancing at where the receptionist stood.

In the receptionist's place was vacant air, and in the distance was her quickly retreating figure. "O...okay?" Tracey muttered, heading toward the office.

The hall's light filtered into the office, falling just short of the imposing figure which sat behind the desk. Tracey paused. From what she could see, there were two hands flying across the typewriter in front of them. Attached to these hands were arms clad in a navy-blue jacket, a neck tightly wrapped in a starched collar and necktie, and two piercing eyes looking at her from the darkness. "Well? Are you going to stay there and block my light?" the figure gruffly said.

"O-oh, I beg your pardon," Tracey said, quickly stepping into the room. "Constable Berkley, I suppose—"

"*Mr.* Berkley will suffice, miss, and please take a seat," he said, typing all the same. His eyes returned to his paper.

Tracey blinked. *Well, then!* She obediently took the offered, or rather vacant, seat and waited for him to finish. She watched as he dutifully worked, occasionally pausing to look at some notes beside him. Steam silently puffed out of the side of the typewriter, keeping pace with his typing.

"I am not the High Constable nor even a constable. I am a records keeper," he finally said, breaking the heavy silence. "Name?" he asked.

"Tracey Higgenbottom."

The typewriter's keys continued to clack away. Tracey restlessly pulled at her gloves, waiting for him to continue. "Well?" he snapped, his eyes darting up to her. "For what reason are you here today?"

Tracey bit back a rather biting remark. "I'm here today," she started, "I'm here today to report a break-in and kidnapping." Silence. Mr. Berkley continued typing. Finally, he stopped and took the paper out of the typewriter. He then rolled it up and put it into some sort of tube behind him, then pulled the lever.

Mr.
Bentam Berkley

In a puff of steam, the paper was carried elsewhere. He turned to face her again.

"Is that all?"

For the second time that day, Tracey Higgenbottom was speechless. "I-is that all?" she stammered. "What do you mean, 'Is that all?'"

Mr. Berkley sighed. "Do you have any more information, ma'am? It was a break-in. Where, what time, and what was taken? There was a kidnapping. Who, any suspects, and what leads you to believe so?"

"Well," Tracey said evenly, "the break-in was at my place of employment. I don't know when it occurred, perhaps from last night or earlier this morning? The kidnapped is my..." She paused. "My employer, Mr. Porter. I don't know who would kidnap him, but it possibly could be because he's a keeper."

"A what?"

"A keeper. It's a popular profession in Mondon nowadays. They're in charge of keeping things for customers, like jewelry, money, or even just a note—"

"Oh yes, non-bankers," he interrupted, his interest flitting back to the stack of paper next to him. "Our constables are very familiar with the sort." He took up a nib pen and scribbled. "Break...in...at..." He looked up. "What's the establishment name?"

"Porter Keeper Shoppe."

"Porter...Keeper...Shop." He put down the pen. "All right, I'll send the document through, and you'll have constables at the business in about an hour. Thank you."

Tracey waited, watching as Mr. Berkley loaded a fresh sheet of paper into the typewriter and began typing again. He paused, glancing up at Tracey. "Thank you, Ms. Higgenbottom."

"That's all?"

Mr. Berkley paused, raising an eyebrow. "What do you mean, 'That's all?'"

"What about the kidnapping report?"

"What kidnapping? As far as I can tell, there's only been a break-in."

"...why do you think so?"

"Did you try calling him via steamphone?"

"W-well, no—"

"And even if there was no answer, did you check at his residency for him? Perhaps he's ill."

"That would not be normal for h—"

"All right, and even so, what could possibly cause you to jump to your conclusion?"

"Well—"

"Do you know how many kidnapping cases are reported here in Mondon?" Mr. Berkley leaned forward. "Five. Hundred. A week. Every week we have 'new' kidnappings reported." Bentam rolled his eyes in disdain as he said "new." "Do you know what would have happened if we followed each lead without evidence? A vast majority of these reports end with the person popping up as if nothing happened! And do you know what that means?"

"But—"

"A waste of resources. Constables sent out on wild goose chases while there are *real* cases to pursue." He pointed to a paper on the wall behind him. "Take him, for example. Famous actor. He's been plagued by someone advertising fake performances using his name." Tracey paused to look at the poster. On it was a picture of Jon Starr, a well-known stage actor at the time. "We should be spending our research finding *this* out, but instead we spend time on cases like yours."

"Yes, but I have evidence!" Tracey held up Mr. Porter's glasses. "I found these under his desk."

Mr. Berkley squinted at them. "What's the significance of these?"

"He can't see without them. He never leaves anywhere without them!"

"Has it ever occurred to you that he may have a spare?"

"Well...no."

"Mhm." He leaned back in his chair. "Is that all? That's hardly enough proof for me to open a case."

"I..." Tracey hesitated. Dare she mention the note? It was evidence, but it was also potentially illegal. She sized up the man in front of her. "I...received a note, saying he would be on vacation," she ventured.

"Well, that solves it! He's merely on vacation. Thank you, Ms. Higg—"

"He didn't make arrangements for a vacation today, Mr. Berkley. I'm his secretary."

"Things can change—"

"It was typed on combustible paper."

Mr. Berkley paused, his eyebrows flying up. He leaned forward, the silence deafening. Tracey shifted nervously in her seat. She knew bringing up the paper would be dangerous, especially when she thought of its questionable history.

"I-it evaporated in my hands," she said. "Right after I finished reading it."

His icy stare seemed to penetrate straight through Tracey. She shivered. "Ms. Higgenbottom," he frigidly said. "You do realize what you are saying?"

"Yes, sir," Tracey said, the poor woman beginning to regret having mentioned the note in the first place.

"It is *impossible* to get combustible paper. The High Constable destroyed any remaining sheets of it years ago. And yet, you now claim that you had one in your possession?"

"Y-yes, sir."

Mr. Berkley squinted, sighed, then pulled the paper from the typewriter. He then rolled it up and put it into the tube behind him, pulling the lever and sending it away. "I'm going to pretend I did not hear you say anything about the paper," he said, turning to face Tracey. "I've just filed a break-in report. Constables will be out at Porter Keeper Shoppe. Ms. Higgenbottom," he said, his gaze fixed on her, "I would be very careful to whom you mention this paper. You may find yourself in prison. Or worse."

Tracey gulped. "Yes, sir." She stood with a quick curtsey. "Thank you. Your help is much obliged."

But Mr. Berkley was already back to typing. Without another word, Tracey Higgenbottom left the office. As she descended the stairs of the High Constable office, she felt even more helpless than she had that morning.

CHAPTER 3

# In Which a Surprise Arrives

TRACEY PACED about the shop as the constables took a few images with their strange machinery. She watched as they aimed the small device at each heap of disorder, and with the crank of a handle, sent steam everywhere. "Photographs," they had explained to her earlier. "Much like having a painter on scene, but faster."

She had spent a better part of her noon turning away customers and answering questions from the constables. *I'm beginning to wonder if this robbery report will be of any use!* Tracey thought with an impatient sigh.

"Almost done, ma'am," a constable said, a little startled by her injection of impatience. "Apologies for the delay. We'll wrap up the photographs and be right out in a jiffy."

"Thank you," Tracey said. She glanced at the clock.

It was 12:40 p.m. and still no sign of Mr. Porter. She had stopped by his home (to which she had the key) but found no one inside. She then called him on the steamphone but got no response. Tracey tapped a finger on her crossed forearm. It'd been almost six hours and nothing. Not even a single lead.

"Is this yours, ma'am?" a constable asked, handing her a handkerchief.

Tracey jumped. "I'm sorry, I didn't see you there," she said.

"No worries," he pleasantly replied, tipping his hat.

Tracey took the handkerchief. She squinted. *I don't recognize this at all!* It was a simple silk square with small cream rosettes embroidered around the edge. On the corner were the initials *RN*. "No, I—" She stopped herself. *This could be the evidence I've been looking for! My first lead!* She looked at the inquisitive constable. "Now that I think of it," she slowly began, "I believe this could possibly be my friend's. She may have dropped it when she visited."

Tracey swallowed. The only friend she had was far away on the other side of the country; they hadn't visited in years.

The constable hesitated.

Tracey blinked, keeping her expression clueless and innocent. Finally, he nodded. "Very well, ma'am," he said.

"Report, sir," the other constable said, handing him a piece of paper. "I'll wait for you outside." With that, the other constable left the shop.

The constable with Tracey read over the paper before handing it to her. "All right, ma'am, here's your report," he said.

She scanned it, noticing that there was only vague information, hardly enough to open a case. She frowned.

"Something wrong, ma'am?" he asked, leaning forward in concern.

"No," she blurted. "Although, I hardly see this being enough information to open a case."

"How so?"

"You didn't even spell the location correctly! How am I supposed to expect proper help if this is riddled with typos?"

"Riddled with what, now?"

"There's a typo in the shop's name. It's Porter Keeper *Shoppe*, with 'ppe' ending shop. You have on here 'Shop,' with only one 'p' ending it."

The constable looked at the sheet. "Will you look at that. Suppose there was a typo somewhere. I'll get that fixed when we get back." He fished a notepad from his pocket and scribbled. "Thank you for alerting us. As for this case, we'll be in contact with you *if* we find any leads."

"If?" she echoed.

The constable paused, then cleared his throat. "You see, ma'am, there's quite a bit a' robberies in Mondon, and oftentimes we can't find the culprit..."

"I see." Tracey looked at the paper again. *Mr. Porter's entire life hinged on this paper*, she thought, a sense of despair growing within her. It felt as if everything were a dead end. Rustling herself, she quickly shook the constable's hand. "Thank you, sir."

"Any time," he said with a smile. With the tip of his hat, he turned and left.

Tracey's shoulders sagged, her fake demeanor slipping away. "Well, Tracey," she muttered, "you've got two pieces of evidence now: a handkerchief, and spectacles... And a city full of people who could have both a motive to take Mr. Porter and the initials RN."

Due to the nature of a keeper's job, it was natural to assume they would be in possession of many enemies. Keepers did as their title suggested—they kept things. Anything, really. For a fee ranging from frugal to exuberant, a keeper could hold anything from a sheet of paper to priceless furniture. The keepers of Mondon lived with the creed of discretion: ask not, know not. As such, it was not uncommon for a keeper to hold stolen contraband or incriminating evidence unbeknownst to them. For this, keepers were unpopular with the High Constable. And as Tracey already feared, they made Mr. Porter's case a low priority.

Tracey paced the room, her steps speeding with each turn as frustration built.

"*What* am I supposed to *do* with these?" she yelled to the ceiling, flinging the report down. "This is hopeless. I can't find Mr. Porter at this rate."

Behind her, the door's bell jingled.

"I'm sorry, we're closed at the moment," she said, not bothering to turn around. "Excuse the disorder."

"Sorry if I'm interrupting, but that's why I'm here, miss," an unfamiliar voice replied.

Tracey straightened, then turned around. There stood a woman, not more than twenty-five and of average height. Her cocoa brown, tightly coiled hair was styled into a fashionable bun, and the deep violet of her ensemble complemented her dark skin. The dress's bodice and jacket looked as if it had seen its share of traveling. Her skirt—or absence of it, rather—surprised Tracey. In the place of a skirt were a pair of bloomers, cuffed with a smart pair of brown boots.

"Bloomers!" was all poor Tracey could say.

"I prefer 'knickerbockers,' miss," the woman said comfortably. "These always cause quite a start, but, ya know, when you travel by steamship by yourself, it can be pretty impractical to wear skirts around machinery. Believe me," she chuckled, "I've learned the hard way."

"I see," Tracey replied. "Y-you said that you're here for...what reason, Miss...?"

"It's just Mittie," the woman said, offering a hand. Tracey shook it. "Pleased to make your acquaintance."

"Tracey Higgenbottom, but Tracey will suffice," she replied. "Pleased to meet you as well."

"All right, Tracey," Mittie said with a smile. "Now, I do see the 'disorder,' as you said. And I also saw you've had a couple o' constables around?"

"Yes. Were you watching?"

"A little." She shrugged. "I've only just returned to see if anyone would come. I supposed someone found the mess and called in the constables, so here I am dropping by."

"'Returned?' When were you here last? I don't remember ever seeing you visit our shop." Tracey's interest was piqued. *Could this possibly be a witness?*

Mittie sized her up as if she were debating what to reveal. "I had just arrived in Mondon last night and had passed by this shop," she began. "There were a couple a' people inside sometime past midnight. Looked a little suspicious, considering the mess, but I didn't think much a' it. I mean, this *is* Mondon, after all."

"What's that supposed to mean?" Tracey said, taken aback at the quip to her hometown.

"Nothing," Mittie said, raising her hands in a surrendering stance. "Anyway, I passed again this afternoon and saw you here with those two constables, so I figured I'd see what happened."

"Why didn't you report it yourself, when you saw people here last night?"

"Like I said, didn't think much of it," she said with a shrug. "Besides, I didn't stick around. I didn't have any o' my self-defense mechs with me, and I didn't want to linger long enough to find out if I would need it or not."

"Did you..." Tracey hesitated. "How many people did you see?"

"Two, I think." Mittie squinted around the room, nodding her head. "Yup, two looks 'bout right."

"Was one of them burly? With spectacles?" Tracey's heart pounded in her chest.

"Spectacles, no. Burly, yes. And...a burgundy vest and a small bit a' brown hair on top a' his head." With the latter part of her statement, she reached her hand above her head and made a scratching motion.

"Yes, that's him! That's what Mr. Porter wore yesterday."

"Mr. Porter's who you're looking for, miss?"

"Yes," Tracey said, nodding enthusiastically. She could now place when he was last there: sometime around midnight. "And the other person," Tracey ventured. "Could you see their face?"

Mittie paused. She looked up at the ceiling. "No."

Tracey released a breath. This wasn't ideal, but at least she now had an eyewitness.

"But they were tall," Mittie helpfully added. "And slim. 'Fraid I didn't see that person's clothes, though."

"Thank you, thank you so much," Tracey said. And now a suspect!

"Is...is something wrong?" Mittie asked. "Were those men robbers?"

"No, no, one of them was my employer. He hasn't shown up all day."

"Oh! A kidnapping then! Or as I like to say," she added with a small smile, "a case o' plagium."

"A case...of what?"

"Plagium! One a' those big words I read in a book once. Means kidnapping," she said with a wink. "Always was hopin' I'd get a chance to use it—it's rare when you can use all those fancy words ya learn! Except maybe at dinner. But at that time, the company can be so droll—" Mittie paused and blinked. "A-anyways," she continued, "I went off on a tangent there. Sorry!"

"No worries," Tracey said.

"Ey, cheer up!" Mittie said, trying to give a reassuring smile. "I can help you out. Seemed like the constables weren't much help, were they?"

Tracey shook her head. "Thank you," she wearily said. "I was beginning to think I'd have to start searching aimlessly!"

"Glad to help!" Mittie cheerfully said. "And ya know, I know where we can start looking for your Mr. Porter."

"You do?"

"Yep." Mittie nodded. "I heard the two a' them leave behind me as I continued down the street. Checked behind my shoulder to make sure they weren't following me—for safety, you see—and saw they were going in the opposite direction."

"Oh...depending on the direction, that could make the search easier or more difficult."

"Over this way?" Mittie said, pointing out the shop's front windows toward an alarmingly dark section of the street.

"Oh. I was hoping it wouldn't be there." Tracey deflated. "But of course, why not?"

"Where's that?"

Tracey sighed. "The Undertown."

# CHAPTER 4

# In Which Tracey and Mittie Explore The Undertown

THE UNDERTOWN was not a place where any person, alone or accompanied, would want to find themselves. From the unkempt and damp sidewalks to the impossibly thick night and gloom that seemed to hover over the entire sector (likely due to the suspiciously protected factories to the south of the area), The Undertown was apt to leave even the bravest of persons unsettled after a short trip through it. Rampant with an abundance of criminals and suspicious characters, the High Constable soon gave up on ever calming down the growing crimes occurring there, focusing instead on the equally devious, yet more infrequent crimes of the other sectors of Mondon. As a result of this, the notorious sector of The Undertown created its own group of crime control: Vigilantes—residents who kept up their own patrols—would nab a criminal, promptly carry them to the High Constables, and much to the delight and mutually agreed-upon payment of the High Constable, would use the earned bounty to hire more residents to join their league.

Porter Keeper Shoppe's close proximity to this sector was no mistake on the part of Mr. Porter. In a place like The Undertown, there would almost certainly be people who would need their secrets kept. And by being the first keeper shop that a person would see after escaping the said sector, Mr. Porter was almost guaranteed to receive eager customers. Tracey and Mittie found this to be the case, as it seemed all too soon before they found themselves out of Mondon's typically cheerful sunniness and instead amid The Undertown's gloom.

Tracey and Mittie haltingly walked into the sector, each taking a cautious look about her with every step.

"In all a' my traveling, never have I seen sucha gloomy place," Mittie said, nervously eyeing the dark clouds above. "Was that a rat?" she exclaimed, pointing to a dark shadow quickly disappearing down an alley.

"I'm sure that was just someone taking a shortcut," Tracey said. "I hope," she added under her breath. Tracey scanned the dismal surroundings, attempting to find something more encouraging on which to begin a conversation. Unsuccessful, she turned to other topics. "Traveling, you say," Tracey said. "You've mentioned that a few times earlier. What sort of places have you been to?"

"Can't even count 'em!" Mittie replied. "Must've been to 'bout three or four continents, more or less."

"Oh!" she said.

Tracey and Mittie turned a corner.

"I've never traveled much myself," Tracey said with a sad smile. "I suppose I'm just comfortable where I am. Traveling is far too expensive, anyway." Mittie watched Tracey's face and raised an eyebrow.

"I see," she responded. Mittie paused, as if she were about to say something, but then stopped again. "Well," she started, "for someone who doesn't travel, look at you now! This here area is so dark and twisted, I've no clue of how you're just leading us 'round these streets without us gettin' lost and goin' in circles."

"O-oh. Yes," Tracey said, looking away. "You could say I suppose I've had a bit of...experience in The Undertown. This is still a part of Mondon, you know. And," she quickly added, "I know this city well."

"Seems like it," Mittie casually said.

The two continued to walk in silence as Tracey lead them through the ever-narrowing streets.

"So!" Tracey said, breaking the uncomfortable silence. "We're on the lookout for a tall, slim person. Which is about three-quarters of the sector's population."

"Why don't we go where we can find lots a' people? A shop, maybe? I haven't seen many people out yet."

"People in The Undertown are not exactly daytime people," Tracey said with a nod. "That's why I'm taking us to the center. Anyone who's up will be there."

Tracey scanned her surroundings. The crooked homes had fallen away to equally crooked shopfronts—tired buildings with crumbling brick facades, broken, boarded-up windows, and roofs with missing shingles. "Here we go! Some shops!" she said, observing the signs.

*Joe's Curious Goods! Rare and Off-Market Mechanics!*

*Harold Shop. "General" Goods.*

*Steam Gearitry: Steam Gauges, Pipes, and Levers*

*Shrimp Reginald—Finest "Seafood" Away From the Sea!*

"I could do for some shrimp, actually," Mittie said as Tracey read the signs aloud.

"Trust me," Tracey said, "what they serve there can hardly be called 'seafood.' I've tried it before." She shuddered. "I wouldn't recommend."

"Oh...ya've tried them before?" Mittie said.

"I...yes. I have," Tracey abruptly said.

Mittie flinched. "Sorry," she said, before quickly changing the subject and scanning her surroundings. "How about that store down there?" she said. "Seems to be many people over there. And look! I even see a tall n' slim person!"

Tracey's eyes followed where Mittie was pointing. Down the street was a crowd gathering around what looked like a disturbance.

In the center of the crowd was a tall man with a bushy mustache. He wore a shiny dome of a hat on his head, not unlike a cooking bowl (in fact, it very well may have been one). On his chest was an equally shiny circle, with words too small for her to make out.

Tracey froze, her vision narrowing on the man. Her blood ran cold. "That's a vigilante," she said, her voice dropping to a hush.

"Vigilante?"

"Yes, they're The Undertown's version of constables," Tracey quickly explained. "I think we should move on from here—"

"Fascinatin'! Let's get closer. I need ta see if he's the same person from ya shop last night. What's he lookin' at?" Mittie urged, pulling Tracey along with her.

"Wait—" Tracey began to protest. But it was too late. Tracey soon found herself near the front of the crowd with a good view of the incident occurring.

There was The Undertown vigilante. By his side was a young boy—not more than twelve years old—caught by the scruff of his neck. The boy clutched a loaf of bread, his body clad in mere rags of clothes. Tracey could see his face under his matted hair and rugged cap.

"Again, I ask ya," the vigilante growled, shaking the boy and leaning closer to his face. "Young man, can ye let the bread go?"

The boy silently shook his head, hugging the loaf all the closer. His eyes blazed as he defiantly returned the officer's gaze.

The vigilante sighed. "Look 'ere. Ye've already attracted quite a buncha people here. It'll do us all good if ye just leave the bread. I can let ye go if you just leave the bread!"

The boy ignored him still, turning his eyes resolutely to the ground.

"This has been going on for ten minutes now, poor boy," a nearby person said.

"Poor man!" someone else replied.

"Poor us!" yet another person piped. "I just want to buy my bread. They've been blocking the entrance!"

Mittie squinted at the vigilante, slightly tilting her head, as if in thought. She sighed. "Tracey, can't we do somethin' to help the poor lad?"

Tracey shook her head. "With a vigilante? Oh, no. Say the wrong thing and you could end up in the High Constable's office." She quickly averted her gaze and tried to squelch the growing disquiet in her. "Or worse."

*Don't bother, Tracey*, she told herself. *After all, he did steal something.* Somehow, however, she couldn't convince herself of that conclusion.

"Oh, all right," Mittie said, disappointed. "I really just came to see if that might've been the person I saw last night. It isn't." Mittie started to leave. "You were right, we should'a moved on."

"Wait," Tracey said, grabbing Mittie's sleeve.

Mittie paused and looked at her. "There's nothin' we can do, right? Didn't ya say so?"

Tracey steeled herself, bunching up her shoulders and taking a deep breath. "This isn't right. I cannot stand to the side and watch this happen, Mittie."

"Then let's leave," she replied with a shrug. "Can't watch it if ya ain't there to see it."

"No, we have to do something. Well, not you, if you don't want to. But I can't ignore this."

"But what's your plan?"

Tracey smiled, gritting her teeth against her thumping heart. "Something I hope won't backfire."

## CHAPTER 5

# In Which There is a New Ally

TRACEY COULD HARDLY believe herself as she entered the center of the crowd, confronting the vigilante. He seemed much larger than he had from her spot on the sidelines. She felt very small in comparison. "S-sir," she started. He ignored her, still lecturing the boy. "Sir," she said louder.

"What's that, miss?" he gruffly asked, glaring at her. She steeled herself against a shudder.

"That young man there is my brother."

He paused, slowly looking between her and the boy. "Is that so?"

"Yes." She could hardly stand her ground under his piercing stare. Perhaps this was not a good idea, she nervously thought.

Around her, the crowd began to murmur.

"I-I can pay for the stolen bread and any damages he may have done. I apologize for his mischief. You know how children can get!" She ended with a nervous chuckle.

Now both the boy and the vigilante stared at her.

Her cheeks flushed. "C-come, dear. Come to Tracey." She held out a hand. The boy looked at it, then up to the vigilante. The vigilante looked once more between the two, shook his head, then let go of the boy. In a flurry, the boy rushed next to her.

"Sorry, ma'am," the vigilante said. "Don't worry 'bout the money, I'm just tryna' catch a group a' littl' thieves in the area. Thought he mighta been their ringleada'."

"Oh, dear, I do apologize for any trouble he may have caused," Tracey said graciously. She looked at the boy. "Come along now, let's go."

He nodded and took her hand, avoiding her gaze. All the while, he still held on to the loaf of bread.

"All right, all right what're ye all goggling about for?" the vigilante said to the crowd, waving them off. "Go on now! Nothing goin' on here! Out, out!" His voice carried after him as he coursed through the throng of people, breaking apart the gathering. Tracey watched as everyone left, and the vigilante disappeared from sight.

"Are you all right?" Tracey asked the boy. He nodded, this time barely meeting her gaze.

"That was amazing!" Mittie said, bounding up to the two. "I always sized ya up for a timid type. Gonna have t' keep my eyes peeled around you, ha! And you said you've done this before, huh?"

"I don't like seeing children in trouble, that's all," Tracey said. "What's your name, young man?"

The boy hesitated before meeting her eyes. This was the first time she saw him so close. Patches of coal were smeared on his face in various spots, from his cheeks to his forehead. Out from the ashes stared back a pair of bright, inquisitive eyes, so large they made his nose look curiously small. His tiny mouth was pursed.

"It's all right, you can count us as friends," Tracey gently said, patting his shoulder. Her gloved hands returned coal on them, of which she discreetly wiped into a handkerchief she had on hand. His clothes were just as full of coal as his face. Over his tattered shirt, he wore a worn vest, his baggy pants sported some patches, and his feet donned a smart pair of shoes. He shuffled.

"Name's Charlie, miss," he muttered. He shook his hand loose from Tracey's, cautiously stepping away. "And I'm no crim'nal. I just was gettin' bread for me and Harrie, miss. She's my sister!" Charlie stopped, giving Tracey a slow, up-down look. "My real sister," he finished.

"Who's calling you a criminal?" Tracey said, taken aback by his forwardness. "I never called you a criminal!"

"You look like an earnin' gentleman t' me," Mittie piped. "That's a lot a coal ya have there—you must've seen your fair share of chimneys, I thinks!"

The boy's eyes widened. "How'd ya know?" he exclaimed.

"The coal, for starters." Mittie winked.

Charlie's face slowly broke into a smile, a burst of sunshine on his previously gloomy face. He looked between the two of them. "Say," he started, "what brought the likes of you two here, anyway? I hardly see anyone quite as 'spectable as you 'round here. Well," he said, pausing and looking at Mittie's knickerbockers. "Almost 'spectable, I guess."

"Mind your manners, young man," Tracey quickly corrected.

"Don't worry," Mittie said. "I'm used to the stares. You stared, too, when I first greeted you today, didn't ya?"

"Ah, I suppose so," Tracey conceded.

"At any rate, I'll take the stares!" Mittie continued. "They're great for traveling."

"You travel?" Charlie said, his eyes brightening. "Aw, gears! I've always wanted to travel the world. Likes a real gentl'man does!"

"I might be in need of a traveling partner one day," Mittie said with a wink. "I'll have to keep you in mind."

His smile widened into a beam. "Would you, really? Gears!"

Tracey smiled, then paused. We're getting sidetracked, she realized. "To answer your question from earlier," she said, steering the conversation back, "we're here on the search for a missing person, Charlie. My name is Tracey."

"And I'm Mittie!"

"Mittie said she saw this person disappear somewhere into The Undertown."

Charlie frowned. "Gears! Ya know it's really hard ta find anyone in the Unda'town. But I suppose I can try. You've both been more than kind t' me already. What did the fellow look like?"

"A man," Tracey said, "who's fairly large and wide, with a mustache and slightly balding. He was wearing a burgundy vest when I saw him last."

"There's at least five of 'em I can think of," Charlie said. "Nothing else interesting about them?"

"The other person," Mittie said, "was tall and skinny. A man, I believe. Can't give much more than that, sorry!"

"That's better—one big man and a skinny man seen together last night. That rules out the ones I'm thinkin' of. I think I might can work with this," Charlie said, thoughtfully looking around. "I know just who you can ask. Follow me!" With those words, Charlie spun around and, bread in hand, ran off down the crooked streets of The Undertown. Tracey and Mittie could barely give each other exasperated looks before they ran deeper into The Undertown, following the young boy.

Tracey and Mittie stood in a small room, awkwardly scanning the space. The floors were bare, worn wood save for a burlap bag that served as a makeshift rug. The door was left ajar, and a glimpse of a narrow staircase could be seen within. On the wall behind them was a solitary window, showing an exciting view of a decrepit alleyway. Beside it was the front door, the entrance to the home. We must be in a waiting room of sorts, Tracey thought. Charlie had disappeared somewhere up the stairs after having let them in.

Soon enough, he returned, swinging the stair door wide open. "After you!" he said, gesturing within. The two women followed and mounted stairs of questionable integrity, their every step shaking the very tread on which they stood. They exited into an equally small and decor-less room.

A shaky wooden table stood in the center, adorned with nothing but a stub of a candlestick, a small broken jar with some dried flowers inside, and the loaf that Charlie had carried with him sitting proudly on a chipped plate. The only chair in the room was already occupied—a girl of no more than thirteen stared expectantly at Tracey and Mittie. Tracey blinked.

The girl's hair was pulled up into a tight, prim bun, save for a few rebellious black sprigs that escaped. Her dress was just short of her ankles and full of patchwork. A small apron covered a majority of the patches. Her shoes were tattered boots, seemingly held together with nothing but the lace that closed them. Her clothes were as full of coal as Charlie's.

Tracey noticed that her hands were shaking.

"How do you do?" the girl asked stiffly. "My name is Harriet."

# CHAPTER 6

# In Which Tracey Sees Something

THE GIRL SAT tense in her chair, fidgeting with her hands as she greeted them. She tried to muster a smile.

Tracey returned the smile, sympathetically tipping her head. "My name is Tracey Higgenbottom," she said. "Pleased to meet you."

"And I'm Mittie," Mittie added.

"Charmed," Harriet said. She shifted in the seat, her forced smile wavering a bit. "I-I'm sorry," she stammered. "I suppose I'm not too good of a hostess, there being no seating for you." She quickly stood. "You can have my seat!"

"That's quite all right," Tracey reassured her. "I don't mind standing."

"Oh, I've never had people in here before, let alone fancy ladies!" Harriet groaned.

"I wouldn't exactly consider myself upper class, dear," Tracey said.

"I'm just a traveler," Mittie said. "This is a nice home you have here!"

Harriet relaxed. "O-oh. Thank you...Miss Mittie—"

"Just Mittie will do."

"Oh. Thank you, Mittie." She closed her eyes and nodded. "So," Harriet began, her voice gaining more confidence, "Charlie said that you both are lookin' for some men?"

"Correct," Tracey said.

"A fat man with a mustache, and a skinny, tall man?"

"W-well I couldn't exactly call Mr. Porter fa—"

"Funny pair, if you ask me!" Harriet said, pacing the room. "Definitely something you wouldn't forget seein'. I'm guessing the kidnappee is the skinny man?"

"No, the fa—" Tracey stopped herself. "The larger one is the victim."

Beside her, Mittie stifled a snicker.

"Charlie was right to carry you to me," Harriet said thoughtfully. "Y' see, 'im and I are a couple a' chimney sweeps, and since I'm older, I'm in charge of scouting new customers. I meet lots of faces in this kinda work."

"I see!" Tracey said.

"When did your Mr. Whatzit go missing, Miss Higgn'bottom?"

"His name is Mr. Porter. The time may be an issue," Tracey said. "It happened late last night. A child your age wouldn't be out so late, would you?"

Harriet shrugged. "Some customers call late at night, so yes, I'm out late occasionally, Ms. Higgenbottom."

"You may call me Tracey, dear."

"Thanks, Tracey!" Harriet said with a toothy smile. Her confidence bloomed by the second. "I think I have just what you're looking for."

"Do you?" Tracey glanced at Mittie, who raised her eyebrows in turn.

"Yep! Last night, I was walking through one a those nice neighborhoods, ya know, not in The Uppertown, but pretty close. I was just headin' back from one a our chimney jobs. Charlie had already gone home, and I had stayed behind to discuss payment. Gears, you shoulda seen how much coal was in their chimn'y! I'm surprised the house didn't go up in flames years ago!

"Anyway, I was headin' back home when all a sudden a couple o' people came barreling past me—reeked of alcohol, too. Nearly shoved me off the sidewalk, those two. I never saw their faces, but one was large n' round, and the other one tall. I wouldn't say the tall one was skinny, though..."

"That's rather vague. They may have just been some men heading back from a gear pub," Tracey said with a frown. "Could you see what they were wearing?"

"No," Harriet said, shaking her head. "The steamlighter hadn't reached that area of the street yet. I saw which house the men went into, though. That's what struck me as funny, ya see?"

"Which house?"

"Mrs. Pinot's home. She's one of our reg'lars. Kinda grumpy, if ya ask me. What's so funny is that she's a pretty lonely widow. I didn't think she knew anyone!"

"Mrs. Pinot," Tracey echoed. "I'm not sure if she'd know Mr. Porter—I don't remember filing any widow clients, per se. Do you know her first name? Pinot is fairly common in Mondon."

Harriet shook her head.

"Oh, that's too bad." Tracey touched the handkerchief in her pocket. *At least that name couldn't match with RN,* she thought.

"Maybe we can check her place to see if she's a client or not, Trace?" Mittie said with a shrug. "Never know if we'd find some other lead there. This is the best we've got so far, besides my testimony."

Tracey flinched. *Trace?* she thought in alarm. "From when has my name been Trace?" she asked, squinting at Mittie. Mittie shrugged.

"Dunno. Just matches you, I guess?"

Tracey sighed. "May we go see this Mrs. Pinot, Harriet?"

"Sure!" Harriet said enthusiastically. "You know, this could be a chance for me to get her to clean her chimneys again. Mrs. Pinot pays 'handsomely,' as she always says."

"How far is she from here?" Mittie asked, wearily looking at the front door. "It was a rather long walk to get here."

"She's 'bout an hour's walk, I guess," Harriet said. "Maybe two."

"Two?" Mittie replied in alarm.

"Charlie!" Harriet yelled. "C'mon, we got anotha chimn'y to clean!"

"Gears!" Charlie's voice distantly said. Somewhere above Tracey and Mittie, Charlie's footsteps pounded on the floors as he ran around. Dust shook from the ceiling as he pattered down the stairs and burst into the small room. His vest was gone, and in its place he wore a jacket and scarf. "Ready, Harrie!" he said with a grin, chimney brush in hand.

As the group filed out, Tracey's eye caught something glittering under the burlap bag door mat. Without thinking, she bent and snatched it up.

Closer examination of the object caused her to start. *Mr. Porter's ring?* she thought in alarm. She checked the engraving inside.

*Remington L. Porter*

It was indeed his ring. She hesitated. *Just how did these two get their hands on his ring?*

"Trace? Comin', aren't ya?" Mittie said, poking her head back inside.

"O-oh, yes, of course!" Tracey said, cramming the ring inside of her pocket. "I...I just thought I dropped something."

Mittie glanced at Tracey's hand in her pocket before slowly nodding. "All right, then," she said, "don't get left behind." She ducked back outside.

Tracey's stomach felt unpleasantly queasy as she followed suit. *I'll ask them later*, she told herself, pushing the pressing question to the back of her mind.

# CHAPTER 7

# In Which They Meet Mrs. Corsetta Pinot

"WE'RE CLEANING Mrs. Pinot's chimney?" Charlie asked in dismay, stopping short of the house's walkway of which Harriet had led them to. "If I knew we was comin' here, I would've stayed home!"

"That's exactly why I didn't say anythin'," Harriet sniffed. "Besides, Mittie and Trace asked nicely. Mrs. Pinot doesn't let just anyone into her house. We're just making it easier for them to find their Mr. Porter." She turned to Tracey and Mittie. "The plan is that you, Trace, are our visiting cousin, and Mittie's a friend who decided to join you, okay?"

"Right," Tracey and Mittie said with a serious nod.

"All right," Harriet said.

She mounted the ivory stone stairs and approached the large mahogany doors, reaching her hand to a strange piece of machinery. The tubular shape was filled with a complex array of interlocking gears, and a copper crank (equally ornate) protruded from its base.

"Here goes nothin'." Harriet closed her eyes, nodded, and then quickly turned the handle, starting a chain of gears into motion. As it clacked away, little puffs of steam emitted from a pipe at its top. Finally, it ended in a tinny "ding."

"Ooh, that's a fancy doorbell if I'va eva seen one!" Mittie said, watching the mechanism with great interest.

"Eh. That's just a steambell. Most fancy people 'round here have 'em," Charlie said.

They waited.

Without warning, the door unlocked with an alarming amount of aggression, causing Harriet to yelp and flinch away. It swung open.

There stood a woman of tall stature, looking down at the group. Her dark hair was pulled tight into a severe bun. Around her throat rested a gear brooch. Her sleeves came out in billowing puffs, cuffing close to her wrists, and her dress dramatically flooded the floor around her. Her sharp eyes, not to be forgotten, darted between Harriet, then Charlie, then Mittie—pausing briefly on her lack of skirt—and finally Tracey. "Harriet," she said, her voice surprisingly gentle. "Who are these? Why are you here?"

"Mrs. Pinot, ma'am! At your service," Harriet replied with a tip of her head. "We're checkin' round on our customers for follow ups. Do you mind if Charlie an' I have a look at your chimney?"

"For you two, of course!" Mrs. Pinot replied. "However, for these two—"

"I'm Harriet's cousin, visiting from..." Tracey's mind raced. She hardly knew anywhere outside of Mondon, let alone her own sector and its neighboring ones.

"From?" Mrs. Pinot prodded, her eyebrows raising.

"Strattengear," Mittie interjected. "Sorry 'bout Tracey, she can get nervous 'round new people. I'm her friend and had wanted to meet her cousins—she speaks 'bout them so much, y' know!"

Tracey squinted at Mittie. *She lies too easily.* "Yes," Tracey continued, "and Harriet said she'd like for us to meet her best clients. Which included you."

"Isn't that sweet," said Mrs. Pinot rather flatly, before turning her attention back to Harriet. "Why didn't you just say so, dear?" she said, noticeably warmer as she looked down at the girl. "Come in, all of you. Charlie, you can leave your broom by the door."

The group gathered into the large foyer, their eyes darting around from the tall cream ceilings and grand chandelier to the iron staircase and the glistening checkered floors—so shiny one could see their reflection in it. "All right, what are you really here for?" Mrs. Pinot asked, spinning to face the group as she closed the door, poising a dainty hand on her hip. "Harriet, I know you and Charlie have no family other than each other, and...ah...Tracey, is it?"

Tracey started. "I never said my name—"

"Hm, yes. It is Tracey. Ms. Higgenbottom, if I'm not mistaken."

Tracey's mouth hung agape. "I-I-I'm sorry, but do I know you?"

"For a secretary, you're not very quick at recognizing regular customers." Mrs. Pinot sniffed. "Perhaps my full name will pique your memory? Corsetta Pinot."

Tracey blinked. *Corsetta?* she thought. *I do know that name!*

Mrs. Pinot's attention next flitted to Mittie. "You, however, I haven't seen before."

Mittie looked to each member of the stunned group before bursting into laughter. "Suppose the gig is up, eh? It was fun while it lasted—as short as it was," she said. "I just came into town. The name's Mittie."

"Hm," was all she sounded.

Mittie's peals of laughter faltered into a chuckle. "Ahem," she coughed. "Sorry."

Mrs. Pinot glared at the group.

Tense silence filled the foyer. "Harriet," she finally said, "I do believe an explanation is in order, don't you think?"

Harriet stared at the ground, her ear tips a flaming red.

"Never mind that," Mrs. Pinot said. "Come now, all of you. There's hardly any use in us standing here when I have a parlor ready for guests, now is there?"

"You're expecting, then?" Tracey asked politely as they all entered the parlor.

"Yes," Mrs. Pinot replied. "Have a seat, feel free to take any snacks," she said, gesturing to the prim sofas. Everybody sat.

The room had bright wallpaper decorating the space and tasteful furniture and lamps lived by large windows that reached the ceilings. A low table sat in front of the group. The table was covered in all sorts of treats—pickled cookies and sugared carrots. Needless to say, no one took a snack.

"Did she get all a' these treats from that nasty Shrimp Reginald shop o' somethin'?" Charlie whispered to Harriet, who discreetly stepped on his foot in response. "Ouch!" he yelped.

"Is something the matter?" Mrs. Pinot said, looking at the two of them.

"N-no, ma'am," Charlie stuttered, "Meant to say 'gears,' just a slip a' the tongue..."

Mrs. Pinot raised an eyebrow, then took a seat. Charlie and Harriet promptly sat on one sofa, and Tracey and Mittie took the other sofa. Hesitantly, Tracey reached out and took a cup of tea, the most palatable item on the table. Mrs. Pinot nodded in approval.

"Now," Mrs. Pinot said, her voice slicing through the silence, "Harriet, can you explain to me why you've brought Ms. Higgenbottom and Miss...ah...forgive me," she trailed off, looking helplessly at Mittie.

"Mittie's the name," she said with a friendly tip of her head.

"Yes. Thank you. Why have you brought Ms. Higgenbottom and Ms. Mittie here under the guise that you were here to chimney sweep? I've never known you as the type to lie."

"Apologies, ma'am," Harriet quickly said, looking earnestly at the woman. "We thought the only way we could get you to talk to Trace would be if she tagged along while we cleaned!"

"I'm just here 'cause I thought there was a chimney ta clean," Charlie muttered.

"I'm afraid my chimney is in no need of service, dears. You could have just sent them this way—I would have had them! It would hardly be the polite thing to do to turn away guests, after all," Mrs. Pinot said with a warm smile to them. Her smile dropped as her attention refocused on Tracey. "Do you remember me yet, dear?" she asked, noticeably harsher.

"I recognize your face, yes," she said. *But as for her face...*

Tracey squinted. From the striking lady's silhouette, she would have been certain to remember someone like her. *After all*, she thought, *I am the only one in charge of Mr. Porter's documents!* "I," Tracey began. Her eyes flitted to Mrs. Pinot's gear brooch. "I remember that brooch," she said in surprise.

"Ah, this?" she replied airily, her fingers brushing the gear. "My late husband gave this as a gift one year.

He was an engineer, you know. He used to make the most impressive inventions. Very successful." Mrs. Pinot sighed.

"Sorry for your loss," Mittie said sympathetically.

Tracey looked at her hands, her voice caught in her throat. She blinked, surprised at her uncertainty.

"Oh, it was a long time ago," Mrs. Pinot quickly replied. "Is that all you remember, Ms. Higgenbottom?"

"I apologize," Tracey said. "We have a lot of customers at Porter Keeper Shoppe." She cleared her throat. "But that's actually why I'm...we're here today, Mrs. Pinot."

"Oh?"

"Regrettably, there was a burglary of some sort at the shop—"

"Burglary?" Mrs. Pinot asked in alarm, rising from her chair. "Was anything stolen?"

Tracey forced a smile. "I understand that, as a customer, you may worry about your documents. But no, I can confirm that no major documents were compromised. It appears whatever they were searching for, they didn't find."

"I see," she said, lowering into the seat again. She shakily took a pickled cookie, took a bite, frowned at said cookie, then placed it on a napkin beside her. "Continue," she said.

"Mr. Porter has not been seen since last night, and I've been looking for him since this morning. I thought you may know something."

"Hm," Mrs. Pinot said. "But how did you know to come to me? You clearly did not remember me, and I'm certainly not Mr. Porter's only customer." Mrs. Pinot's mouth pursed into a thin line, and her eyes narrowed to a squint.

"That's why Harriet and Charlie are here, miss," Mittie said. "We met Charlie and asked him 'bout Mr. Porter, and he led us to Harriet. Harriet thinks she saw Mr. Porter in this area last night!"

"Is that so?" Mrs. Pinot swiveled to Harriet, who shriveled under her scrutiny. "I'm sure you were mistaken, dear."

Harriet stared at the ground.

"To answer your question, Ms. Higgenbottom," Mrs. Pinot said, her attention flitting back to Tracey, "no. I had nothing to do with whatever happened to Mr. Porter. Although it's unfortunate, I'm sure he's just away on some unexpected business or something. I heard non-bankers are usually quite busy with those kinds of things."

"Even if you have nothing to do with it," Tracey evenly said, "I would simply like to know if you saw Mr. Porter on this street last night?"

"Dear, how should I know? I go to bed promptly at nine o'clock," Mrs. Pinot said. She stood. "Now, I do believe I've taken up enough of your time. I'm sure you'd like to continue your search elsewhere, hm? Harriet, Charlie?"

"Yes, ma'am?" they said.

"You may come next month to clean. I anticipate I'll be firing up the chimney by then," Mrs. Pinot said as she ushered the now-standing group to the door.

"Aw, gears," Charlie said dejectedly.

"Thank you for visiting. I do hope you find Mr. Porter," Mrs. Pinot quickly said as she stepped toward the door.

As the group reached the foyer, however, the steambell rang with a tinny "ding." "Oh, he's here so soon!" she muttered impatiently. She wrestled with the locks and swung open the door. "I'm sorry, I was just seeing some guests out, sir," she said, her voice taking on a fake, cheerful pitch. "They'll be out in no time. Come in, please!"

"That is no issue, Mrs. Pinot. The documents will be strictly confidential," the man replied. Tracey stiffened, peering closer at the doorway. *I know that voice!*

"It will be fine if they leave before I bring the papers—" The man froze as he stepped inside. He stared. "Ms. Higgenbottom?" he blankly said. Mittie, Harriet, and Charlie stared at Tracey.

"He knows ya? How d'ya know so many people?" Charlie loudly asked, to which Harriet discreetly bumped his shoulder, hushing him.

"Hello...Mr. Berkley," Tracey said.

## CHAPTER 8

# In Which a New Direction is Found

TENSE SECONDS PASSED in the foyer as Mr. Bentam Berkley stood in the doorway. Tracey remained frozen, Mittie, Charlie, and Harriet stared, and Mrs. Pinot observed with bemused silence.

"I was not aware that you were of acquaintance to Mrs. Pinot," he finally said, stumbling over each word as if he were uncertain of his statement.

"I'm not," Tracey replied. "I was inquiring after Mr. Porter."

"Ah, yes. Mr. Porter," Mr. Berkley sighed. "I presume that you did check his residence—"

"*Yes*, and I steamphoned him as well," Tracey retorted.

She could hardly stand the first meeting she and Mr. Berkley had, and this current meeting appeared as if it would end as badly as the last one.

"Hm," he sniffed. "And who are these?" he said in an almost dismissive tone, his wave to the others looking more like a gesture one would use to shoo a gnat away.

"They're witnesses," Tracey said evenly. "Mittie here saw Mr. Porter when he was kidnapped from the shop, and Harriet saw him in this area last night."

"To which I said that she was mistaken," Mrs. Pinot interjected, fixing an unfriendly gaze on Tracey.

Mr. Berkley looked at each person. "Witnesses, you say?" He shuffled a stack of papers that Tracey had just noticed he was holding. "So, you've become a detective now, haven't you?"

More tense seconds passed as he engaged in a silent debate with himself. Tracey sighed. *I don't have time for this!* she thought. *At this rate, I'll never find...* She stopped herself, pushing away the negativity. *No. I will find Mr. Porter.* Upon looking up again, she found Mr. Berkley's icy gaze fixed on her.

"Wait outside for me, please," he finally said. "I may be of some use, but I have some business to attend to here first." With that, he abruptly walked past the group into the parlor.

"Good day," Mrs. Pinot said.

"And that's our cue to leave," Mittie said, bobbing her head.

Mrs. Pinot suspiciously watched the group as they shuffled out of the house and onto the sidewalks.

"Are we really gonna wait for that rusty man?" Charlie said as they stood by a lamppost near Mrs. Pinot's residence.

"Watch yourself!" Harriet said, pinching his arm. "We don't call people rusty."

"Well, it's true!" he retorted. "I neva' saw a stiffer man in my life!"

"How do ya know each other, Trace?" Mittie asked. "He seemed t' know about the case already."

"Yes and no," Tracey said, shrinking under the sudden attention of everyone. "I've only met him this morning. When I was trying to report about Mr. Porter."

"Porter?" Charlie piped. "Is *that* who we're looking for?"

"We've been saying his name all afternoon, Charlie. How are you just now realizing that?" Harriet said with an unamused raise of her eyebrows.

"Something just clicked," he said, shrugging.

"Do you know him?" Tracey asked.

"No," he slowly said, "but I've seen his shop a few times 'ere and there..."

"I see," she replied. "You'd like him. He's a very kind man."

"Doubt that," Charlie sullenly said, kicking at the post. "Most people change their 'pinion once they getta look at me."

"Oh, no! Mr. Porter would be the last person to look down on someone," Tracey said. "I should know," she quickly added.

"You?" Mittie said, raising an eyebrow. "How?"

Tracey's cheeks flushed, and she crossed her arms, her fingers drumming on her forearm. "His work, of course!" she sputtered. "Mr. Porter takes all sorts of clients. Anyway," she abruptly said, "we should discuss what we know so far. I don't think we have had a chance to thus far."

"Good idea," Mittie said, nodding her head in approval. "So, I saw Mr. Porter sometime last night. Midnight."

"Midnight?" Harriet said with a frown. "Where did you see 'im?"

"Near The Undertown, I s'pose?" Mittie said with a shrug.

"It was at the shop," Tracey supplied. "The edge of Burberay, close to The Undertown."

"That can't be right!" Charlie exclaimed. "Harrie saw 'em round twelve thirty o' so!"

"Well, what's the matter with that?" Tracey asked.

"That side of Burberay is at least an hour's walk away from this area in The Borough," Harriet explained. "It'd take especially long if they went through The Undertown to get there. Unless..."

"Unless?"

"Unless...they had a steam car?"

Tracey started. Steam cars were a recent marvel to grace the city of Mondon. Bright and fast, they easily outpaced even the fastest of horses. There were a number of problems that plagued this invention, however. Its immense speed was a cause of many accidents, and the clouds of scalding steam it left in its wake were a hazard to any passersby. Regulations soon followed to keep it out of the possession of the general public. "That can't be," Tracey said. "Hardly anyone owns a steam car."

"Not unless they're rich..." Charlie said, looking out to the carriage-filled streets.

"Say..." Mittie said, her eyes drifting to Mrs. Pinot's townhouse, "Would ya think that Mrs. Pinot there would be rich enough to afford something like that?"

"Oh, yes!" Harriet said.

"Yes, I agree," Tracey said thoughtfully. "Mr. Porter's keeper services are not something an average person could easily afford."

"Lemme make a note of that," Mittie said, snapping out a small pocketbook from her knickerbockers. "Our first suspect, Mrs. Pinot." She finished writing out details from their earlier conversations and closed the book with a flourish. "Now—"

"'Scuse me," a gruff voice sounded.

The group turned around.

There stood a gruff-looking woman, donned in a cap with her hair loosely pulled back into a rather messy ponytail. Her vest and skirt closely resembled Charlie's and Harriet's own patch-filled attire, minus the coal dust.

"Can we help you?" Tracey asked.

The woman held out a pamphlet. Tracey peered at it, noting the woman held a considerably large stack in her other hand.

"Come one, come all," she said flatly, "Jon Starr himself, performing at the Baldgrass Theatre. Tickets only five springs. You don't want to miss it."

"Who's Jon Starr?" Charlie asked.

"Only the biggest actor in town! And only for five springs?" Mittie gasped, her eyes beaming. "Are tickets still available?"

"Yes, ma'am," the woman replied.

"Oh, I've heard practical *legends* of this man—I've neva' gotten a chance to see him act in the flesh! Lemme see this," Mittie said as she took the pamphlet. "In two days. That's plenty o' time for me to conjure up some sorta' outfit to wear. Have you ever heard of Jon Starr, Trace?"

"Me?" Tracey asked, startled. Outside of her comfortable bubble of work and home, Tracey had hardly had time to go out to plays or performances, nor had she ever cared much for those sorts of things. "Perhaps? We may have had him as a client; his name sounds familiar... Maybe Mr. Porter had him as a client recently. I'll need to check, though—"

"Really?" Mittie exclaimed. "You've seen *the* Jon Starr, in the flesh?"

"Well...perhaps?" Tracey slowly said. "I really can't say, Mr. Porter has a lot of clients—"

"To think I've been walking around all day with someone who's met *Jon Starr*! What was he like? How could you just be standin' there knowin' you've met Jon Starr himself?"

"I-I wasn't aware—" she stammered.

"No, no. I need information! Did he laugh the same way he does on stage?"

"Well, um—"

"Or does he really wear his red brooch in his left pocket? Or what about his hair? I've heard it glows gold as if it's under the stage lights, even when he isn't! Oh!" Mittie gasped. "Maybe we can pop into his performance and see if he has any clues leading up to Mr. Porter's disappearance!"

Tracey nodded, rather disorientated by the onslaught of questions from Mittie. "I suppose we may be able to find out...something? Perhaps we can speak to him after the performance...if that's even a possibility." She frowned. "But what does he have to do with Mr. Porter's disappearance? Are you sure you're not just trying to see his performance?"

"I'm a big fan o' him, Jon Starr," Harriet piped, an impish grin growing on her face. "Do you think I could join you both when you go?"

"I don't see why not!" Mittie replied.

Yes, reader, Jon Starr was a famous figure in their country of Dnalgne. So famous, it's a wonder that Tracey Higgenbottom did not hear of him. An extravagant actor known to dazzle the stage with his passionate speeches and moving performances, he was often on the front cover of the daily gossip papers for his latest feats: international performances, surprise appearances, and even a private play for the queen.

"All are welcome," the woman said with a nod. With that, she walked away in the direction of Mrs. Pinot's residence.

However, the woman suddenly froze and backed away.

"Is something the matter, miss?" Tracey began to say.

The woman turned around and ran.

"What was that about?" Charlie said.

"Strange..." Tracey said.

"Why does it feel like it's gotten colder?" Harriet said with a small shiver.

"I feel that, too!" Mittie replied.

"Hello, there," a familiar, icy voice sounded behind them. The group turned to find Mr. Berkley. He stood alarmingly close to them and clenched his stack of papers. "Was that woman bothering you?" he said.

"No..." Tracey slowly said. "She was just inviting us to a performance—"

"Jon Starr, I suppose."

"Is somethin' wrong?" Mittie asked, looking at the pamphlet in her hand.

"May I see that?" he flatly asked. Mittie hesitantly handed the paper to his extended hand.

He glanced over said pages, sighed, and handed it back to her. "I would not go to that performance if I were you."

"Why?"

"Yeah! Why can't we?" Harriet blurted, before stiffening and biting her lips. "Sorry," she whispered.

"Nothing to apologize for," Tracey reassured her. "But I do believe an explanation is owed to us, Mr. Berkley. Why did she run? Was she running from you?"

"Perhaps. I've been following Ms. Halpin for months, Ms. Higgenbottom."

"Ms. Halpin. Is that who just invited us?" Tracey echoed. "Why, exactly, have you been following her? Are you a stalker?"

"No!" he exclaimed, his nose wrinkling in disgust. "What sort of man do you take me for?"

"I don't know," Tracey dryly replied. "You've clearly told me before that you weren't a constable, so I'm not sure what to think of this now."

"Ms. Halpin happens to be a major lead on Jon Starr's fake performances, and I've been tasked with recording her testimony," Mr. Berkley indignantly said.

"And shouldn't the constables be the ones bringing her in for you?"

"Our resources are limited," he said indignantly. "At any rate, there's proof she's actively inviting victims."

"Fake performances?" Mittie said, her eyes widening as she raised the pamphlet. "You mean to say this is fake?"

"There's only one way to tell," he replied, trailing off. Mr. Berkley stared into the distance, his eyebrows furrowed.

The ensuing silence lasted for several long seconds.

"Well?" Charlie finally asked, bewildered. "What's the way?" He frowned. "Has he gone mad?" he muttered under his breath.

"Charlie!" Harriet sharply whispered.

"What?" he whispered back in dismay.

Mr. Berkley blinked, then nodded. "Yes..." he muttered. "I may need to go and confirm this performance."

"What? Now?" Tracey asked.

"Yes, of course," he replied, weaving through the group and striding past them.

Tracey looked at the confused others before following him. "Why did you want me to wait for you?" she said, falling into step with him. "You told me to wait outside, and now you're running off to who-knows-where for some quest or the other?"

He stopped and turned to her, squinting. "Oh. Yes." He glanced at Mittie, Charlie, and Harriet, then turned back around, gesturing with his hand and continuing his walk. "I'll get to you after I deal with this. You may as well come along. I need to catch Mr. Starr before he leaves for rehearsals. Or I can meet you at Porter Keeper Shoppe. Up to you."

"He knows Mr. Starr, too?" Mittie squealed. Her smile broke into a grin. "Trace, do you mind if we take a little detour?"

"Let's!" Harriet said enthusiastically.

"But—" Tracey started.

But alas, poor Tracey was outnumbered.

"C'mon, Trace! When's the next time we'll get the chance to meet someone like him? Besides," Mittie said as she trotted off, "you never know what clues you may find!"

Before she could respond, Mittie, Charlie, and Harriet were off, following close behind Mr. Berkley. Tracey sighed. *Search for more clues, it is,* she thought.

# CHAPTER 9

# In Which the Group Is Starrstruck

TRACEY TRAILED BEHIND the group as she took a moment to herself. Things were finally looking up—she found a first suspect, a last sighting of Mr. Porter, and it appeared as if she found a group willing enough to help her in her search. Well, she thought, not including Mr. Berkley.

She fished into her pocket and pulled out Mr. Porter's spectacles and ring. It was nearly impossible for him to have reached two distant locations so quickly, and yet both were undeniably his own. She studied the carriages in the street, watching as an occasional steam car sped by in the distance, leaving panicked horses and fleeing pedestrians in its wake. She shuddered. *I hope none of those machines come close to here*, she somberly thought as she secured the spectacles and the ring safely back into her pocket.

Tracey hastened her pace to catch up to Mittie. "Mittie?" she said as she fell into step with Mittie's brisk walk. Mittie turned to her, her eyes beaming with excitement.

"Can you believe it?" she squealed. "We're going to meet Jon Starr! *The* Jon Starr! Oh," she gasped. "I wonder if he's going to be wearing his red brooch? I've always wanted to see it in person! I can keep in this excitement!"

"Yes, ah, about that," Tracey slowly replied.

"Somethin' the matter, Trace?"

Tracey hesitated, her hand touching the embroidered handkerchief. Mittie glanced at the pocket before fixing an inquisitive gaze back on Tracey. Dare she say anything about the handkerchief? *After all,* she thought, *this is my only solid lead, and I don't know anyone very well...* "No, never mind," she finally said.

Mittie frowned.

"Actually, yes!" Tracey quickly corrected. "Do you think that he'll have us for tea? I know he may be busy, but I am rather curious about this man, with all this fanfare and everything."

"Oh!" Mittie said, her eyes brightening again. "If ya were embarrassed ta say so, don't be! I don't mind talkin' 'bout 'im."

*Good, I've distracted her.*

"I hope he does! I can only imagine Reggie's reaction when I tell 'im I met Jon Starr!"

"Reggie?"

"Oh, yes, I don't think I told ya 'bout 'im, huh? Suppose we've only met each other a couple a' hours ago, anyway," Mittie said, blinking. "Reggie—Reginald—is my beau. I had stopped here in Mondon to pick up some supplies before I sail off to meet 'im on the southern coast. Never thought I'd stop here longer than a half day or so, but he'll understand. He's a big fan of Jon too, ya know; he was the one who got me into his acting in th' first place." Mittie's face softened as she spoke of her fiancé, a smile tugging at the corners of her mouth.

"Oh! I see," Tracey said.

"Say, Trace," Mittie said, curiously peeking at her, "do you have a beau?"

Tracey blinked. "Me?" she squeaked. "I-I've never thought much about dating—"

"Ah, no worries. I see I took you off guard there," Mittie amiably said with a bump to Tracey's shoulder.

"We're here," Mr. Berkley said, pointing ahead to a prominent townhouse.

It wasn't the towering windows nor the grand staircase that made the home so prominent. Nor was it the fact that it was a full story taller than the surrounding buildings. Nor was it its trees that flanked the front, nor ivy that climbed the facade. And not even the fact that this stark, baby blue home stood on its own large property, making the surrounding beige apartments look cramped and dark by comparison. No, for it was what sat glittering in its driveway, sitting dormant, waiting to roar to life. "A steam car!" Tracey gasped.

Yes, dear reader, as this invention was only owned by the rich (as Charlie earlier stated), it was of no surprise that a famous actor like Jon Starr would be the owner of such a contraption. Tracey shuddered.

"What? You don't like 'em?" Mittie said with a surprised glance. "This is the second time I've seen you react like this to 'em."

"No, I'm not fond of steam cars," Tracey stiffly replied. "The less time I spend around them, the better." She carefully averted her gaze from the car. "I had a...rather horrid run in with one when I was a child."

Tracey briefly closed her eyes against a memory of scalding steam.

"Ah, I see," Mittie said with a sympathetic nod. "You don' have to talk about it if you're not comf'table with it."

"Thank you," Tracey said with a small smile.

"Ladies?" Mr. Berkley's voice sliced through the air. "I would appreciate it if you kept pace. Now," he continued as they hurried forward, "Mr. Starr is a rather peculiar person. As I was telling these two over here—" He paused. "I don't believe I've gotten your names?"

"Oh, I'm Harriet," Harriet said, "and that's my little brother Charlie."

"Yes, as I was telling Harriet and Charlie, he does not appreciate fanfare." He stared at Mittie. "Your name, please?" he said.

"Mittie—er, Mitilde?" Mittie stammered, taken off guard by the sudden attention. "But I prefer Mittie, if ya may."

"Thank you," he responded. "Mittie—I'll call you as you prefer—I noticed you seem to be an enthusiast of Mr. Starr?"

"A big fan? Yes, of course!"

"Hm. This won't do at all. Mr. Starr does not like fanfare in the least. No cheers, no bouncing in excitement, and for the love of all things good, *do not ask for an autograph*."

"Why not an autograph? What happens when you ask for one?" Mittie asked.

Mr. Berkley raised an eyebrow. "Let's just say it would be best if you do not know."

"Oh."

"No fanfare. Understood?"

The group solemnly nodded. Mr. Berkley dipped his head in approval.

"Now, I don't believe I've introduced myself," he said. "I am Mr. Bentam Berkley, a records keeper from the High Constable office."

"Wow, a real constable!" Charlie said, his eyes lighting up.

"No, a records keeper," Mr. Berkley coolly corrected. "For the sake of visiting Mr. Starr," he continued, "you may call me Bentam. Now that we've all met each other—"

"I'd hardly call this meeting each other..." Tracey said with a frown.

Bentam squinted at Tracey before continuing. "Now that we've met each other," he resumed, "we can now proceed to Mr. Starr's home."

"What do we call Mr. Starr, sir?" Harriet piped.

"Mr. Starr, unless otherwise told," Bentam said as he approached the stairway.

Beside the massive double doors was a gear handle far grander than Mrs. Pinot's—a large, golden tube with emerald-encrusted gears and an equally encrusted gear handle. Bentam turned the ornate handle, starting off its chain of gears. It soon produced little puffs of steam from the pipe on the top and ended in a melodious "ting ting."

"Impressive doorbell!" Mittie said, her eyes full of curiosity. "And the second one today! I wond'a why I haven't seen these kinda ones until now!"

"They're very common here in Mondon," Bentam replied. "I'm not certain if you'll find steambells like these outside the city."

"No," Mittie said with a shake of her head. "I've been all over the country—this is the first place in Dnalgne I've seen these!"

Bentam nodded. "Undoubtedly because of the demands to create them. As far as I can tell, the inventor creates them himself, so the supply is limited. Marvelous contraptions, those things."

"You're very knowledgeable about these things," she replied.

"The inventor of it is an acquaintance of mine."

"Really? I must meet 'em some time!"

Bentam started as if to speak again when the door opened.

A tall and slim man stood in the doorway. His dark hair was neatly parted and combed flat against his head, and he wore a neat beard. He sported a sharp outfit—everything from his bow tie to his shoes was pristine and orderly.

"Gears!" Charlie whispered to Harriet. "I can see my reflection in those shoes!"

"Wouldn't expect anything less from a butler," Harriet whispered back.

The butler's thick eyebrows furrowed as his mouth formed into a perplexed frown. "May I be of assistance to you?" he said as he looked at the dysfunctional group, the corner of his mouth curling into something between a scowl and a sneer.

"Yes," Bentam said, gesturing to the group. "They're with me on business. You may remember me: Mr. Bentam Berkley? I've been here several times to help Mr. Starr with tracing false fliers on his performances?"

The butler nodded. "Of course. Please, enter," he said. He stepped away from the door. "You may already know, Mr. Berkley," he said as they shuffled into the entry, "but for the new visitors, Mr. Starr does not like...dirt or dust."

Charlie and Harriet shuffled.

"Please, take these complimentary house slippers. You may take them with you when you leave." He turned to a console by the entryway and pulled out a box of slippers, handing a white, fluffy pair to each guest.

"Look at the quality of these things, Harrie!" Charlie whispered, grinning.

As she finished changing from her shoes, Tracey turned her attention to the room about her. It was surprisingly darker than the exterior's light paint had suggested. The room stretched into a distant set of stairs, from what Tracey could see. The tall ceilings reached up toward an enormous chandelier situated on a black ceiling. Below it, the walls were covered in deep burgundy, offset by dark wooden wainscoting closer to the ground level. Topping it off, the floors were a dizzying checkered pattern, so polished, she could see her reflection in it. "I'll say..." Tracey said in quiet awe.

"Please, follow me," the butler said as he rearranged everyone's shoes into a neat line by the door. He whisked away into an adjoining room.

This room resembled the outside of the apartment far more than the foyer. The walls were a matching baby blue, and the wainscoting—similar style to the one in the foyer—was painted to a cheerful white. The group cautiously perched on an assortment of cobalt chairs that sat about the room. "Mr. Starr will be with you momentarily," the butler said, whisking out of the room.

Tracey sat near the exit, her back to the foreboding foyer. Mittie, on the other hand, sat in a chair adjacent to her with an optimal view of the doorway. Bentam busily sorted through stacks of paper from his seat on a long sofa, using the extra cushions as a makeshift desk. Harriet sat in a chaise near a window, looking as if she were trying her best to be at ease, and Charlie sat nearby her on a bench, sullenly looking out of the window. "I thought we were gonna eat..." he sighed.

"There was food at Mrs. Pinot's," Harriet replied.

Charlie wrinkled his nose. "Pickled cookies? And worse, sugared carrots?" he scoffed. "I'd hardly call *that* food."

"Charlie, don't be rude," Harriet said.

Mittie leaned close to Tracey. "Spiffy place, eh?" she said with a smile.

"Yes," Tracey agreed, leaning away. "It's quite different from what I expected to see, based on the foyer."

"It was kinda dark, don't you think? It reminded me a bit of a dungeon."

"Oh, or a funhouse!" Charlie added.

"You're right!" Mittie said. "It looks just like one!"

"A...funhouse?" Tracey blankly repeated.

"You've nev'a been to a funhouse, Trace?" Mittie gasped. "The steamchairs and gear-mirrors?"

"Yeah, and those spin-y walkways!" Charlie added. "Harrie an' I been to one a couple a' years back. Blazing fun!"

Mittie nodded enthusiastically. "My fam'ly went every summa' when I was a girl. Don't see 'em as much nowadays with all the travel'ing, but you can bet we'll go to one the next time we're together!"

"So, what is it exactly?" Tracey asked, feeling rather lost.

"It's a building you enter and try to walk through!" Mittie said, waving her hands to form the crude shape of the building.

"That's it?"

"No, of course not!" Charlie exclaimed. "They make it all colorful—the floors are purple or red or yellow, and the walls are green or blue or—"

"In other words, it's a big mash o' colors," Harriet summarized.

"An' you can't forget the mirrors!" Mittie said.

"Mirrors?" Tracey repeated, feeling rather queasy at the mental image of the disconcerting place.

Mittie nodded. "Mirrors all over the walls—some of them make you tall, some make you small, some make you wiggly!"

"Goodness!"

"Harrie, can we go again this year?" Charlie said, his eyes pleading. Harriet frowned. "We can save up some extra spigots, take a few jobs here an' there—"

"Say no more," Mittie interjected. "I can take all 'a us!"

"Really?" Charlie and Harriet exclaimed.

"Ah..." Tracey said in confusion. "Now?" *I'd rather not.*

Bentam merely looked at them, then resumed sorting through papers.

"After we find Mr. Porter, of course," Mittie added, much to Tracey's relief. "Don't think I've forgotten! And you're invited too, Bentam!"

"Funhouses have never been my sort of scene," he replied, pausing again to look up at Mittie. "I went once...as a child. We never went back."

"Oh, well, maybe ya haven't been with the right group a' people!" she cheerfully answered.

"I doubt it," he sighed. "But I suppose I—"

"Bentam, my friend! Fancy finding you here!" a sudden voice sounded from the dark foyer. All eyes turned.

There, in the wide entryway, stood Jon Starr.

# CHAPTER 10

# In Which They See a Twinkling Starr

JON STARR WORE an elaborate costume of a fur cape, clasped about the neck with a heavy golden chain, and an equally detailed suit of black and gold. Be it the rumored radiance Mittie said he had or the literal radiance of sunlight pouring onto him from the room's many windows, the actor was absolutely covered in brilliant light—a sharp contrast to the gloomy foyer behind him. His broad smile added to the effect. Tracey found herself hardly able to see his face past all the splendor.

"Jon," Bentam said with a simple nod, unfazed by the celebrity before him.

Harriet's face beamed in wonder as she leaned forward to take a better look at him.

Charlie, on the other hand, stared blankly about the room, his eyes finally meeting Tracey's before looking back at Jon Starr. He sighed, unimpressed.

Tracey herself felt similarly bewildered, partially from the blinding lights, and partially from the presence of such a well-known figure. *Is he really that big of a deal?* she wondered. *He looks mostly normal to me...minus all this light—where is all of this light coming from?*

Mittie, as expected, was positively captivated, her eyes radiant. "He's wearing the brooch!" she quietly squealed to Tracey.

Tracey spotted the red brooch as he strode into the room. Jon held his arms open in a welcoming gesture. "And you've brought guests as well!" he said, his smile somehow breaking wider yet. "Welcome, welcome!"

As he fully entered the room, Tracey could now see his face. She raised her eyebrows, surprised he looked so familiar. His golden hair was split in the middle, the front's parting strangely resembling a mustache. His face, on the other hand, did not sport any sort of hair (in fact, it was alarmingly smooth). His light blue eyes matched the baby blue walls, and they danced with warmth and laughter.

"You must pardon my attire," he said, gesturing to his clothing. "Usually, I'd sit guests down to tea, but you've just caught me before I leave to rehearsals."

"Rehearsals? Is that for your play *And Then the Summer's Eve Cried?*" Mittie blurted, scooting forward in her chair.

"A woman of taste, I see," he laughed. "Yes, you are correct. Who *are* these friends of yours, Bentam?" Jon said, turning to him with a flourish. "It's lovely to be in such company as those who know stage plays."

"That is Mittie. Next to her is Tracey. And these two children are Harriet and Charlie," Bentam said, pointing to each person.

"Charmed, a pleasure to meet all of you. Really," Jon said, flashing a warm smile to each person.

"Pleasure's all mine, Mr. Starr—" Mittie started.

"Oh, *do* call me Jon! Mr. Starr is far too...stuffy for my tastes."

"Well!" Mittie said. "Pleased to make your acquaintance...Jon!" If Mittie could burst, she may have in that very moment, judging by the level of pure, unbridled joy on her face.

"Hm," Jon hummed in a pleased manner, closing his eyes and tilting his head. "Now," he said, turning to Bentam, "how may I help you? I know you're a very busy man, and knowing that I'm a busy man myself, you must have had something of *great* urgency to tell me, no?"

"Yes, Jon. These people here with me have had the unfortunate event of encountering a pamphlet distributor. Mittie?" he said, holding out his hand.

"'Course!" she said as she pulled out the pamphlet from the pocket of her knickerbockers.

"A woman of taste *and* fashion, too?" Jon said, with an impressed raise of his brows. "I dare say those knickerbockers are the finest I've ever seen. Please, do tell, where did you get those from?"

"Made 'em myself!" she proudly said. "Y'see, I do a lot of traveling as a tradeswoman."

"Practicality too—I like this one, Bentam!" he said, turning back to Bentam. Mittie beamed, ducking her head.

"Lovely," Bentam grunted, unfolding the paper. "This pamphlet," he continued, louder, "directs the guests to Baldgrass Theatre two days from now. I'm here to confirm if this location will be correct?"

"May I see that?" Jon said, taking the paper. His face stilled into a frown as he examined the sheet. "No...no, this isn't right. I'm performing at the Stateshire Theatre."

Bentam sighed. "I was afraid that was the case. I'll add this to the case record set."

"Oh, dear," Jon groaned, dropping the paper as if it burned his hands. "Was it that same woman passing it out?"

"Yes. And elusive as ever."

"This won't do." Jon sank into a seat near him. "I'm sure each of you were looking forward to my performance in a few days?"

"No, not partic—" Bentam started.

"Yes! I was taking Harriet, Charlie, and Trace with me to see you!" Mittie said, leaning forward. "And Bentam, of course, if he'd be interested."

"No, no, that won't be necce—"

"Oh, you poor *victims*! Yes, I know just what to do," Jon said with a clap, standing up. "Hassan!"

Almost immediately, the butler appeared. "Yes, Jon?" he said.

"Please draft up some tickets for them, VIP, front row."

"Right away." With that, he ducked out of the room.

"I do apologize for any confusion or disappointment this may have caused," Jon said. "I hope this small gesture may suffice."

Mittie stared at Tracey, speechless.

"Oh, dear," he groaned, his excitement slipping once more from his face. "I ought to go on another tour, anything to get out of this place. It seems as if the longer I stay here in Mondon, the more frequent these false performances become."

"I assure you that we are doing our utmost to catch the perpetrator and bring you peace of mind," Bentam gravely said.

"Thank you, Bentam," he replied with a smile. "I appreciate your dedication. But this situation is rather stressful, you see. Imagine my reputation—ruined!"

"With such a reputation as large as yours, I doubt that," Bentam answered.

"I suppose, but—"

Before another word could be spoken, a clock in the foyer rang.

"Oh, is it five already? Dear me, I'll be late!" Jon hurried to the foyer. "Hassan will see you out. I'll ask Rollo to bring you some refreshments to go."

"Rollo?" Charlie whispered to Harriet, looking around.

"My cook!" Jon said as he ran out the front door. "Can't be late, ta-ta now!"

The door slammed shut.

"Well..." Tracey said. "That was—"

The front door swung open again. Jon poked his head back in. "Dear me, where are my manners?" he called from the foyer. "I almost forgot we've already met, Ms. Higgenbottom!"

"M-me?" Tracey replied, raising her voice to be heard from her far distance.

"Yes, it was lovely to see you again. Please let Mr. Porter know that I'd like to set up a follow-up appointment with him later this week."

"A-a-appointment?" Tracey stammered. "I don't recall seeing you before?"

"Must be the costumes," he said as he waved his hand. "I must steam away now, or I'll be late! Ta-ta again, all! I'll see you at the performance!"

With that, the door slammed shut once more. A few moments later, the once-idle steam car could be heard as it roared to life (along with a few startled neighs from nearby horses). The group watched as the vehicle sped past the window, leaving a billowing cloud of scalding steam in its wake.

"Gears, look at it go!" Charlie said, running to the window and watching as it swerved around the corner. "Neva' seen one so close up before!"

"Yes," Tracey said, anxiously crossing her arms. "That's lovely for you, Charlie."

Tracey's hair on her neck stood on edge. Her eyes snapped to Bentam, surprised to find his gaze unnervingly focused on her. "Yes?" she inquired.

"Jon is a client of Mr. Porter?" he slowly asked.

"That's what he said, yes. But he could have been mistaken," Tracey replied. She frowned. "Come to think of it, I might have written his name down in our appointment book..."

"Strange," Mittie said. "We just found out Mrs. Pinot is a client of his, too! How come you have so many clients you don't remember, Trace?"

"Hm." Bentam stood and entered the foyer. "Strange, indeed," he muttered as he changed his shoes. The rest looked at each other, shrugged, and joined him. Tracey trailed behind, snatching the now-abandoned advertisement to the fraudulent performance. She tucked it into her pocket and rejoined the group.

"I can't believe it," Mittie said as she pulled on her boots. "I met *the* Jon Starr! He's so much friendlier than I thought, based on what Bentam here said."

"Hey—" Bentam said.

"And he likes me!"

"You're a very likable person!" Charlie said as he stowed his and Harriet's newly acquired slippers into his baggy vest.

"Thank you, Charlie!" Mittie squealed. "Oh, I must be dreaming! Wait 'til Reggie hears of this!"

"Reggie?" Harriet said.

"Her beau," Tracey chimed in. She forced a smile. "I'm glad that you were able to meet your favorite actor."

"And to think I wouldn't have met him today if I hadn't—" Mittie cut herself off, her excitement draining away. "Oh, yes. There're more important matters on hand than my little fanfare, isn't there? I'm sorry, Trace."

"No, you're quite entitled to your joy," Tracey replied. "Who knows, maybe I can find a lead yet while we're here!"

"Ladies and gentlemen, your tickets," Hassan said as he whisked into the room. He held out a tray with five golden tickets.

"Well, if that isn't just squeaky?" Mittie exclaimed. Each, except for Bentam, took one.

"Thank you, sir, but I will not be needing it," he said.

"I insist. Jon and I are good friends," the butler said. "We've been close for years. To see him give you his tickets so easily...not to mention: front row? Or VIP? I had to cancel a few reservations to get these to you. This must mean a great deal to him. Please, do take it."

"If you insist," Bentam said as he carefully took the ticket and placed it in his breast pocket.

"He must admire all of you greatly for him to have made such a tall order. Really."

"I just happened to drop by to help further a case of his."

"Thank you," Tracey added. Bentam narrowed his eyes at her before looking away.

"Yes. Thank you," he said.

"The cook will be here momentarily," Hassan said, before leaving the room.

"Now that this is done," Bentam said, "I will need to have all of you to my office for statements on your case."

"You've decided to open it?" Tracey said, perking up.

"Merely push it higher on their priority list. As I see, you have three witnesses here." Bentam gestured to Mittie, Harriet, and Charlie. "It should be more than enough to get some action going."

"Here's your food," a booming voice said from behind them. "I've packed them in a box."

"Oh, my! How long have you been there?" Tracey gasped, spinning around.

There stood a towering man, his large stature dwarfing the group. His thin mustache matched the thin line that his mouth formed. A tall white hat sat on the top of his head.

*The cook, I suppose*, Tracey nervously thought, trying to ignore his scowl.

"I've been here long enough," the cook grunted. "Here," he said, thrusting the box at them. Tracey snatched it mid-air, saving it from an untimely demise on the ground. She handed it to Harriet.

"You can take these," she said.

"Gears!" she exclaimed, hugging the box close to her. "Thank you, Trace!"

"I'll see you out," the cook said as he stepped closer. Tracey and the group backed away, closer to the front door.

The chef reached past them and swung open the door, nearly knocking Harriet over in the process.

"Hey!" Charlie exclaimed, jumping toward the man.

The chef stepped closer yet, forcing the group to pile out onto the top step. "Don't come back," he abruptly said. Rollo slammed the door shut.

"What a brute," Mittie sniffed as they turned to dismount the stairs.

The group froze.

There, at the base of the stairs, was none other than Ms. Halpin herself. Much tidier in appearance than earlier, but undoubtedly her. In her hands was a considerably smaller stack of flyers. She gaped, looking strangely akin to a fish blowing bubbles. "Ah," she choked out.

"Ms. Elizaveta Halpin," Bentam said as he advanced down the stairs, his eyes narrowed. "I've been looking for you. May I have a word?"

Elizaveta stayed frozen at the base of the stairs. "Ah," she repeated. "Um—"

As Bentam reached her at the bottom of the stairs, she turned and bolted, disappearing down a nearby alley. Rather than giving chase, Bentam sighed and turned back to the group.

"You're not chasin' her?" Charlie exclaimed.

"No, no. Mondon's only so large before a constable finds her," he said.

"I thought you said constable resources are limited?" Tracey pointed out.

"Yes—well, ah," Bentam quickly said, shaking his head. "Was that not strange, however? Here she is at Mr. Starr's residence, and earlier she was around Mrs. Pinot's residence?" He frowned. "This can't be a coincidence... Ms. Higgenbottom, can you absolutely confirm that Jon was a client at your establishment?"

Tracey hesitated. With all the clients Mr. Porter received on a daily, it was hard for her to pinpoint if Jon had been there. Especially if he was in costume or disguise. Her eyes met the expectant gazes of the group. *It's technically against Porter Keeper Shoppe standards to let constables see client information...but if this can be a connection to Mr. Porter's disappearance, it should be fine, right? Besides, he's not a constable...* "I'd have to check the record books first," she said, "but yes, I should be able to. Follow me."

## CHAPTER 11

# In Which (Some) Truths Are Revealed

"Wow, will ya look at this place!" Charlie exclaimed as they stepped inside Porter Keeper Shoppe. Since the eventful morning and afternoon, Tracey had no chance to tidy the office from the evidence of the previous night's incident. The group looked about in shocked silence at the piles of paper everywhere.

Bentam cleared his throat.

"I...can see why you had cause for concern," he finally said, looking embarrassed. "I apologize for not taking your case gravely enough, Ms. Higgenbottom."

"All of this mess...what were they after?" Harriet asked as she tried to straighten a misshapen stack of papers on a table.

"I wish I knew," Tracey sighed. "Considering we handle mostly paperwork, it could have been anything."

"Is there no inventory?" Bentam said.

Tracey shook her head. "That would defeat the entire purpose of a keeper. We keep secrets. There's no use keeping secrets if we document what they are in easy-to-find files."

"Then why don't you keep the inventory in a safe?" Charlie said, carefully stepping over a toppled chair. "Your business is flawed."

"I don't make the rules, Charlie," Tracey said, feeling rather affronted. "I've tried convincing Mr. Porter to keep a written record for years now!"

"Now, shall I gather statements?" Bentam said as he set down his stack of papers on an open corner of a table. He pulled a pen and notepad from his pocket. "Let's start with you, Ms. Higgenbottom, as you were the first to find the scene. Time and description."

"Sometime this morning—I'd say around seven—I found the room in this condition. Every door was open."

"I see...including the front door?"

"Yes. Lights on, shutters open."

"Did you find any suspicious people near the scene or any objects left behind?"

"People, no, objects..." Tracey hesitated. This could be the moment she revealed what new evidence she found! Tracey touched her pocket where she had stashed Mr. Porter's ring. She glanced at Harriet and Charlie. *But I don't want to reveal too soon, in case they run before Mr. Berkley can get their statements.*

Bentam raised an eyebrow. "Objects left behind?" he repeated.

"His glasses," Tracey finally said, pulling out the spectacles from her pocket.

"Mhm, and did you—"

"And this handkerchief," she hurriedly added, pulling the cloth out.

"All this time, you've had more evidence?" Mittie said. "That could'a helped narrow down our search!"

"It never came up," Tracey replied. "Besides, your leads were far more concrete than these."

"The spectacles are not news to me, Ms. Higgenbottom," Bentam said. He leaned forward, looking closer at the cloth. "However, that handkerchief is. Where was this when you came in this morning?"

"Here, I presume. The constables gave it to me. I suppose he had assumed that it was mine. I took it because I thought it might provide a clue."

"Proceeding with cases without the High Constable's approval could land you in prison, Ms. Higgenbottom."

"It wasn't as if the High Constable was about to open my case either, was it?" Tracey retorted.

Bentam blinked. "You may have a point." He reached forward and took the handkerchief from her hand. "This kerchief has initials on it...RN. Do you know who this could be?"

"No," she said with a shake of her head.

"Did you check your register list to see if there're any clients who share this initial?"

"No," she replied.

"I'd have asked you that if you'd've mentioned that handkerchief earlier!" Mittie said indignantly, putting her hands on her hip. "Is that what you've been hiding in those pockets o' yours?"

"Partially," Tracey said. "Although I fail to see why this would matter to you?" *Why does she care so much?*

Bentam turned to Mittie. "May I get your statement, Mittie?" he asked. "I suppose you were the next person?"

"No, I was the first one around the incident. I actually was there at the time of the plagium," she gravely said.

"Beg pardon?"

"Plagium?" she repeated. "Ya know, kidnapping? Thought that was an official term…"

"Oh, yes," he said with a slow nod. "However, plagium means the crime of kidnapping a *child*."

"Ah. That makes sense. Well, anyway, I was there at the time of the kidnapping."

"Good, an eyewitness." He scribbled on the paper. "What time did this occur, and what did the perpetrator look like?"

"Ehm, it was 'round midnight," she started. "An' the perpetrator was tall an' slim. I think I saw 'im today, in fact."

Tracey froze. *Did we come that close to Mr. Porter's kidnapper?* "Why did you not say anything?" Tracey said. "And to think you were getting upset with *me* for not mentioning the handkerchief!"

"Well, he was a little different close-up than when I saw 'im from a distance," Mittie said. "Actually, he was a lot more intimidatin' close-up. And not as slim as I'd thought."

"What is his new description?" Bentam asked.

"Still tall," Mittie continued, "but I'd say he's rather burly."

"Mhm. And can you tell us who exactly you saw, and where?"

Mittie shuffled, her eyes darting around the room. "At Mr. Starr's residence."

"Really?" Harriet exclaimed from a corner, where she had situated herself and begun tidying up disorganized papers.

"Was it Mr. Starr?" Charlie asked from his seat at the window, where he had sat shortly after their entering the shop.

"No." Mittie shook her head. "It was...what was his name? The chef."

"Rollo?" Charlie offered.

"Yes, that's it! It really startled me to see 'im there all a sudden—I was a little frighten'd... Sorry for not sayin' anything sooner."

"Interesting," Bentam said. "I believe we have a solid case here. Did you see where they left to?"

"According to where I pointed out to Trace, it was The Undertown. That's how we met Harrie and Charlie."

"You've been doing a lot of legwork, I see," he said, nodding to both Tracey and Mittie.

"And all before a case has even been opened," Tracey sniffed.

He glared at Tracey before continuing. "Now, Harriet and Charlie. Can you both tell me what you saw?"

Charlie shrugged. "I didn' see anything. It was really just Harrie."

"Right," Harriet started. "I think I saw Rollo in The Borough, near Mrs. Pinot's residence. Actually, I suppose I should be more specific—I saw him going *into* Mrs. Pinot's residence. With a man that matched Tracey's description of Mr. Porter."

"The Borough?" Bentam frowned. "At what time?"

"Twelve thirty."

"That can't be right..."

"That's what I said," Charlie said with a shrug. "It's an hour away from here. There's no way they could have reached over there unless they had a steam car or somethin'."

"Mittie," Bentam said, turning to her, "did you hear any loud engines in the area when they left?"

"No...unless they'd parked down the street?"

"Is it possible for steam cars to be quiet?" Tracey asked.

"Yes, but steam car silencers are difficult and dangerous to install. There are very few, if any, installers in Mondon," Bentam replied. "Not to mention, they are illegal."

"Kidnapping is illegal, too," Charlie pointed out. "Don' think they'd care 'bout somethin' like that."

"That is true," Bentam sighed. "Is that why you were at Mrs. Pinot's residence?"

"Yes, we were following Harriet's lead," Tracey said.

"And can you confirm if he was there?" Bentam said.

"No," Tracey replied. "She denied him ever being there."

"So conflicting testimony," Bentam said, lowering his pencil. "I cannot take either word without evidence to back a claim."

Tracey hesitated, her hand hovering over her pocket. "I think I can confirm that Harriet saw Mr. Porter last night," she said, reaching inside and pulling out Mr. Porter's ring. Harriet's face paled.

"Where did you get that?" she said, a quiver in her voice.

"Under your rug."

"How much are you hidin' in those pockets of yours?" Mittie exclaimed.

"I was afraid they would run if I revealed this too soon," Tracey said.

"But I'd never!" Harriet exclaimed.

Mittie leaned closer. "That says *Remington L. Porter.* Is this Mr. Porter's ring? How d'ya get your hands on this, Harrie?"

"He dropped it," she said, tears forming in her eyes. "I'm sorry! I was going to pawn it and try to get some spigots. Maybe twenty or thirty spigots. That would have gone far. A few months, if I stretched it. I didn't think it was terribly important. I mean, I *did* tell you I saw him. Isn't that enough?"

"This is the evidence I need to back your statement," Bentam said. "Without it, your world would have been useless."

"You didn't see the inscription inside?" Tracey asked.

Harriet lowered her gaze. "I did," she mumbled.

Tracey frowned. "I understand why you may have done this, dear, but I wished you'd have said something sooner rather than try to hide it. This ring is very important. I—" Tracey stopped herself.

"You what?" Charlie asked.

"I gave this to him myself," she quietly finished.

"Were you close to Mr. Porter?" Mittie asked.

"You could say that, yes. I'm sure this may sound strange, but he was my guardian when I was a child."

Tracey looked at everyone, half expecting disapproving stares or, worse yet, more questions. Instead, she was met with understanding gazes and polite nods. She blinked, taken aback by the courteous reactions. "Ah..." she awkwardly started. She shook her head. "But yes, the ring is important. I'm just glad we can pin down Mr. Porter being in Uppertown around twelve thirty last night."

"I find it surprising that Rollo took Mr. Porter to Mrs. Pinot's place, however," Bentam said.

"Why's that?" Mittie asked.

"Mr. Starr and Mrs. Pinot have an ongoing feud. It's rather public in the high-class social circles, actually."

"A feud?" Charlie asked. "What's it about?"

"I'm not sure. It's simply public knowledge that neither of them gets along. For his cook to be going to her home...it's rather strange."

"It could be that the feud only goes as far as Mr. Starr. Why would his staff be involved?" Tracey wondered.

"Perhaps that may be the case."

"But wait," Charlie said. "Why were you at Mrs. Pinot's, anyway?"

"Just some bank issues in her records," he waved off. "Nothing important." Bentam scanned the notes on his pad. "So, for suspects, there's Mrs. Pinot, Rollo the cook, and perhaps the pamphlet distributer, Ms. Halpin. Between the three of them, however, I believe that Rollo may be a more solid lead." He raised the handkerchief in his hand. "Do you see these initials?"

"RN," Harriet said.

"Correct. Mrs. Pinot's first name is Corsetta, and Ms. Halpin's is Elizaveta. The cook, however, is Rollo. If we can figure out his last name, we may be able to tie him here."

"And how are we supposed to do that?" Charlie asked as he continued his journey across the shop, navigating to the back of the room.

"Well...we *could* ask him—" Tracey started.

"No!" everyone replied in unison.

Tracey blinked. "Or not."

"Ms. Higgenbottom, both Mrs. Pinot and Mr. Starr claimed to be your clients, and yet you don't remember either. Could you verify if they are your clients or not?" Bentam asked, handing the handkerchief back to her and walking to a small desk. "Is this your desk? Perhaps we may find something here."

"Yes, it's mine," she said. "Let me see if my ledger is still intact." Tracey approached the desk and unlocked the top drawer, rifled through its contents, and pulled out a clipboard. The two of them silently scanned the pages of names, dates, and times, flipping through each sheet.

"They don't appear to be on here," Bentam murmured. "Would they have gone by any different names? Anything that matches 'RN'?"

"No, none of these names share the initial."

Bentam's frown deepened.

"What if Mr. Porter had private clients?" Mittie offered. "They could have seen you without you signing them in, then?"

"That's a possibility," Tracey slowly said. "It *has* happened a few times, where the customers would enter without stopping at my desk—"

"I did it!" Charlie exclaimed, popping up from behind a large walnut desk in the back of the shop. He raised his hands over his head in a cheer, a letter opener gripped in one of them.

"Charlie!" Tracey gasped. "What are you doing at Mr. Porter's desk?"

# CHAPTER 12

# In Which a Curious Event Occurs

CHARLIE'S SMILE FADED as he was met by shocked—and borderline disapproving—stares. He set down the letter opener.

"Ehm...I mean," Charlie stammered, "I was just lookin' to see if he might've had any paperwork. An' this drawer here was locked...so I thought I could just, ya know, jimmy it open?"

"Gears, Charlie," Harriet exclaimed, jumping from her seat. "How many times have I told you not to pick locks?"

"Is this a common occurrence?" Bentam asked, raising an eyebrow.

"No," Charlie and Harriet quickly replied. They exchanged surreptitious glances.

"Hm," Bentam grunted, his eyes narrowing.

"But, uh, look at this!" Charlie said, quickly reaching inside of the drawer and pulling out a strange book. "This fancy book was in here!" Tracey sighed, pushing away her annoyance before joining the modest crowd that gathered around Charlie.

In Charlie's hands was a book unlike anything Tracey—nor anyone else in the room, for that matter—had seen before. On its cover was an elaborate design of gears, inlaid in a thick wooden surface. The pages were gilded, and its spine sported an equally intricate design of gears, intertwining in a spiralling pattern.

The book was locked.

"Is this Mr. Porter's record book?" Mittie asked.

"I don't think I've ever seen this book before," Tracey said. "Why would he hide a book like this?"

"Perhaps you can break this lock as well, hm?" Bentam said, staring harshly at Charlie.

Charlie gulped and shook his head. "I've never seen a lock like this. That drawer was a piece of cake in comparison. Really, look at all a' those gears!"

"Why would Mr. Porter hide this from me?" Tracey said in bewilderment.

"I suppose that even a keeper has secrets of their own," Mittie said as she leaned closer to the book. "Maybe we can turn the gears?"

Tracey grappled with the gears, to no avail. "They're not moving," she sighed.

"Question," Harriet said from the front of the room. "Have you already checked motor-mail for any clues?"

"Yes," Tracey said. "I received a combustible note earlier today."

"Combustible paper?" Charlie gasped.

"Why?" Tracey continued, ignoring the ripple of shock from the group.

"I thought—I just thought you may have missed this piece of mail here," Harriet stammered, holding up a peculiar brown sachet. "This was in the motor-mail."

Tracey frowned. *I may have missed that, with the shock of the combustible paper this morning and all.* "May I see it?"

Mittie crossed her arms. "You got your hands on *combustible paper*? And ya never thought of mentioning *that*?"

"I was simply following Bentam's advice—"

"He's in on it too??" Mittie spun to him.

"No, Mittie, she merely informed me of this when she requested a case opening this morning," Bentam calmly responded.

"It's the only reason why you even bothered opening the case, is it not?" Tracey sniffed.

Bentam stared at Tracey, a flash of annoyance in his eyes. "It appears as if we've gotten off track," he said. "Let me continue gathering information for this report." He furiously scrawled on a sheet of new paper procured from his stack.

Tracey took the sachet from Harriet and examined it, frowning. "There's no return address, nor any labeling," she said.

"Kinda thick for an envelope, don't ya think?" Mittie said, her interest flitting back to Tracey and Harriet.

"How do you open it?" Charlie asked as he set down Mr. Porter's book and joined them.

"It says 'rip here'," Tracey said, straining to read the impossibly small type on the envelope. She tore the sachet.

"What's inside?" Harriet asked as she craned her neck to get a better view.

"A piece of paper," Tracey said as she pulled out the small sheet. On it was a crudely written—if it could be called written (the words more closely resembled chicken scratch than an alphabet) note:

*Talk to William Matthews. 9 AM. Bank of Mondon. Come for*

*more information on your precious Porter.*

Tracey gasped and dropped the paper.

"What's wrong? What does it say?" Mittie cried, snatching up the paper. "'Talk to William Matthews, nine a.m., at the Bank of Mondon...for more information...?' Tracey, this is blackmailing."

"And the clearest lead yet," Bentam said, quickly putting down his notepad and rushing over. "Let me see this. I can add it to the case record."

Bentam took the piece of paper and scrawled the message onto his own sheet. "Now, let me file..." he trailed off as he stared at the paper in his hands, his eyes widening.

"Why's he lookin' at the paper like that?" Charlie whispered to Harriet.

The paper in question smoked in his hands before suddenly dissolving into smoke. The plumes filled the room. Tracey recoiled, covering her nose from the familiar sickly-sweet odor.

"That wasn't combustible paper, was it?" Mittie nervously asked.

"Yes. And 'the crime for being in possession of, or in the presence of, combustible paper is immediate imprisonment'," Bentam quoted. "A passage from our Major Felonies Coursebook."

"You mean to say I could still land in the slammers just for standing near one a' those things? I didn' even touch it!" Charlie exclaimed.

"I'm too young to go to prison," Harriet wailed.

Tracey found herself speechless. A quick glance at Mittie showed a reaction mirroring her own.

Bentam dusted the powdery remains of the paper from his hands and cleared his throat. They watched him in tense silence as he took up the new sheet of paper he had been writing on.

To their surprise, however, he reached for a half-melted candle on Mr. Porter's desk, grabbed a nearby match, and proceeded to set the paper afire.

"Wha—" Charlie said. "What's he doin'? He's burning the paper! Why's he burning the paper?"

"Isn't that the case file?" Tracey gasped. "What are you doing?"

Bentam stared at the flames as they licked up the paper. He dropped it into a metal candle tray as the tongues of flames reached his hand. He then methodically rubbed the ashes between his fingers. "That parcel never arrived," he evenly said. "None of us saw that sheet of paper."

"Beg pardon?" Tracey asked.

"It would be prudent if we proceed without the case file," he continued, taking his notepad and holding it up. "I just burned the case file application. These are the notes from your testimonies."

"I don't know if I should be relieved or afraid," Harriet said. "You're *not* arresting us, then?"

"What's all this 'bout, Bentam?" Mittie said.

"Arresting you would arrest me," Bentam said. "If the High Constable catches wind of this paper—let alone the one found earlier by Ms. Higgenbottom—imprisonment is imminent. So, we'll pretend this never happened."

"On the other hand, he continued, "we cannot turn a blind eye to the fact that Mr. Porter has likely been kidnapped by someone dangerous. There are only a few people who could have combustible paper, and those few are better suited for prison."

"All the more reason to give it to the High Constable, this case!" Mittie replied. "This is too dangerous for us. I'm sure they'd understand once we explain."

"They'll imprison you first, then ask questions later. Only after they clear you are you able to leave, and that may take one or even two weeks later. Do you think that Mr. Porter will still be safe by then?"

The air hung heavy in the room, the late evening sunlight casting a right golden glow across the chaotic and somber scene. "Then what's the next plan of action?" Tracey finally asked.

"We all go home," Bentam said. "They may be watching us as we speak, especially since we've already met someone who was here at the time of the crime. We go home as normal to avert suspicion."

"And then what?" Mittie asked. "I'll go back to the ship, you all go to your homes, and then?"

"We do as the paper says," Bentam said, gathering his sheets of paper. Tracey noticed his hands trembled as he straightened the stack. "We reconvene tomorrow at the Bank of Mondon. I'll be there from eight thirty as I have some work balances to deposit."

"S'pose I'll take this book with me and see if I can open it tonight," Charlie said as he grabbed up Mr. Porter's book from the desk.

"Be careful with it," Tracey said, anxiously watching as the boy stuffed the book into his vest.

She watched as everyone shuffled out of the office, each going on their own way. As the sun set over the towering buildings of Mondon, Tracey couldn't help but wonder if the following day would prove to be successful in tracking down Mr. Porter or not.

# CHAPTER 13

# In Which There Is Adverse Action

THE BANK OF MONDON was one of the few reputable banking establishments within the large city of Mondon. Due to its trustworthiness, and ability to prevent the theft of customers' money (unlike other similar establishments), it soon anchored itself as the High Constable's number one source and trustee of its funds. Its efficiency was like no other, with processing speeds rivaling the fastest of motor-mail transport.

It was of no surprise to Tracey, then, that Bentam was ready and waiting for them as they arrived that morning, already done with his business. "I've been finished from 8:35," he had claimed. It was also of no surprise that, considering their business was of no affiliation to the High Constable, their group was low priority to the bank. It was a full hour later than the combusted note had arranged for them, and there was still no sign of William Matthews, despite Tracey having requested for him precisely at 8:45 AM.

Charlie, who had just given up in his pursuit of unlocking Mr. Porter's book, sat with his head in his hands. His legs restlessly kicked as he let out a loud sigh. "What time is it?" he grumbled.

Mittie's attention snapped from a book that she had carried with her, her head swiveling to the glowing gearclock that hung prestigiously on a far marble wall. "Look at that, it's already half past ten," she said. Mittie closed her book and stood. "D'ya think we should go ask again?"

"The more inconspicuous we can be, the better," Bentam said with a shake of his head.

"Right," Mittie said, slowly sitting. "How's that locked book comin' along, Charlie?"

"A bunch of rust, that's what," he growled.

"Charlie," Harriet said with a warning glance.

"Well, it is. Can't make heads or tails o' this lock."

Tracey scanned the bank, her eyes flitting on the bustling activity of businesswomen and businessmen scurrying about on their daily tasks, crisscrossing to the point that she couldn't tell if anyone was walking toward them or simply crossing to the other side of the foyer. "It has been quite a while, Bentam," she sighed. "You were able to get your business done rather quickly."

"That's right," Mittie joined, "How's it you were able to get in so fast?"

Bentam waved a hand nonchalantly. "The Bank of Mondon doesn't tarry with High Constable business."

"And yet, they would tarry with a customer appointment," Tracey said. She sighed and settled back in her seat, staring listlessly at the teeming masses. "I wonder if this William Matthews knows where Mr. Porter may be," she said.

"Hopefully so," Bentam replied. "The sooner we find your Mr. Porter, the sooner we can close this case."

Harriet straightened in her seat. "Is that the William Matthews fellow?" she asked. "He looks like he's walking over here."

Tracey's eyes followed her gaze. *There!*

From the crowd of people strode a small man, his most notable feature being a mustache stretching from ear to ear— or rather sideburn to sideburn. His sharp attire indicated his being a banker, from his high collar and pearl-white cravat to the vest and sharply starched burgundy suit. His polished shoes clacked against the white marble floor as his eyes locked with Tracey's. His pace quickened. "Ms. Higgenbottom?" he boomed as he drew nearer.

"Y-yes," she stammered, taken aback by the deafening volume of his voice.

"Please follow me."

Tracey and the group stood, gathering around him.

"*Only* Ms. Higgenbottom," he snapped.

"What?" Charlie cried indignantly. "We're together!"

"I'm following instructions," was his response before he whisked back toward the crowd.

"Wait!" Tracey called, dashing after him. "Let me keep up with you first!"

"If you need us, yell!" Mittie said as Tracey wove through the crowd. She steeled herself and bunched up her shoulders as she spotted Mr. Matthews' burgundy suit among the throngs of people. *This might be it!* she thought. *He must know where Mr. Porter is!*

The banker led Tracey through a grand corridor, down a set of stairs, across a perilous catwalk, down another set of stairs, and finally to a pair of two dark, imposing doors. He swung the doors open to reveal an equally dark and imposing room. With confident steps, he marched down the length of the long room before sitting at a desk at its far end. Tracey squinted to see the desk in the murkiness of the room, let alone him sitting behind it. "Do close the door behind yourself, Ms. Higgenbottom," he said, his voice somehow just as loud as when he was right beside her.

Tracey closed the door and made the long trek through the room before nearly tripping over a set of chairs that sat in front of the banker's desk. "Oh!" she exclaimed. "I do apologize. I couldn't see these here from the door. Nor right in front of me, for that matter."

"I prefer the dark. It's comforting," the banker said, his voice echoing in Tracey's ears. "Take a seat, please." He took a key from underneath a desk lamp and unlocked a cabinet behind himself, pulling out a thin, black portfolio. "I understand that Mr. Porter has sent you here?" he said as he opened the portfolio and placed it on the table.

Tracey blinked. "No?" she said. She bit her lips, uncertain of how much to reveal. *He doesn't seem to know much.*

The banker stopped mid-page turn and raised an eyebrow. "I see." With a flourish, he closed the portfolio and placed it back into the cabinet. "I hope you understand what your coming here implies?"

"No, I'm just following some instructions I had received yesterday."

"Oh." The banker frowned and rubbed his chin. "Of course, Remington wouldn't tell you," he sighed. "I'm sure you're aware of what sort of strained relationship banks have with non-bankers?"

"Yes," Tracey replied, taken aback by this banker using Mr. Porter's given name. Mr. Porter's position as a keeper (or non-banker) placed him as a competitor to local banks, especially to a bank like the Bank of Mondon. Oftentimes, customers who used keeper shops in the city of Mondon were trying to avoid laws that would otherwise penalize them with taxes and fines had they chosen to take their business to a traditional bank. With these circumstances in mind, it was understandably uncommon for bankers and keepers to be on any sort of friendly terms.

"Well, there's a shared client Remington and I personally account for," the banker continued.

"That's hardly uncommon," Tracey said in surprise. "Some of our customers have accounts at banking establishments. Not many, but enough for me to have heard of it."

"This client," he replied, "is different." He squinted at her, scrutinizing her from head to toe before taking the portfolio out again. "I don't believe I've introduced myself to you yet," he said as he flipped once more through the portfolio's contents. "My name is William Matthews. I'm a lead banker here at the Bank of Mondon. What I'm about to give you is a document that I've been holding for Remington as a...favor for him. Under no circumstances may you show this to any staff at this bank." He yanked a sheet of paper out, folded it, and placed it on the desk. He lit a candle.

"I don't understand why I had to come in person just for a sheet of paper," she said. "Couldn't you have sent this via the motor-mail?"

"Motor-mail!" he scoffed as he picked up the candle with one hand and held a block of wax over the paper with the other. "I hardly trust all of this steam technology, let alone *motor-mail*.

Look around you, Ms. Higgenbottom. Do you see any sort of steam technology in this room?"

Tracey looked. "Well, now that you mention that—no."

"Twenty years ago, steam contraptions would have been *unheard of*," he sniffed. "Why, even five years ago, they would have still been a topic of contention!" He took up a stamp and placed it onto the melted mound of wax that had landed on the paper. "We used to use real means of communication!" He removed the stamp and held the sealed paper to her. "Nothing like now."

"You don't use any steam technology?" she said as she took the paper and rose.

"Never." Mr. Matthews stood as well, and the two made the long trek back to the exit.

"Then you weren't the one who sent me the instructions to come here? Via motor-mail?"

"Absolutely not."

"Then how did you know I would be coming?"

"Simple," he said as he opened the door. "Remington sent me a letter yesterday."

Tracey stared. "Mr. Porter...sent you a letter...yesterday?"

"Yes, yes," he waved off. "Of course, there's a couple of days delay sending mail by post and not"—he shuddered—"motor-mail. So, I'd assume he sent this a few days ago, then?"

"The return address was for Porter Keeper Shoppe?"

"I hardly pay attention to that." Mr. Matthews squinted. "Is something amiss with Mr. Porter? Why are you asking so many questions?"

"No—no reason!" Tracey quickly supplied. "Thank you, Mr. Matthews." She bobbed her head and rushed away.

"Ms. Higgenbottom!" he boomed.

Tracey stopped, then turned. "Yes?" she said.

"The lobby is in the opposite direction."

"Of course. Thank you." Tracey bobbed her head again and rushed in the other direction.

"Up the stairs, across the catwalk, up the other stairs, and through the corridor!" he loudly called as Tracey retreated.

"Couldn't you just walk me there?" she asked, exasperated.

"No, no, too busy! These letters won't send themselves."

"They would with motor-mail," she muttered as she continued.

"With *what?*" he yelled. Tracey quickened her pace. "What?" he repeated as Tracey turned the corner. *"Motor-mail?"* She glanced back, relieved to see Mr. Matthews retreated into his office rather than chase after her.

"Ah, Ms. Higgenbottom," Bentam said as she rejoined the group. "We were just going to inquire after you."

"What did he tell ya?" Charlie asked, pausing briefly from tinkering with the locked book to look at her.

"He gave me a document—" she started.

"Can we see it?" Mittie inquired.

"Mr. Matthews..." Tracey lowered her voice as she noticed passersby turning their heads at the sound of his name. "Mr. Matthews requested that no staff here see it."

"Why don't we go somewhere else, then? I know just the place!" Mittie said with a clap.

"Where would that be?" Tracey asked as the group gathered their things and began their walk to the exit. She paused, suddenly feeling a gaze prickle the back of her neck. Tracey turned.

Behind them trailed a rather familiar figure whose eye Tracey met in surprise. Before she could say a word, however, they slipped back into the throngs of people.

"Oh!" she gasped.

"What?" Charlie said, turning around.

"I thought I saw somebody that we met yesterday..."

"Who?" Harriet inquired.

"The...the pamphlet woman?"

"Ms. Halpin?" Bentam said, suddenly alert. "Where did she go?" He took a few steps toward the crowd, an expression of frustration growing on his face. "It really should not be this difficult to bring someone in for questioning."

"Remember, we're looking for Mr. Porter, not Ms. Halpin," Tracey curtly replied.

Bentam sharply turned to her. "Ms. Higgenbottom—"

"Well," Mittie interrupted with a nervous chuckle. "I was going to suggest we visit Mondon Center Park to look at that paper, Trace, but I think I may know somewhere a bit more private."

"Any place private is fine with me," Tracey sniffed as she whisked away. The rest trailed behind her, Bentam lingering back a few paces. "Where is it?" Tracey said as she swung the doors of the bank open and squinted in the bright morning sun.

"I'll show ya," Mittie said, taking the lead. "How does going up a few hundred feet in the air sound?"

# CHAPTER 14

# In Which the Clock Counts Down

"WELCOME ABOARD!" Mittie gallantly said as everyone shuffled out of the shuttle. "Hope the ride wasn't too bumpy on the way up."

The shuttle was a precarious oval tube attached to an equally questionable metal track—two skinny pieces of metal stretching up hundreds of feet in the air. The group had just entered said shuttle, ridden up to its top, and disembarked onto an open-air boardwalk.

"B-bumpy? N...no, not at all," Tracey stammered, trying hard to not look over the edge of the walkway—over the edge, to a view of Mondon and the surrounding countryside.

Over the edge, where the nearest ground was hundreds, if not thousands, of feet below them. "It's not the ride that is the issue," she murmured.

"Gears, I thought we were gonna die!" Charlie exclaimed, finally catching his breath. "I don't like heights, you know!"

Harriet stood stiffly next to him. "I don't either, Charlie," she said.

"Wonderful view," Bentam said in approval, as he leaned over the railing. "You can see the entirety of Mondon from here."

Reader, had Tracey mustered the courage to look over the edge, she would have seen her entire life in a single snapshot. As she had never left the sprawling city, she may have felt a twinge of insignificance—an existential crisis of sorts. Or perhaps she'd simply feel more intense fear than she already was experiencing.

"Right?" Mittie said enthusiastically, brushing past where Tracey remained rooted and joining Bentam by the railing. "It's my favorite part of travelin' by steamship!"

Steamships were as natural to the public majority as steam cars were to the streets of Mondon: tolerated but not fully accepted. Surprisingly, more affordable than a steam car, steamships soon filled the skies of Mondon and the rest of the country. It was a normal occurrence for one to see steamships drifting lazily about in the air, narrowly missing collisions with other ships, and docking off at tall buildings known as vessel-pads (a highly profitable business that works similarly to inns—complete with lodging for weary travelers and access to the building's amenities, ranging from saunas to hot and fresh breakfasts). It was this sort of building they had entered, and from the roof of which they had loaded into the complimentary vessel-pad shuttle to enter Mittie's steamship.

"Can we go inside the ship?" Tracey abruptly said. "To a room, preferably. Away from this boardwalk."

"I wasn't aware you were afraid of heights, Ms. Higgenbottom," Bentam said. Tracey caught a hint of a smirk on his face.

She frowned. "There are many things that you don't know about me, *Mr. Berkley*."

"It has only been about a day since we've all met, hasn't it?" Mittie interrupted with a smile, stepping between the two of them. "How about we go to my study? There's still a nice view, and it's indoors!"

"Fine by me," Tracey said, closely following Mittie.

As the group made their way to the interior of the vessel, Tracey was able to relax and look closer at her surroundings. This was the first time she had ever been on a steamship, and for the first time, she could feel the rush of curiosity and the pull of adventure. Tracey couldn't help but wish that Mr. Porter was there with her, so they could sail away on an exciting journey of their own. She sighed.

Mittie glanced back at Tracey. "Do you think we can open up that paper when we all settle in th' study?" she said. "I'm really hopin' there's some direction to point to where your Mr. Porter may be."

"Of course," Tracey said. She looked at the paper, which she held tightly in her hands. Its wax sported a familiar symbol: a gilded K, interlaced with a lock and a broken key. "Where have I seen this before?" she muttered.

"What?" Charlie said, falling back in stride with her. He leaned over to look at the wax. "Oh, that's the same mark that I'd seen on the book." He waved Mr. Porter's book and turned a small gear on the corner of the front cover, revealing a matching symbol. "All th' gears line up to make a bigga' version of the design, so I thought I'd have to match up the design to unlock it. But nothing!"

"Maybe this paper will give more information," Tracey replied as she followed Charlie into the study. "We must be missing a step."

Mittie's study was filled to the brim with books, some strewn about on her large oak desk and others stuffed on full shelves. It was all Tracey could do to not step on some sort of stray leaf of paper or forgotten pen on the floor. The largest wall was dominated by a massive window, stretching from ceiling to floor. Out of it could be seen a lovely view of Mondon and surrounding skies. "Oh," Tracey said as she carefully stepped across the room and perched on a chair farthest from the window, "your study is very...what's the word..."

"Cozy?" Harriet offered.

"Cluttered," Bentam sniffed.

"Messy," Charlie said, which rewarded himself a pinch from Harriet.

"Yes, sorry 'bout the mess!" Mittie said with a nonchalant laugh as she took up a few books and wedged them into a nearby shelf. The shelf groaned. "It'll be fine," she quickly said. "It's usually not this messy; I've been busy doing some research. Now, Trace!" she said with an enthusiastic clap of her hands. "Let's have a look at this paper, shall we?"

Tracey held the paper in front of herself, examined the seal once more, then broke the document open. "Let's see what we have here," she said as she unfolded the paper.

Across the top of the paper was a scrawled message she could barely make out. She immediately recognized it as being Mr. Porter's own handwriting: *Highly suspicious. Check this, William?*

Below, Tracey read the contents in question. "It appears to be a copy of a deposit record," she said, examining the paper closer. "I see several withdrawals, and all of them are for theaters."

"May I see?" Mittie asked. She took the offered paper. "Strange. These are all locations Jon Starr's performed at—and recent, too! The play names: *Beyond the Starry Sky*, *An Event of Regret*, and even *And Then the Summer's Eve Cried*. Pretty sure that these are his."

"That's hardly remarkable," Bentam said from his seat by the window. "I'm sure Jon has many admirers who follow his plays."

"There must be something wrong with it if it's marked as 'highly suspicious,'" Mittie said. She scanned the paper once more before handing it back to Tracey. "But what's so suspicious about this? Nothin's wrong with someone goin' to all o' his performances."

"Perhaps it's not as much as *why* they're going as it is *who's* going," Tracey said. "Look at the client's name: Corsetta Pinot."

"Mrs. Pinot's not suspicious!" Harriet cried.

"I thought that she has a bone to pick with Jon Starr," Charlie said. "Why would she be going to his performances?"

"That's what I wonder, too," Bentam murmured. "Let me see the document."

Bentam stiffly took the paper from Tracey, muttered a strained "thank you," and returned to his seat. He then took out a device of some sort from his pocket. It appeared to be a tube with black paper wrapped around it. Bentam unfurled the tube and pushed buttons along its top. It made a whirring noise as its miniature gears clacked to life. Soon enough, the black of the paper began to shift and form letters.

"Gears! Look at that!" Charlie said as he rushed behind Bentam to get a clearer look. "What's that? How'd it do that?"

"I can't always carry papers with me," he explained. "So, we use these portable documents. I just enter the motor-mail coordinates of the document I need, and this paper will shape the black into letters. It's really all just a matter of electromagnetics."

"Electr...what?" Charlie blankly echoed.

"Don't worry about it," Bentam said with a wave. "Now, if my theory is correct..." He trailed off as he scanned the document. "Hm," he grunted. "I'm afraid my theory *is* correct."

"What's the theory?" Mittie asked, leaning against her desk.

"Every one of these performances that Mrs. Pinot purchased tickets for matches the location and name of the false performances that Ms. Halpin has been advertising."

"Ms. Halpin," Tracey echoed, thinking back to the gruff woman who had suspiciously been following them the past few days. "I wonder why."

"Maybe Mrs. Pinot is just very unfortunate in her choices of performances?" Harriet offered.

"But that wouldn't explain why she chose his performances in the first place, especially if they have an ongoing feud," Mittie replied. "Plus, she told us that she goes to bed promptly at nine o'clock. Jon's performances end well past then. If she lied to us about that, what else has she lied to us about?"

Harriet squirmed. "I'm certain I saw Mr. Porter go into her house that night," she reminded the group. "So, there's that."

Silence filled the room.

"So, what's the next step?" Mittie asked.

"I think Mr. Porter may be at Mrs. Pinot's," Bentam said. "I suggest we investigate her home ourselves. Ms. Halpin's performance invitation—tomorrow night is when that happens, correct?"

"Yes," Tracey said.

"If she keeps with this pattern, it's likely that she'll be at the fraudulent performance. To be safe, we can go to the performance and see for ourselves, then go to her home."

"What about the tickets Jon Starr gave us?" Tracey reminded.

"Oh, yes. I suppose it would look strange if we didn't take his offer." Bentam frowned.

"How about we go long enough for Jon to see us," Mittie suggested, "then a few o' us—not me, mind you—slip away and check if Mrs. Pinot's at the fraudulent one?"

"That could work..." Bentam said, slowly nodding. "But why not you?"

"There's no way I'm missing *a VIP front-row* performance of Jon Starr!"

"I understand. It's all right," Tracey graciously said. "I could check with someone. If she's there, then we can go to her home and find Mr. Porter!"

"Very plausible," Bentam agreed. "There's only one problem. How will we communicate quickly enough? This is a relatively small timeframe that we're working with, and it is too large of a distance for us to be traversing back and forth."

"Leave that to me!" Mittie said. "I have steamgear to communicate, and steamweapons to protect ourselves."

"Weapons?" Tracey gasped. "I hardly think that would be necessary."

"We don't all need t' carry one. I could carry one as a backup."

"I can also carry one," Bentam joined. "I don't trust anyone who is capable of sourcing combustible paper and kidnapping."

"Come, follow me," Mittie said, striding to the door. "I'll give ya a quick walkthrough of the tech before we go tomorrow."

As the group followed her, Tracey bit back a smile of anticipation. Things were finally looking up, and they may very well find Mr. Porter at long last!

# CHAPTER 15

# Plagium!

IT WAS THE DAY of Jon Starr's performance.

Tracey stood in front of Stateshire Theatre and fidgeted with her dress and necklace. *Why did I let Mittie talk me into buying this?* she thought, feeling scandalously bare. *Imagine this! No collar!* She was unused to wearing such formal wear. In fact, this was the first performance that she had ever attended—such attire was not a thing in her wardrobe. *This is just for Mr. Porter,* she reminded herself, re-examining her dress in the reflection of the theater's windows.

The scoop neckline revealed a simple strand of pearls that Mittie had loaned to her. Her hair was styled into curls that piled high on her head, accented with similar-looking pearls. Her dress pooled on the ground, and its bows were so large she thought it impossible for a dress to hold such weight. "I look ridiculous," she muttered. In her gloved hand was the golden ticket. "VIP, front row," Tracey read with a shudder.

Around her, people of all sorts in equally formal clothing streamed into the theater. Tracey scanned the crowd for any sign of the others.

"See, it looks beautiful on ya!" a voice said from behind her. Tracey spun to find Mittie approaching, with Charlie and Harriet in tow.

Mittie wore a sweeping dress, studded with embroidery and framing a golden necklace of threaded amethyst. Her curly hair was braided into a large, ornate updo, and a pair of matching earrings reached to her shoulders. Her face radiated with excitement.

Harriet wore a prim dress that stopped short of her ankles, revealing lace socks and white shoes, topped with little bows. Her chestnut hair was twisted into bouncy curls and her face was flushed with joy.

Charlie wore a prim suit of black, his jacket swung open to reveal a frilled shirt. His hair was combed back into a prim do, unlike his typically ruddy hair. His black shoes were neatly polished, reflecting the streetlights. His face was in a fixed grimace. "Why do we have t' wear all this?" he grumbled. "It's too stuffy."

"So, we can blend in, Charlie!" Harriet said. "Besides," she added, "didn't you always want to wear something so nice?"

"Not this," he muttered, tugging at the collar.

"You all look lovely," Tracey said with a smile. "And thank you, Mittie."

"Where's Mr. Bentam?" Harriet asked, peeking through the crowds.

"Right here," he replied as he stepped from the theater's entry. Bentam wore a sharp attire: his sleek, black tailcoat matched the polished, smart shoes. His embroidered vest matched his elaborate bowtie, and his neat hair peeked from underneath his tall, top hat.

"You've been here all along?" Tracey said in alarm.

"I was finding our seats," he replied. "Shall we?"

"Wait!" Mittie said, holding up her hand. "Does everyone have their steamgear on them?"

Tracey nodded, touching the small device hidden behind her ears. Harriet and Charlie turned their heads and pushed back their hair to show theirs. Bentam pointed to his own, hidden by the hair.

"Good," Mittie said with a nod. "We'll stay connected to the same frequency 'til you and Charlie leave during the intermission, Trace, just like we practiced. Since you'll be farther from the transmitter," she continued, pointing to a hidden pocket on her dress, "the connection will prob'ly be a tad spotty."

"So, then we connect to our own private frequency, correct?" Tracey asked.

Mittie nodded. "The rest of us will stay and wait for the signal. Make sure that you switch back to the main frequency when you do that. Bentam and I have the steamweapons, so we'll be on standby if you need us over at the Baldgrass Theatre."

"The theater is but a five-minute walk from here, so it should be no issue for us to reach," Bentam added.

"Okay, so we check Baldgrass, find Mrs. Pinot, then go to her home, right?" Charlie asked.

"Spot on," Mittie confirmed.

"And then we begin our search for Mr. Porter," Tracey said.

"Right," Mitie replied. "And since Harriet and Charlie know her home so well, we should have no problem going through it."

"Sounds like a plan!" Harriet cheerfully said.

"Wonderful. The performance is about to start—let's go inside," Bentam said. They joined the crowd filtering into Stateshire Theatre.

Inside, the ceilings were encrusted with ornate gold which encircled patches of fine art paintings. The chandelier cast glittering light onto the paintings' details and illuminated the brilliant gold that followed down the walls. The carpet was a lush red, muting the crowd's murmurs to a pleasant hum. The group weaved through the crowd, made their way past ornate wooden doors, and down the theater's aisle.

Down they went, past the hard wooden economy chairs, the slightly more comfortable still-wooden standard economy chairs (equipped with steam-powered binoculars), and the standard plush, upholstered chairs, before stopping beside a row of luscious, red velvet seats that were as encrusted in gold as the ceilings.

They filed into the row.

In front of the first row was a golden railing, blocking guests from the drop to the orchestra pit below. Slightly above that was the stage, just low enough so that the front row had the optimal view, yet not so high that it would strain one's neck to peer upward.

"Polished chrome!" Charlie said in awe as he sank into the seat.

"It feels like clouds!" Harriet sighed.

Mittie beamed at the stage. "I can't wait for it to start!"

"You won't have to wait long," Bentam replied from his end seat, watching as the audience filed into their respective seating. The gas lights dimmed.

Behind her, Tracey felt someone tap her shoulder. She quickly turned, startled. "I'm sorry, ma'am, didn't mean to disturb you," an older woman whispered, her mouth curled into a small smile. "But I would just like to compliment you on your family!"

"My...family?" Tracey echoed.

"Oh, yes! Your two children and husband, and oh! Look at her hair, how lovely," she said, admiring Mittie's hairstyle. "Is she a family friend of yours?"

"Ah," poor Tracey sounded, at a loss for words.

"Yes, she is," Bentam said, turning around as well. "She's a very good friend of ours and we wanted to treat her to a performance of Jon Starr's."

"Marvelous!" the woman gasped. "You have *very* good friends," she said with a friendly tap on Mittie's shoulder.

"Oh! Thank you...kindly," Mittie haltingly said, raising an eyebrow.

"Enjoy the show," she replied, settling back in her seat.

Tracey turned back to look at Mittie and down the row to Charlie, Harriet, and Bentam. "So, we're a family now?" she whispered as the orchestra began to tune their instruments.

Harriet looked enthusiastically between the two of them. "Are we really?" she asked.

"If it helps our narrative," Bentam evenly said, his gaze fixed on the empty stage. "The guise of being a family makes us less suspicious—don't you think Ms. Higgenbottom?"

Tracey gritted her teeth at the sharp tone of his saying her name.

"Look, they're startin'!" Mittie said, excitedly tapping Tracey's arm, stopping her from shooting back a scathing remark.

The tuning of the instruments fell silent, and a quiet buzz of anticipation filled the room. Even Tracey could feel the tinge of excitement as the lights dimmed even more. The curtains raised.

There in the center of the stage, with the spotlight shining upon him, was Jon Starr. He wore the same attire that Tracey had seen him wear when they last met. He stood at the center of the stage, his eyes fixed to a point past the audience. Slowly, softly, the music began. "Is the summer's eve the time of utmost joy?" he quavered. "For I..." Jon paused and leveled his eyes at the crowd. "I find it as the time of utmost *sorrow*.

"Of whence one dizzily stumbles upon lines...of grief and betrayal, joy in the dawn yet...shunned by friends and called shameful by the day's end.

"By the summer's heat and the sweat of the sun, once words were given, it could not be undone. Never was forgotten, never forgiven. Yet in the summer's eve—ah—cries of remorse, then."

With those words, the curtains closed once more, and the audience broke into polite applause. *He's worse than I thought*, Tracey thought, unimpressed.

"Those were the opening lines," Mittie whispered, leaning over to Tracey. Tracey noticed her eyes were watering.

"Are you quite all right?" she whispered back in alarm.

"Of course! He's just so...touching! O-oh," Mittie straightened, her attention to the stage once more, "they're starting with the first act."

The first act began with similar lengthy speeches, dramatic acting, and, of course, many tears. Jon Starr, fittingly named, stood out among the ensemble with his natural charisma and acting skills. Before Tracey knew it, the curtains fell, and the lights brightened once more. "How d'ya enjoy it?" Mittie asked excitedly, turning to everyone.

"I've never seen anything like it," Tracey said, still staring at the closed curtains. "I couldn't even tell what the plot was, in fact."

"He was wonderful," sighed Harriet.

"Was all right," shrugged Charlie. "Kinda long, if ya ask me."

"Exceptional as always," Bentam said approvingly.

"I loved it," Mittie said. "To think we got front row!"

"I think that he looked at us as the curtains were closing, though," Tracey said, standing. "We need to leave before the intermission ends. Come along, Charlie."

As Tracey guided Charlie from the aisle, the older woman leaned into the aisle and grabbed Tracey's arm. "Really, a lovely family!" she said, shaking Tracey's hand.

"Y-yes, thank you—"

"Do tell me, do you live here in Mondon?"

"Well—"

"I would *love* to invite your family and friend for tea someday! Please, let's sit and talk about the performance and our favorite parts!"

"What's with this lady?" Charlie quietly hissed to Tracey. Tracey discreetly kicked his foot.

"They were just heading to the powder room," Bentam said, stepping behind her. "But we three here would be more than happy to talk with you."

Appeased, the woman returned to her seat and engaged in conversation with them instead. Bentam subtly nodded to Tracey, and the two made their escape out of Stateshire Theatre.

"*Testing the steamgear,*" Tracey said as they stepped outside. "*Can you hear us?*"

"*We can hear you loud n' clear, Trace!*" Mittie cheerfully replied. "*I'm in the phone booth right now. Seemed to be the safest place to wait to hear from you. I'll keep this on, and we're all listening. Just let us know when you find Mrs. Pinot and we'll see ourselves out.*"

"*Got it,*" Tracey replied.

"Well, now that that's out of the way..." Charlie said. He pulled out Mr. Porter's book from his shirt.

"Charlie! Were you carrying that the whole time?" Tracey gasped.

"Sure! The ruffles did a good job hidin' this!" he cheerfully said. "Didn't want to be bored on the walk over, y'see?"

"No, I don't. It's only a five-minute walk."

"I'm going to try open this an' see if there're any more clues that we could use. I think I'm close to openin' it!" he continued, ignoring Tracey's quip. The two slipped into the evening, away from the lights of Stateshire Theatre and toward the lights of Baldgrass Theatre.

By the time they reached Baldgrass Theatre, Charlie had stuffed the book back into his shirt in frustration and claimed "It's impossible to open!"

"Check if your steamgear is working or not, Charlie," Tracey said before they opened the theater's main doors.

The two took a few quick seconds before determining it was time to connect to the private frequency.

*"We're signing off, everyone,"* Tracey said into the piece.

*"Okay, be safe,"* came back Mittie's delayed response.

"Let's go," Tracey said as she swung the doors open.

The atmosphere of Baldgrass Theatre was starkly different from the atmosphere of Stateshire Theatre. Although it was ornate, it was noticeably simpler than Stateshire. Perhaps the dim lights helped with this illusion, as it was difficult to see far. The golden ornate details could very well have been scraps of metal, for all Tracey knew. Perhaps the most noticeable difference, however, was the appearance of the audience.

Their attire was far less formal than those of the other theater, some even donning work uniforms. Tracey and Charlie looked at their elaborate outfits. "Tracey, we stand out like a sore thumb," he said.

"We do," she agreed.

Surprisingly, however, the guests were not focused as much on Tracey and Charlie as they had feared they would. Instead, they were gathered around a man in the center of the lobby— the ticket master, Tracey assumed—angrily yelling at him. "What do you mean, 'Jon Starr isn't here yet'?" a man roared. "The performance was supposed to start at eight!"

"I was here from six in the morning!" another person yelled. "Gimmie back me money!"

"I missed work for this!"

"Can't believe I fell for one a' these scam performances!"

"I'm sorry," the ticket master calmly replied. "No. Refunds."

"Oy! I say that we ransack this place and get every penny back!"

"Riot!"

"We won't stand for this!"

"Now, now," the ticket master interjected. "Let's not riot, shall we. I promise, if you refrain from rioting until at least...hm...ten o'clock, you will see Jon Starr and each get an autograph."

The crowd broke into a humming murmur.

"Really?" someone finally replied.

"Yes, but not so much as a peep from any of you," he said, wagging a finger. "We apologize for any inconveniences this may have caused."

The audience parted, disgruntled. Tracey leaned toward the boy. "Charlie," she said, "be careful. I'll check the powder room, and you check this foyer. Check the crowds, and if nothing, we'll go into the auditorium."

Charlie nodded and trotted off. Tracey slipped into the powder room, scanning the women within. All of them were huddled in front of the mirror, quietly chattering to each other. A quick scan proved that Mrs. Pinot was not one of them. As Tracey turned to leave, however, someone called her back. "You there, miss!" one of the women said, waving to her. "That's a pretty dress you've got there."

"Thank you," Tracey awkwardly replied.

"We're talking about how we're going to get back our money. You look like you might have influence."

"Oh, no. No, I do not—"

"Sure you do," another one interrupted. "With a getup like that, anyone could have influence."

"I'm just looking for a friend."

"Of influence?"

"No," Tracey sighed. "Look, just call the constables if you want your money back."

The women broke into chortles of laughter. "And get ourselves arrested instead? No thank ya, miss!"

"Excuse me," Tracey said as she slipped out, closing the door on the cackling.

"Found her?" Charlie said, weaving through the crowd toward Tracey.

"No," she replied.

"I glanced in the auditorium. There wasn't anybody in there, 'cept for one man." Charlie frowned. "He kept askin' me where the refreshments were. Kinda scary, y'know? Like he was gonna riot on *me* if I didn't give him any refreshments. Do I look like a server to you?"

"No," Tracey reassured him. She paused, looking at his sharp outfit. "Well, maybe? Everyone here is a bit strange, at any rate."

"Well, that leaves us one spot," Charlie said as the two rounded the corner and went down a dark hallway. "Up ahead!" he said, pointing.

A door occupied the back wall of the hall, adorned with a large sign: BACKSTAGE—STAFF ONLY. It was ajar, revealing the plank flooring of the backstage within.

"Good! It's opened!" Tracey said, reaching for the door. Upon trying to open the door, however, she was met with resistance. "Why won't it open further?"

The door remained ajar, but no amount of budging opened it. "That gap looks big. Let me slip in and see what I can do," Charlie offered.

"I don't like the idea of that, Charlie. We shouldn't separate where we can't reach each other." Tracey scarcely said these words before he began squeezing himself in.

"This book," he grumbled, taking it out of his shirt and tossing it to Tracey. "Hold this for me, will ya?"

"Charlie, wait—"

Charlie slipped through the gap in the door. "Huh," he said. "There are locks on the hinge, Trace! Neva' seen this kind before."

He tried several moments of jiggling and shaking before sighing.

"If I had my lockpickin' kit on me, I could'a done this inna snap." He frowned. "Probably wouldn't have been possible, anyway. I could barely fit the book with me as it is with this rusty outfit."

"Charlie," Tracey said, warningly. "Let's just go. I'm sure we can find another way in."

"I think we'll get caught if we try any otha' way to get back here Trace," Charlie replied. "And this might be our only chance at findin' Mrs. Pinot."

"If it means we must separate," Tracey said, exasperated. "Is it really that important to confirm if she's here or not?" *I'm starting to have second guesses.*

"I'd rather we knew for sure, though," he said. "Don't worry, I'll be careful!" Charlie stuck a hand out the door and waved before disappearing deeper into the area. *"Use the steamgear, Trace!"* he said, his voice sounding in her earpiece.

*"What do you see?"* Tracey asked, wincing at the tinny edge that the machine added to his voice.

*"Nothing so far,"* Charlie said. *"But then again, there's a lot of rooms. Let me check down...oh, no, it's just a dead end."*

*"It would be much faster if we were both in there,"* Tracey lamented.

*"Lemme check this room—gears! All these costumes! Wonda' if I could change my out—"*

*"Stay focused, Charlie,"* Tracey said. She sighed, looking around at the dismal hallway. She could hear the crowd

beginning to riot again out in the foyer. *"They're getting pretty unhappy out there."*

*"I'm hurrying!"* he replied. *"Oh, a pirate's hat!"*

*"Charlie, are you* still *in there?"*

*"Sorry, sorry!"* Charlie said. *"It's really big in here, though."*

*"What makes you think that she'd be in a costume room?"*

*"I dunno...maybe for a nice hat?"*

Tracey sighed. *"If only we could have found a key for the door."*

*"Hold on, I think I hear her! I'm hearing some voices 'round the corner."*

*"You do?"*

*"Yeah!"* Charlie paused. *"Wait, Tracey, I think they're coming this way."*

*"What?"*

*"Lemme hide."*

Tracey could hear some rummaging noises.

*"Charlie? What's that sound?"*

*"Tryn'a find a good hidin' place. These costumes in this area are kinda sparse."*

*"Are you hidden?"*

"*Yes,*" he replied, even quieter than before. "*I hope. Oh, that's not Mrs. Pinot...*"

"*Who is it?*"

"*It's—*" Charlie abruptly stopped. From her end, Tracey picked up the sound of heavy footsteps getting louder. It stopped.

"*Will you look at that,*" a gruff voice sounded. "*Got ourselves a hide'way!*"

"*Rollo!*" Tracey gasped, remembering Jon Starr's unfriendly chef.

"*And what's this here?*" The voice grew louder, and the mic muffled with sounds of struggle. "*A little steam talker? Isn't that just the polished chrome?*" the cook boomed. It sounded as if his mouth were right on the speaker. "*Hellooo, who's there?*"

Tracey held her breath.

"*Nev'a mind that. What do you think we should do with the boy, Hassan?*"

"*Don't you think the funhouse sounds like a wonderful idea, Rollo?*" Tracey heard Jon's butler say, his voice somewhat more distant.

Rollo chuckled. "*Of course. Well, boy—*"

"*Let go of me!*" Charlie yelled.

"*Charlie!*" Tracey shouted.

*"We've got a voice!"* Rollo said, his voice once again loud. *"Look here, miss, we've got the boy. Drop whatever you're sniffing 'round in, and we might let 'im go."*

*"Lay a finger on Charlie, Rollo, and—"* Tracey fumed.

*"And what? It's too late,"* he said with a triumphant laugh. *"And that's Mr. Nicolson, to you."*

*Rollo Nicholson?* Tracey thought, her eyes widening. *"So you are RN!"*

*"Whatever ye mean by that...RN are my initials, yes?"*

*"That means—"*

*"Look here, I'm not here to chitchat or solve some puzzle with you or whatever. I've got places to go, people to see. All the best with...whatever you're up to."*

*"Wait, what about Char—"*

Tracey was interrupted by a loud crunch before hearing sickening static come from the other side. She crouched, slowly sitting for a few seconds. *Another kidnapping?* she thought in disbelief. The noise of the riot outside crescendoed into breaking glass.

Numbly, she turned the dial on the device, connecting to the main frequency. *"Are you all still there?"* she said, her voice quiet and hoarse.

A delay.

"*Yes,*" Bentam's distorted voice said. "*I've stepped out. Do we need to go now, Ms. Higgenbottom?*"

"*I've got to leave,*" Tracey said, glancing in alarm at the sound of constables' whistling. "*Charlie's gone,*" she said. "*They've gotten him.*"

# Act II

# CHAPTER 16

# In Which a Familiar Face Appears

TRACEY HIGGENBOTTOM stared listlessly into the unlit fireplace, back at her own residence. In her hands were the few pieces of evidence that she had to work with:

Mr. Porter's glasses and ring.

The handkerchief with the initials of RN.

The document of Mrs. Pinot's ticket purchases.

And the locked notebook that Charlie had hurriedly given her before they had split up.

Tracey sighed and touched the book's cover, setting the other items aside. A gentle knock sounded from the doorway. She looked up. There stood Mittie, holding a small box.

"Hey, Trace, I was lookin' in your cupboards an' found some tea," she said with a sympathetic smile. "D'ya want some?"

"Yes," she gloomily said, dejectedly setting the book aside with the rest of the evidence. "Let me help you find some cups."

The two worked in silence, only broken by a few intermittent discussions of where to find utensils or ingredients. Tracey noticed Mittie stealing glances at her but saying nothing. "So," Mittie finally said. "Looks like it's just the two of us again."

Tracey took her cup and sat, staring once more at the fireplace. Mittie followed her gaze, then looked back at her.

"I'm sure that Harrie and Bentam will rejoin us soon," she offered.

Tracey frowned, thinking about the events of the previous night. "I'm sure Bentam made it quite clear that he will no longer be helping us."

"He was rather upset, yes," Mittie sighed. "A real shame that evenin' should'a ended so sour. Ya know, you even missed Jon! He came after the show and personally thanked us! I could'a dropped right there..."

Mittie trailed off, gazing wistfully at the fireplace. Shaking herself, she directed her attention back to Tracey. "I'm sorry, Trace. I'm sure you're in a terrible state. That was thoughtless of me."

"It's all right, Mittie," she replied dryly. "I can understand why Harriet went with Bentam, however. I'm certain the High Constable will close Charlie's case quickly, especially with Bentam's help."

"Poor Charlie. Looks like we've actually got a case of plagium now," Mittie said, frowning. "Don't you think that it was a bit strange that Jon Starr's staff was there at that fake performance? Why would Rollo and Hassan be there, of all places?"

"I was thinking about that, yes," Tracey said, thinking about her conversation with the chef and butler. "The best I can come up with is that she must've been behind those fraudulent performances. Rollo and Hassan are likely secretly working with her. That could be why Harriet saw them by her house that night, and why Charlie ran into them backstage. She kidnapped Mr. Porter because he discovered she was orchestrating the fake performances. He may have tried to report it."

"Solid theory. But why would she buy the tickets, then?" Mittie said, leaning over and taking up the bank ledger. "It'd hardly make sense for her to buy tickets to fake performances that she made herself."

"To throw off suspicion, perhaps?" Tracey said. "Whatever the case, I have reason to believe that Charlie and Mr. Porter are in the same place."

"Right. The funhouse," Mittie thoughtfully agreed.

"It's strange, though," Tracey said. "Why wouldn't they just call Mrs. Pinot's house for what it is? Why call it the funhouse?"

"Perhaps it's an alias? We should ask around to see if her home has any other names."

"Perhaps..."

"I wish we had a chance to get into her home before this debacle," Tracey sighed. "What if the funhouse is an entirely different place, and they've split up Charlie and Mr. Porter? That means we missed our opportunity to end everything last night."

"Right," Mittie said, her shoulders slumping. She sipped her tea and stared at the pile of evidence. "We don't have much to work with. Mr. Porter's glasses aren't much help, and Rollo's handkerchief won't do much either." Mittie paused. Her eyes lightened. "But we have the book!" she said. "That book could hold loads of information!"

"Unfortunately, Mr. Porter never shared with me how to open his journal," Tracey replied. "And Charlie himself couldn't open it."

"Let's back up a bit. Maybe we don't need the book to find them. We've got the best clue yet, Tracey!"

"What's that?" Tracey wearily replied, taking another sip of tea.

"They said the funhouse, so why don't we make good on that trip and go now?"

"To a real funhouse?" Tracey groaned.

"Why not? They said it themselves." Mittie downed her cup and jumped up. "There's plenty of time for us to look an' come back."

"I suppose—why not," Tracey said. She finished her cup of tea and stood, gathering the evidence into various pockets of her dress.

"Oh, wait..." Mittie said.

"What?"

"No, no it won't work. There are too many funhouses in Mondon."

"Not unless we can narrow it down," Tracey thoughtfully said. "You saw Rollo and Mr. Porter go to The Undertown at one point. Why don't we start back to square one?" Tracey said. "Not many people have the nerve to run a business down in The Undertown, let alone an amusement attraction. Shrimp Reginald, however, has a funhouse attached to it."

"Really? That restaurant that Charlie called nasty?"

"You remembered that?"

"Have a good mem'ry," Mittie shrugged.

"Well," Tracey continued, "I've always heard that the only reason why they can keep running that restaurant is because of the funhouse." Tracey walked to the doorway and turned back to Mittie. "Shall we go?"

"Looks like rain," Mittie said as they made their way into the foyer. She peered through the front door's glass. Thunder rumbled in the distance.

"Here, I have some umbrellas," Tracey said as she handed one to her.

"Wait," Mittie said, squinting as she peered through the door's windowpanes. "Trace, were you expecting guests?"

"No," Tracey replied, donning a raincoat. "Why?"

Lightning briefly flashed, revealing a dark figure through the glass. Mittie and Tracey scrambled from the door. "Maybe that's Bentam?" Mittie said, her eyes wide.

The figure knocked, each pounding hit rattling the poor door.

"Is Bentam the sort of person to bang down doors?" Tracey replied, slowly taking her coat off.

"Should we steam the Constables?" Mittie said, backing toward the steam telephone on the entry table.

"Tracey Higgenbottom!" the figure yelled, banging the door more insistently.

Tracey paused, squinting at the door. "Wait," she said as she edged closer. "I recognize this voice."

"Are you *sure?*" Mittie said incredulously.

Tracey put her hand on the handle.

"Wait, Trace—"

Before she could talk herself out of the action, Tracey swung open the door. A gust of wind swept in the rain as the person scrambled inside, pushing past Tracey and slamming the door behind themselves. "I thought you'd never let me in," the figure gruffly said, shaking their hat and placing their soggy coat over Tracey's on the coatrack.

"Mr. Matthews!" Tracey gushed, quickly moving his coat to another hook and turning to face the banker. "What a surprise!"

"William Matthews?" Mittie said in bewilderment.

"Yes, the same Mr. William Matthews," he said, as he roughly combed through his hair and dusted his jacket. "Now," he said, carefully stepping out of the puddle of water his entrance had created, and looking between the two with distrustful eyes, "where is the book?"

# CHAPTER 17

# In Which Motor-Mail Sends a Clue

MR. WILLIAM MATTHEWS stood before Tracey and Mittie, his bushy mustache quivering with rage, and his eyes sharply darting between the two. "Well?" he demanded. "The book?"

"I'm sorry, Mr. Matthews, but you must explain why you're here," Tracey replied. "How did you find where I live?"

"You should have thought of the consequences when you stole Remington's Keeper Book," he huffed. Mr. Mathews marched into the sitting room and proceeded to rifle through a nearby bookcase, carefully placing books onto the mantelpiece as he flicked through its pages.

"I stole nothing!" Tracey indignantly said as she picked up the displaced books and returned them to the shelves. "And I would hardly think you'd find his book in this fashion. Do you think I've somehow hidden his book inside of another book's pages?" she scoffed.

"So you *do* have it?"

"I never said so," Tracey said, carefully keeping her gaze from the side table where she had earlier placed it.

"Do you know what it looks like?" Mittie said, venturing into the room.

"Of course, I don't!" he exclaimed. "He's never shown it to me." Mr. Matthews moved his search to the neighboring bookshelf, this time carelessly tossing books aside as he looked.

"Mr. Matthews," Tracey said, quickly stepping to his side and grabbing a book mid-air. "Mr. Porter may be a friend of yours, but I've only just met you yesterday. As far as I see it, you're an intruder entering and ransacking my home."

"You are rather forceful about all of this," Mittie quietly added.

"If you knew the importance of a Keeper Book, you'd understand," he replied, moving to the next shelf.

"And why are you so convinced that I have it?" Tracey retorted.

Mr. Matthews ignored her.

"Mr. Matthews," Tracey evenly said. "I've had a long night. Seeing that you will not cooperate, I have no choice but to call the constables."

Mr. Matthews paused, shooting a sharp gaze toward her.

"Wait a minute, Trace," Mittie said in alarm.

"You've somehow located where I live, barged into my home, and proceeded to search for a book that I may or may not have," Tracey listed. "I'm sure the High Constable would enjoy hearing this case of stalking."

Mr. Matthews held Tracey's gaze for a few moments before sighing in defeat. Internally, Tracey let out her own sigh of relief. "I apologize for the abruptness of my arrival, Ms. Higgenbottom," he said as he straightened his suit. "You must understand the circumstances of this situation."

"And that would be?" Tracey asked, raising an eyebrow.

"May I have a seat?"

"Oh, you need permission to sit?" she dryly replied. "Here," she said, pointing to a modest stool.

Mr. Matthews hesitated, his eyes darting to one of the plusher seats.

"Mittie, why don't you join us?" Tracey said, sitting on the plump sofa.

Hesitantly, Mittie entered the room. "Are you sure? Because it seems a bit tense in here."

"No, it's quite all right," Mr. Matthews sighed, perching onto the stool. He frowned as he settled on the wooden seat, then cleared his throat. "Again, I do apologize for barging in here so abruptly. You must be wondering why I'm here," he said as Mittie settled onto the couch beside Tracey.

"Moreso, why you need this book so much?" Mittie replied.

"So you do have it?" Mr. Matthews boomed, eagerly leaning forward.

Mittie glanced at Tracey, who returned the look with a small shake of her head.

"You *must* understand!" Mr. Matthews said, "I should have known something was wrong when you asked about the letter."

"The letter?" Tracey blinked.

"You had asked about Mr. Porter contacting me!"

"Oh!" Tracey said. "Oh, yes. That I did."

"There was a lot that happened since we went to the bank," Mittie said with a shrug.

"What about the letter?" Tracey asked, leaning forward.

"Well, I did find it." Mr. Matthews shifted in his seat as if he made a groundbreaking revelation.

Tracey and Mittie stirred in uncertainty.

"And?" Tracey finally said.

"And I found that he sent the letter to me with *motor-mail*!" he said, his emphasis on the final words almost at a roar.

"What's wrong with motor-mail?" Mittie asked before Tracey could bump her foot in warning.

Mr. Mathews whipped his head around to face Mittie, his eyes ablaze. "What's wrong with *motor-mail*?" he spat. "I'll tell you what's wrong with motor-mail! Those nefarious abominations are a threat to the very existence of good, well-cultured letters! *Real* letters, miss, not these excuses of paper that come through those atrocious pip—"

"Mr. Matthews is not a fan of steam technology," Tracey interrupted.

"I see," Mittie said with a slow nod, casting a surreptitious glance at Tracey's motor-mail receiver in the other corner of the room.

"Don't you see?" he continued. "Remington would never send me letters through motor-mail!"

"How did you not realize this sooner?" Tracey asked, narrowing her eyes. "Surely you would realize it was motor-mail if you took it from the machine's receiver?"

"I'm a lead banker—I don't sort my mail myself," Mr. Matthews said, waving his hand. "I should have known something was strange when he sent you in his stead for our weekly meetings."

"Weekly meetings?" Tracey asked, frowning. She would have remembered if Mr. Porter had meetings with anyone, considering she made his schedules for him. "What meetings?"

"Our Keeper Embassy meetings, of..." Mr. Matthews trailed off. "I've said too much. Please," he said, rising from the stool with a grimace, "I need the book, Ms. Higgenbottom."

"Does this book have anything to do with these...meetings?" Tracey asked, her suspicions rising.

Mr. Matthews paused, his jaw clenched. "The book, Ms. Higgenbottom."

"We never said we had it," Mittie said with a nonchalant shrug.

"This book seems rather important to you," Tracey said. She tilted her head and squinted at him. Mr. Matthews seemed to shrink under her gaze. "And thus far, you've been avoiding answering our questions. Why do you need this book?"

He frowned, then, once more, sighed in defeat. "The Keeper Embassy," he said quietly (or rather, as quietly as his booming voice allowed). "That book contains important information on it."

"And what is this 'Keeper Embassy?'"

At the mention of those words, Mr. Matthews flinched and cast a glare at Tracey. "I've already told you too much," he growled. "Remington was supposed to have given me that book at our last meeting. It was a very important meeting as this would be the first time I would get my hands on his Keeper Book.

"I thought that when he sent you in his stead, you would have brought the book. But you didn't." Mr. Matthew shook his head. "I really should have known something was wrong. I'm sorry I've wasted your time. I'll see myself out."

"Wait," Tracey said, jumping from her seat. "Why did you give me that document on Mrs. Pinot?"

Mr. Matthews hesitated. "That's what Remington told me to give you."

"In that letter?"

"Yes."

"But we know now that wasn't Mr. Porter," Mittie chimed in, her eyebrows furrowed.

"Yes?" he said, more perplexed.

"I wonder who it could have been," Tracey said. She shook herself, whisking past Mr. Matthews into the foyer. "We'll evaluate that later," she said, squinting out of the window. "It appears it's still raining. Would you like an umbrella? I'm afraid they're steam-powered, however."

Tracey cringed, waiting for his booming response.

"Mr. Matthews?" she said, turning around.

Much to Tracey's bewilderment, she saw Mittie desperately pointing to the other side of the room. Tracey moved her gaze in the direction of Mittie's finger. There was Mr. Matthews standing by her motor-mail, his face expressionless.

"O-oh, I do apologize for that!" she exclaimed, rushing over. "I know how you feel about steam technology—"

"Ms. Higgenbottom, do you know who sent this?" Mr. Matthews interrupted, holding up a small object in his hand.

Tracey noticed he held a familiar brown sachet. On it was extraordinarily small text. "Rip here," it read.

"Say, isn't that combustible..." Mittie started. She stopped, glancing at Mr. Matthews.

"Where did you get this?" Tracey quietly asked, taking the envelope from him.

"Where else but from this confounded junk of technology?" he spat. "I ask you again, Ms. Higgenbottom, do you know who sent this? There's no return. Of course," he added with a disgruntled mutter, "*real* mail would never have this sort of problem."

"I don't know who sent this," Tracey said, "but whoever did is the same person who sent me to you."

"Really?" he said, his voice near yelling volume.

"We had gotten one a' those sachets a couple o' days ago," Mittie said, walking over to look closer at the sachet. "Believe it said something like: talk to William Matthews for more information on your 'precious Porter.'"

"What?" he boomed, louder yet. "Is that what they sent you? I have no information on Remington—I thought he was out of town on business. What is going on here?"

"Well—" Tracey started.

"You know," he barreled on, distracted, "this is the same sort of envelope that Mr. Porter supposedly sent me his letter in!"

"You didn't notice anything...strange with the paper?" Tracey asked.

"Of course not! He always types his letters," he replied. "And unlike this parcel, it had a return address. To his shop. Which is why I saw nothing out of the ordinary."

"So the paper didn't..." Mittie slowly said.

"...didn't what?"

"...you know..." Mittie said, miming out a plume of clouds.

Mr. Matthews stared inquisitively.

"Did it combust?" she finally said with a frustrated sigh.

"Why would it?" he said, his eyebrows furrowing. "Have yours?"

"That's not important," Tracey quickly said.

"If yours have, you may want to check Shrimp Reginald."

"Thank you, Mr. Matthews," Tracey said, ushering him to the foyer. "We're actually quite busy. I hope that we answered your questions, and..." Tracey paused, her hand on the doorknob. "Did you say 'Shrimp Reginald'?"

"Yes, that's where you can buy the stuff, combustible paper. Only seller in the entire city."

"How do you know that?"

"I know many things, Ms. Higgenbottom."

"How many things does that restaurant have?" Mittie exclaimed. "A funhouse, and now illegal goods?"

"Funhouse?" he repeated in surprise. The foyer shook with his laughter. "Is that what you think it is?"

"What's the funhouse? Isn't it a funhouse?" Tracey asked.

"Oh, it may *look* like a funhouse, but I assure you: if you know where you're going in that place, you can find The Marketplace."

"The Marketplace?" Mittie and Tracey echoed.

"You can find anything you need there," he said with a nod. "Even...steam technology." Mr. Matthews said the final words with a shudder.

"How would we get into The Marketplace?" Tracey asked.

"Just ask Reggie for"—Mr. Matthews paused, glancing out the door. His voice lowered to a whisper (or, rather, a rumble)—"'The Mirrored Funhouse.'"

"Reggie?" Mittie repeated, perking up.

"Do you know him?"

"N-no, just happens to be my beau's nickname."

"I see."

"So we ask for 'Mirrored Funhouse' then—" Tracey started.

"*The* Mirrored Funhouse," he corrected. "Very important."

"Right," Tracey said, nodding.

"Now!" Mr. Matthews said with a flourish, gently moving Tracey's hand off the door and opening it himself. "I came here for information and ended up revealing everything myself!" he chuckled. "My lunch break is almost up, so I must return to the bank."

"This is how you spend your lunches?" Mittie said in bewilderment.

"If you have the book, please be certain to keep it away from prying hands," he said as he leveled a glare at the two of them, ignoring the remark. "I hope to see you soon."

With that, Mr. Matthews stormed out the door, unbothered by the wind, rain, and occasional lighting brewing around him.

Tracey turned to Mittie, propping the door open. "Well," she finally said.

"Looks like we were on the right track," Mittie said with a shrug.

"If this 'Mirrored Funhouse' is the same place as the funhouse Rollo mentioned, we may be able to find Charlie." *I hope I'm wrong about Mr. Porter being at Mrs. Pinot,* Tracey thought. *I hope he's with Charlie—then we could find the both of them!* "And figure out who's sending these combustible notes once and for all!"

"Guess we should really head out now?"

"Yes," Tracey said, reaching in and taking her coat from the coat rack. Mittie grabbed some umbrellas. In short order, the two ladies were once again off to The Undertown.

# CHAPTER 18

# In Which We Return to Shrimp Reginald

If The Undertown was already gloomy on Mondon's sunniest of days, rainy days were downright dreadful. Tracey and Mittie darted through the twisting streets, narrowly missing bouts of water as rain converged and rushed off the crooked roofs above. "Somehow, this feels much longer than the last time we were here," Mittie panted as the two darted into yet another alcove. "It's a shame we lost the umbrellas so quickly."

"Yes," Tracey agreed with a solemn nod. She scanned the streets ahead for another shelter before darting out to another spot. "I've forgotten how easily they're stolen in The Undertown."

"I'm not sure if you'd call ripping an object from someone a theft. That was more like an attack," Mittie grumbled. "My hair's ruined with all this rain."

"It's impossible to stay dry in this weather," Tracey sympathetically said. "Thankfully, we should be there soon." She scanned the streets. "If I could see anything in all of this rain..."

"Wait."

"I think I see it up there!" Tracey said, taking a few paces toward her next target.

"Trace, wait!"

"What?" Tracey said, turning back.

"Is that the back entrance for Shrimp Reginald?"

She glanced to the alleyway where Mittie pointed, barely catching a glimpse of a blonde figure ducking into the doorway. As the door slammed shut, a sign swung into view: *"Shrimp Regina-"* (the last two letters were worn from age, unfortunately). "Yes, it is," Tracey agreed.

"Who do you think that was?" Mittie said with a frown.

"If I didn't know better," Tracey dryly jested, "I'd say that was Jon Starr."

Instead of an expected chuckle, Tracey turned to see Mittie staring at the back door, her face still fixed in the frown.

"Is everything okay?" she slowly said.

"Just wonderful!" Mittie abruptly said, her usual cheerful smile flashing on her face. "Why don't we go in? Don't know why we're still standing 'ere in this rain."

With those words, Mittie trotted around the cluster of buildings. "But..." Tracey started. She sighed. "Never mind," she muttered to herself as she followed Mittie through the crooked alleys of The Undertown.

Tracey and Mittie coughed as they entered Shrimp Reginald, batting away the plumes of dust kicked into motion from the movement of the front door.

"Welcome to *Shrimp Reginald*, where you can find the finest 'seafood' away from the sea," a woman said, standing from her seat by the door.

"Why are you doing air quotes?" Mittie asked, bewildered.

"For 'seafood,'" she flatly replied, making the quotes again. "The food's not too bad, though. Today's special is pickled cookies. May I seat you?"

Tracey observed her surroundings. The restaurant was largely empty, save for a lone diner who stared in dismay at their dish. It did not take much investigation to see the lump of charred food on their platter was the 'seafood' in question.

Mittie discreetly bumped Tracey's shoulder, pointing to another corner. There stood a sign leaning against the wall. She squinted to read beyond the buildup of dirt and grime on its surface.

*Please do not feed the rats. Thank you.*

"Ah," Tracey said. "N-no, that won't be necessary. We're here on inquiry, as a matter of fact. May we talk to Reggie?"

"What if I were to tell you *I* was Reggie?" the woman responded.

"Oh!" Tracey blinked in surprise. "Are you?"

The woman blankly stared. "No," she finally said. "But I can show you to him. Please follow me."

The woman whisked past them to a small door in the back of the space. Tracey and Mittie followed suit, stepping through the doorway. Tracey glanced down, noting that the wooden floors of the restaurant had given way to worn, gray stone.

"So many people come for Reggie, I begin to wonder if anyone comes here for the food anymore," the woman mournfully said, as they turned another corner and opened another door. "No one ever comes in and says, 'Louise, can you seat me?' No, it's always 'Where's Reggie?', 'Show me where Reggie is!' 'I've got business with Reggie!'"

Mittie cast a side glance at Tracey, who grimaced in return. They entered yet another set of doors.

"Here we are," the woman sighed. "Please, wait here."

"Thank you, ehrm..." Tracey paused.

"Just Louise is fine," she mournfully supplied.

"Yes, thank you, Louise."

Louise entered a thick set of doors opposite them, slamming it shut behind her. Tracey glanced about at the dark and cramped space.

Other than four, towering walls made of rocks, it was empty. The floors were made of dirt—or perhaps stone (it was difficult to tell past the thick layer of grime)—and littered with scraps of paper and trash from visitors past. "This is depressing," Tracey said. "It's like a prison."

As a matter of fact, the room was indeed strikingly similar to a dungeon.

"This restaurant is bigger than I thought it'd be! Who'd think all this is back here?" Mittie said, kicking a stray piece of paper into a corner. A dark object darted from the corner and into a crack at the base of the stone wall. "Well, I'm ready to leave," she squeaked, shuffling away from the walls. "How 'bout you?"

"The sooner we get into this Marketplace, or funhouse—or whatever this thing is—get a lead on who bought this paper, and maybe find Charlie, the better," Tracey said, carefully patting her pocket, where she had stowed the unopened combustible note.

Louise ducked back into the space. "You can leave," she said unceremoniously.

"What?" Tracey asked in dismay. "Why?"

"He ain't taking any customers. Terribly sorry."

"Why not?" Mittie said.

"He didn't say."

"Can we at least go in to see him?" Tracey asked, stepping forward.

"No," Louise responded, stepping out and closing the door behind herself. "You're welcome to have a late lunch at Shrimp Reginald, however—"

"No," Mittie and Tracey said at the same time.

Louise sighed. "Well, I can't help you, then!"

"Will Reggie take a message?" Mittie said.

"I guess," she replied with a shrug. "But I doubt he'll listen. I've never seen him this adamant before."

"Can he direct us," Tracey slowly said, encouraged by a supportive nod from Mittie, "to The Mirrored Funhouse?"

Louise paused, her eyes darting between the two. "The...Mirrored Funhouse, you say?"

"That's right," Mittie said.

"I see..." she slowly said. "Just one moment, please." Louise reentered behind the large wooden doors.

"I was hoping she would let us in," Mittie sighed.

No sooner did she say this than the doors swung open once more. "You may enter," Louise said as she pushed the door wider and gestured in.

Tracey hesitated, trying her best to catch a glimpse of what lay beyond the entry.

"Come on, Trace!" Mittie said, stepping forward. "What're we waitin' for?"

"It's quite safe, miss," Louise nonchalantly said. "Then again, if you made it this far into The Undertown, the funhouse should be the least of your worries."

"Well," Tracey hesitantly said. She paused. If she were to get any closer to finding Mr. Porter and Charlie, now was not the time for her to hesitate. *And this message*, she thought, once again patting her pocket. *I need to find who's sending these.* "Well," she started again, more decidedly, "let's go. Standing around won't get us anywhere."

The two walked into the room, each squinting as their eyes adjusted to the even darker atmosphere. On the back wall were a couple of small candles, hardly large enough to illuminate the patch of wall immediately behind them, let alone the room. Between the meager candles hung a large portrait, the subject's face unfortunately obscured in the gloom. Other than these simple decorations stood a desk and stately chair, absent of the said Reggie. "Where's Reggie?" Mittie asked, turning back to Louise.

"He told me to lead you there myself," she replied. "Rather strange, if you ask me. He's never done that before. Reggie's always the one to lead customers to The Mirrored Funhouse. Say," she said as she carefully closed the door again, "do you two know him? That would make sense as to why he was acting the way he was..."

"I wouldn't know," Tracey said. "We know many people, and this is our first time coming here. Could you describe him?"

"Well...he looks a lot like him over there," she said, pointing to the painting. "I'm not very good at describing people. Sorry."

"I can't even see what color his hair is," Mittie muttered, squinting and leaning forward. "Can we look closer?"

"No," Louise said, shaking her head. "Reggie always says no one can go behind the desk except for him."

"Can you at least tell us how tall he is? Eye color? Hair color?" Tracey asked, exasperated.

"Anything?" Mittie added.

"Hm," Louise tilted her head in thought. "I guess you could say he's blond...or is he a brunet?"

"Okay," Tracey said, slowly nodding.

"Ehrm," she continued, "his eyes are blue—no—gray. Wait, no—black? Huh, I never paid attention to his eye color before."

"I see," Mittie said with a sigh.

"And I'd say he's around this tall." Louise vaguely waved in the air.

"I don't think I could tell anyone from that description," Tracey said.

"Me either," Mittie agreed, her face unamused and borderline annoyed.

"Oh, well, I tried," Louise said with a carefree shrug. "Let's get going to that funhouse, no?"

"Will we get an opportunity to talk to him later?" Tracey asked.

"Doubt it. Unless you catch him in the funhouse. He said he had to do some runs in there before you arrive...or something like that. Anyway, follow me!"

Louise walked past the two of them to one of the candles. With a pull of its base, the entire wall pivoted outward, revealing a well-lit hallway leading to a path that ran beside—but not behind—the desk. Tracey and Mittie exchanged surprised glances before following her down the mirrorless hallway.

# CHAPTER 19

# In Which a Brief Chase Ensues

"AND HERE WE ARE," Louise nonchalantly said as the three approached a dead end.

"Where?" Tracey slowly said, looking around. Besides the long, twisting halls that stretched behind them, there was nothing but the three walls ahead—bland, gray, and decidedly solid.

"The Mirrored Funhouse," she stated in a matter-of-fact tone.

Tracey and Mittie stared at the walls and ceiling surrounding them.

"I believe we've walked ourselves into a trap, Tracey," Mittie said, darting a glance at her.

"I believe so, too," Tracey responded, taking a few cautious steps back.

"What trap?" Louise said, confusion casting over her face. "That's a first. Sure, we may or may not be a...'front,'" she said with a roll of her eyes and a gesture of air quotes, "but we certainly don't *trap* our guests."

The three stood in uncomfortable silence.

"Then why are we here?" Tracey finally said.

"To go to The Mirrored Funhouse, of course!" Louise responded, shrugging her shoulders. She then turned around and pushed at the wall in front of her, slowly revealing a hidden space. "I was just testin' ya, ya know. Usually shows people's true colors when you postpone what they're expecting."

"Right..." Tracey replied with an uncertain glance.

"Welcome to The Mirrored Funhouse," Louise said. "Or as I'm sure you're more familiar with: The Marketplace."

Louise stepped aside to reveal a sprawling room, its farthest corners seemingly nonexistent, disappearing into oblivion. Surprisingly, the space was well-lit with what seemed to be steam-powered lights (albeit there was a suspicious lack of steam for it to be steam-powered). In the center were booths and makeshift tents bustling with people bartering and selling. Although not crowded, it was still busier than Tracey had hoped for. "Do you need help with where to go?" Louise asked.

"If you could just point us toward the combustible paper seller, that'd be great," Mittie said.

"Straight for the contraband, huh?" Louise said, a small frown forming on her face. "If you go down this way," she said, pointing at an aisle, "you'll end up straight at it. Can't miss it. Big black tent."

"Thank you," Tracey and Mittie replied.

"You'll have to excuse me," Louise said with a nod. "Must get back to the shop—can't keep those hungry customers waiting!"

"Right," Mittie said with a bright smile (although Tracey noticed it looked rather strained). Louise turned back and closed the wall, leaving the two in the cavernous Marketplace.

"Wait," Tracey said. "How are we supposed to leave?"

"I'm sure we'll figure it out," Mittie replied with a shrug. "C'mon, Trace, let's go!"

It was not soon after the two began their journey into the space before Mittie became distracted by the booths. "Hallo, madam!" hissed a vendor from his booth. "Would you care to test our newest steam technology?" He held up a strange-looking object. "With this tool," he said, "you can speak to anyone, from any*where!*"

Mittie paused, with Tracey closely following behind. Tracey squinted at the object.

It resembled a large brick, if a brick was lumpy, covered in multiple pieces, and had one long rod sticking from its top. The face of the brick-like device was covered in dials, each dial having a number box above it, not unlike a luggage lock.

"What is that?" Mittie said, peering closer at the object.

"This is an *inter-latitudinal confabulator*!" he replied, raising his head as if to give a dramatic effect.

"A what?" Tracey asked.

"What does it do?" Mittie said.

"I've told you already," he hissed. "You can speak to any*one*, from any*where*!"

"All right, that's fine and all," Mittie said, "but how does it work?"

"*First*, you must have the person you wish to converse with own an inter-latitudinal confabulator themselves. *Then!* You can speak."

They stared at the man. The man returned the stare, lifting his head even more, his chin high in the air. "Okay, so you simply talk into it then," Tracey said.

"Yessss," he replied.

"Can you demonstrate?" Mittie asked. "I could see this being useful."

"Unfortunately, no."

"But I thought you invited us to test it?"

"Yes."

"And now you're saying we can't?"

"No. I simply said I couldn't demonstrate it. This is the *only* inter-latitudinal confabulator in existence."

"Then how are we supposed to test it?"

"See!" he suddenly yelled, cranking a small handle from the side of the contraption. Small puffs of smoke steadily streamed from its top, and a dim light shone from within.

"Oh...it looks like Bentam's fancy record paper!" Mittie exclaimed. "Except it glows!"

"It does, doesn't it?" Tracey agreed, thinking back to the record keeper's portable document...and then back to Charlie. She sighed. "Come on, Mittie," she said. "We've got to find that vendor."

"Oh, all right," Mittie reluctantly replied.

"But wait!" the man exclaimed. "Do you not want to see what other wondrous technologies of the steam world have come to light?"

"Are they fully functional?" Tracey asked.

"Well...they're still works-in-progress, you see—"

"Then no," Tracey said, walking away.

"Some other time!" Mittie graciously said, before jogging after Tracey. "We should come back here sometime!" she said to her. "Ya know, when we actually have some more time...and we're not searching for two kidnapped people."

"Perhaps," Tracey said. "Although you do realize this place is riddled with illegal technology?"

"Right," Mittie said, deflating a bit.

The two wove through vendors and buyers, deftly avoiding the catchy calls of salesmen, and dodging the attempts of merchants trying to stop their journey. Many a time, Mittie was nearly ensnared by yet another seller, but Tracey's determined steps deterred her from stopping. Finally, the row of tents stopped—or, rather, intersected—at another row of tents. There, at the center of the adjacent row, was a large black tent. The dark atmosphere hanging around it rivaled even the gloominess of The Undertown's outdoors. "I never thought it would be so..." Mittie said, stopping a few paces behind Tracey.

"Foreboding?" Tracey offered.

"I was thinking ominous, but same difference."

"Considering that they're selling something as forbidden as combustible paper, I'd expect it to be looking this seedy." As Tracey spoke, she noticed passersby turning to stare at them.

"Combustible paper?" one of them whispered to another, before hurrying away upon meeting Tracey's gaze.

"I guess even a place like The Marketplace has its undesirable products," Mittie said in surprise.

"Maybe we shouldn't call the...you know...by its name anymore. What about a codeword, like—"

"Butter biscuits," Mittie immediately said.

Tracey blinked. "Why?"

"I was thinking about tea. We never did finish our tea," Mittie said. "Sorry. What's the next step after this? We find out where all this paper is coming from, and then what? Look for Charlie and Mr. Porter? This place is bigger than we thought!"

"Actually, I'd rather we find who exactly is buying these...butter biscuits first," Tracey replied. "I'm certain that whoever is sending them must buy them from here. What are the odds that Mr. Matthews was wrong and there's actually another seller of combustibl—"

"Butter biscuits!" Mittie loudly interrupted. A few passersby cast suspicious glances at them.

"Ehm. Yes, butter biscuits. Because that recipe was..." Tracey nervously looked at a particular passerby who had stopped to stare into their conversation. They held her gaze for an unnervingly long amount of time. "Because," she continued, "that recipe was delicious. Right, Mittie?"

"What are you looking at?" Mittie replied.

"Never mind," Tracey said, breaking eye contact with the stranger. "We'll find who's buying out the butter biscuits, then stop by the keeper shop. We might've missed a clue."

The interior of the tent was as dark as its exterior had suggested, and it took some time for Tracey's eyes to adjust to the dim steamlights barely illuminating the space. "Hello?" she called out.

"Hello," a surprisingly friendly voice sounded from the back of the tent. Tracey could make out the figure of a person behind a slew of furniture. "How may I help you? Do you need...anything?"

"Yes, actually," Tracey responded. She crept closer into the tent. "We were wondering if you sell any rare goods?"

"It depends," the voice responded. The figure stood from behind a desk and approached, the closing distance defining the figure's features.

The man's face was narrow—his face covered in the shadow of a beard. His long hair was slicked back on his head in a wavy pattern. He wore a simple attire of black and gray: a black shirt and pants, a pair of black shoes, and a gray vest.

The man's tall stature made the tent feel rather cramped and small. As he came closer yet, his bright and cheerful brown eyes came into view, a stark contrast to his gloomy clothing. He smiled, his trimmed mustache nestling beneath his pointy nose. "What is it that you seek?" he said.

Without hesitation, Tracey whipped out the small, unopened, brown sachet that contained the combustible paper. "Do you sell these?"

"Oh," he said, his voice laced with disappointment. "Yes," he said, turning around. "We sell envelopes—"

"We don't want the envelope, sir," Mittie interrupted. "We want what's inside of it."

"I'm afraid you'd have to open it to let me see," the man said, lifting a box, placing it onto a crammed display table and sorting through papers.

"I'm afraid that won't be possible," Tracey said. "We might...lose it. If you're following what I'm saying."

He paused. "Oh?" he said, slowly setting down a set of envelopes that he had just fished out. "By lose, do you—by any chance—mean that it may...disappear?"

"Paper has a strange way of doing that, don't you think?"

The man stared at Tracey and Mittie, thoughtfully holding each woman's gaze before walking to the back of the tent. "I see," he said, smiling once more. "How long must your notes last before they disappear? One hour? Ten minutes?"

"It depends," Tracey said with a thoughtful tilt of her head. "How many types do you have available?"

"Virtually any," he replied. "This sort of product is rarely asked for, after all."

"Really, now? Has anyone recently bought something like this?" She waved the sachet. "After all, it appears as if you're the only seller of this in all of Mondon."

"Who are you?" the man asked, his eyes squinting.

"Just a couple of women who've received one too many of these notes."

"I'm sorry, I cannot help you," he dismissively replied. "Thank you for visiting."

"Can you at least tell us where you got this paper from?"

The man remained silent.

"C'mon Trace," Mittie finally said. "Let's go. We can find out who keeps sending these notes to the keeper shop elsewhere."

The man stirred. "Did you say...keeper?" he said.

"Yes?" Mittie replied in confusion.

"You know a...'keeper?'"

"Yes," Tracey replied. "Why?"

He frowned. "Well, if you know a keeper—"

"I work for one."

"Ah, I see." His eyes darted around as if searching for a hidden shadow. "I was told not to say anything unless the person asking for this...paper...was affiliated with keepers."

Tracey frowned. "Who told you to?"

The man avoided her gaze. "I was simply told to tell you that the buyer was a woman. Tall. Dark hair in a bun. And sharp eyes."

"That sounds a lot like..." Mittie started.

"Corsetta Pinot," Tracey grimly finished. "Thank you, sir. That will be all."

Tracey turned to leave the tent, with Mittie in tow. "Do come again!" the man cheerfully called as they ducked out into the still dark but relatively brighter Marketplace.

"So, what now?" Mittie said. "Do we still look for Mr. Porter and Charlie here? Or should we go to Mrs. Pinot's house instead of the shop? I'd say that we have enough evidence to confront her."

"I don't know," Tracey said with a frown. "Somehow, I don't think Mr. Porter and Charlie are here. Why would they take kidnapped victims to such a public place as this marketplace? This is no funhouse. And with Mrs. Pinot...there are too many loose ends that are not adding up."

"Like what?"

"Well, for starters, why would she buy tickets for performances that she already knew were fraudulent?"

"Oh. Well..."

"And all of these clues pointing to her. Why would she ask Mr. Williams to give us documents that incriminate her? Or even this man here in that tent? Why would she tell him to tell us about her buying these combustibl—"

"Butter biscuits."

"Buying these butter biscuits."

"I guess you have a point," Mittie sighed. "Say, why don't we open the note? We haven't had any time to do so yet."

Before Tracey could answer, however, they were interrupted by a loud clattering noise, and voices raising in yells. The two spun around to see a cart full of boxes collapsed and spilled in the walkway. The yells were coming from both shoppers and sellers alike running to the pile of goods and grabbing items— sellers defending their spilled goods, and opportunistic shoppers snatching what they could. In the midst of the chaos, however, one person ran in the opposite direction, away from the debacle. "That's the person who was running from us outside of Shrimp Reginald!" Mittie gasped.

"Why, yes, it is!" *The man who looked like Jon Starr!* she thought. *Maybe he has a connection!* Tracey darted through the crowds, jumping over a box and narrowly missing a seller bending to protect his merchandise. "Follow him!"

"Finally, some action!" Mittie called back, following close behind.

Ahead, the man rounded a corner. The two quickly pursued, only to find that the path split in two directions.

"You go right, I'll go left," Mittie said, dashing off.

Tracey sped through the walkway, her feet throbbing as they pounded against the hard concrete floors. Wisps of hair flew in her face as her bun undid itself in the rush. Her own exhausted gasps were all she could hear past her pounding heart—and the yelling of merchants trying to flag her down to make a sale. *I can't remember the last time I've run like this*, she thought as she scanned ahead, her chest wheezing.

Other than a few sensible buyers that darted out of her way as she charged through, there was no sign of the blond figure. *And this path stops just ahead*, she inwardly groaned.

The blond figure burst from an adjacent pathway, knocking over unsuspecting pedestrians and toppling display carts. Close on his trail was Mittie, her eyes blazing in a determined glower. "Mittie! Corner him!" Tracey yelled, wildly pointing to a sidewall that appeared to be an outer extent of The Marketplace.

Mittie nodded and passed near to the man's side, while Tracey closed in behind him, blocking any path to turn back. "Stop!" Mittie called as they slowed down to the edge of The Marketplace. "We've got you cornered. We just want to talk."

The man stood hunched toward the wall, his back to them.

"Why is he just standing there?" Tracey said, stepping forward.

The walls in front of the man shook and slid open. He raced inside, almost immediately closing the walls behind him.

Without a second thought, Mittie and Tracey lunged forward, forcing their way through the gap and landing in a heap inside—just as the walls rolled shut. "Stop!" Mittie called again, scrambling to her feet. Tracey brushed herself off and stood.

"Sir, we will not stop so easily next time," she called after the man as he ran down the steam-lit hallway, her voice echoing against the stone walls and floors. "Please, we just have a few questions. You're the Reggie who wouldn't see us, aren't you? How else did you know how to open that wall just now?"

The man's sprint slowed into a jog, then a defeated stance. He sighed. "Oh, what's the use?" he said. The man turned around. Between his large, rather fearful brown eyes, his youthful, round face, and his bushy sideburns, Tracey wasn't certain of what to focus on. Despite the similar-looking profile from behind, his face looked nothing like Jon Starr's.

"You are that Reggie?" Tracey reiterated.

"Yes," he said, his eyes fixed miserably on the ground.

"Why were you running from us?"

"Because—" He stopped himself.

"Because this is *my* Reggie, Tracey. My beau," Mittie finally said, her voice more subdued than usual. "I had a sneaking suspicion it was you, Reggie, but I didn't think it'd be so. Weren't we supposed to meet on the southern coast?"

"Mittie..." Reggie started, his voice trailing off in a weak waver. He looked at a loss for words.

211

"It's Matilde to you."

"Well…" Tracey started, feeling rather awkward, "I thought that you might've been Jon Starr posing as a 'Reggie,' but seeing that this is not the case, I can leave you two to…ah…"

"No, no, Trace, it's fine," Mittie sighed. "Reginald, we can talk later. I had taken a detour from the south coast to help out Ms. Higgenbottom here."

"Oh," was all he said. "What would bring you to a place like this though, Mitti…Matilde? The Marketplace is hardly the kind of place I thought you bought your goods from."

"I could ask the same of you, Reginald."

"It's a family business. I was going to tell you about this…eventually…but it looks like the gear's out of the mechanism, as they say." Reggie let out a weak chuckle.

The two women stared.

Reggie swallowed. "I…I was just dropping off a special shipment," he continued. "My father couldn't cover it this week, so I was standing in for him."

"Was he the Reggie we were supposed to talk to in order to enter The Marketplace?" Tracey ventured to say.

"Typically, yes," Reggie confirmed. "I'm Reginald Jr." He turned to his beau. "Mittie, I'm really sorry, but this was a shipment that was supposed to be absolutely confidential!"

"I'm a trader, Reginald," Mittie curtly said. "I'm quite familiar with confidential shipments."

"But you don't understand. This couldn't be delayed. Combustible paper is very volatile and has to be quickly shipped. Those keepers can be very demanding—"

"Wait," Tracey interrupted. "Did you just say you delivered combustible paper?"

"Forget I said that."

"And keepers?"

"Also forget I said that."

"It's fine. I work for a keeper," Tracey said. Reggie squinted.

"You can trust her, Reginald," Mittie said.

He hesitated.

"Look, I have a Keeper Book," Tracey said. "Will that make you believe that I really am working for a keeper?"

"Yes, actually," he said with a nod. "Those books are hard to get a hold of."

"Well, it's right..." Tracey started to say. She froze, patting her pockets. "Mittie."

"What?" Mittie asked. "Where's the book?"

"Mittie, we forgot the book at my house."

"Really?" Her eyes widened. "What if Mr. Matthews went back into the house?"

"You're right!" Tracey gasped. "Uh, Reggie, is it?"

"Reggie's fine," he sighed.

"Could you point us to the exit? Preferably out the back, away from the restaurant?"

"Up that way—wait! Mittie, aren't we going to talk?"

"Later, Reginald!" Mittie called as the two women dashed off.

"I...I'll send you a motor-mail!" he called out, his voice echoing in the cavernous halls outside The Marketplace.

# CHAPTER 20

# In Which the Book Is Retrieved

"OH, NO," Tracey groaned as the two skidded to a halt in front of her now sunny home. The earlier rain had already begun to lift from the ground in drifts of mist.

"What?" Mittie said. "You didn't forget your key, did you?"

"No, it's right here," she replied, holding it up for Mittie to see. "But it appears we won't need it. Look," Tracey said. She mounted the stairs and pushed at the front door. It swung open without a sound.

"Did we forget to lock?" Mittie touched the door's striking plate. "It doesn't appear to be tampered with."

Cautiously, Tracey peeked into her foyer. A quick inspection showed nothing out of the ordinary. She silently nodded to

Mittie, who followed and quietly shut the door. Mittie made a gesture to the stairs at the end of the foyer, moving her fingers in a walking motion. Tracey, in turn, pointed to the sitting room, then to herself, then back once more to the room. Mittie nodded, and the two split ways.

Tracey crept into the sitting room, her eyes adjusting to the dark. Although she couldn't see anything out of the ordinary, she could not shake the feeling that something was amiss in the room. *I shouldn't turn on the lights just yet*, Tracey thought, looking at the switch. *I have the upper hand here. Mr. Matthews doesn't know my home as I do.* A dark mass (of which Tracey had originally thought to be her sofa) at the end of the room shifted. Tracey soundlessly scrambled back, putting distance between herself and the figure.

The figure straightened out to show a silhouette of a tall person. *A man?* she thought, peering closer. In their hands was the golden Keeper Book. Tracey bit back a gasp. Instead, she slowly reached for a fleece throw on a nearby chair and crept toward the figure. Step by step, she approached them. The figure remained unaware, focused on opening the book. Tracey willed her breaths to quiet, desperately hoping they would hear neither it nor her pounding heart. Thankfully, the person seemed to be engrossed in the book, twisting away at the dials on the cover, the gears noisily clacking away. She steeled herself, lifted the large blanket over her head, and then quickly tossed it over the figure's head.

"What!" the person exclaimed, stumbling forward.

Tracey took no time to think and charged forward into them, snatching the book from their hands as they unsuccessfully flailed their arms to regain balance. The figure landed in an unceremonious heap on the floor. They groaned.

"Next time, you should run once you find what you're searching for," Tracey said, "rather than linger at the scene."

"Next time," the person growled in return, slowly pushing themselves up into a sitting position. "You should check to see if an intruder is armed."

"Oh," Tracey started. She blinked. "Are you?"

"No," they slowly replied. "But I can run!"

"What?"

Within the short span of a few seconds, the figure sprung to their feet, stumbled over a table, paused to toss off the blanket, and dashed through the foyer and out of the house. Tracey stared, mouth agape.

"Tracey?" Mittie called. She pounded down the stairs. "I heard something. Is everything all right?"

"No," she dazedly replied. "Well,"—Tracey looked down at Mr. Porter's book in her hands— "I suppose it could be worse?"

"What happened?" Mittie said as she ran into the room. She quickly located the switch and turned on the light, looking around at the mess in the room. "Gears, you'd think someone attacked you, Trace!"

"I wouldn't quite say that—more so the other way around. Someone was here. They were trying to steal this book."

Mittie gasped. "Where did they go?"

"They ran out the front."

Mittie ran into the foyer, swinging open the ajar door. "They must be fast. That's a long street to disappear from!" she said after a moment, closing and locking the door. Mittie returned to the sitting room. "Did you catch a glimpse of their face?"

"No. But they spoke. It was a man. Who—I don't know. They ran before I could think of what to do."

"Did you recognize the voice? Was it Mr. Matthews?"

Tracey shook her head. "I've never heard that voice before."

"At least we've got the book."

"But it's useless unless we figure out how to open it!" Tracey replied. She sighed. "It feels like we're hitting roadblock after roadblock!"

"We must be missing something." Mittie sat in a nearby seat. "What evidence do we have again?"

Tracey located the stack of evidence she had placed earlier and sorted through the items. "Mr. Porter's glasses, which he can't see without."

"Which tells us he couldn't have just left on his own," Mittie said, slowly nodding.

"His ring."

"That Harriet had found outside of Mrs. Pinot's home..."

"Hence why he may be there," Tracey added. She looked at the stack again. "There's also the document of Mrs. Pinot's ticket purchases from the banker."

"Which points the evidence toward Mrs. Pinot trying to throw suspicion from herself for hosting those fraudulent Jon Starr performances..."

"The Keeper Book."

"Locked, and not much help right now."

"And the handkerchief with the initials of RN."

"Which we still haven't pinned to anyone."

"Actually, yes."

"Yes?"

"I-I must've forgotten in all the chaos of yesterday." Tracey rubbed her forehead. "It's Rollo's."

"Really? The chef?"

"Yes...Rollo spoke to me through Charlie's steam device before he kidnapped him. He referred to himself as Mr. Nicholson, and did confirm that his initials were RN."

"Huh," Mittie said, her face twisted in confusion. "I guess that would mean that Jon Starr's employees really are working with her, aren't they?"

"It does seem that way, yes. But this doesn't get us any closer to finding them!"

"Why don't we look through our notes again?" Mittie offered.

"We just did that earlier today!" Tracey groaned, plopping onto the couch. "I'm beginning to regret our group splitting."

"I hate to admit it, but yes," Mittie said.

The two women sighed, each staring out of space. The clock ticked, seemingly deafening to Tracey's ears. She fidgeted, looking at the book in her hands. "Why don't we open the note?" she said, breaking the silence. "That's probably the only bit of clue we haven't examined yet."

"Have at it," Mittie sighed.

Tracey pulled the small envelope out of her pocket and observed the parcel. Like the other combustible note, it was unlabeled. She ripped the packet open.

"Let's see," Tracey said, unfolding the parchment.

*I'm rather disappointed in you, Tracey. Four days, and still no closer to finding Mr. Porter. I'm beginning to doubt your sleuthing skills. Allow me to give you a hint: don't forget the funhouse.*

"Are they taunting me?" Tracey huffed in indignation after reading the note aloud.

"The funhouse?" Mittie said with a frown. "Lemme take a look at that."

As Tracey held out the paper to her, the document already began to evaporate, leaving wisps of smoke in its wake.

"Oh…" Mittie said as she grabbed in the air at where the paper was.

Tracey wrinkled her nose at the familiar, sickly-sweet smell of the paper as it dissipated.

"At least ya got a chance to read it, I s'ppose," Mittie said. "The funhouse wasn't at Shrimp Reginald like we thought, so I wonder where it would be at?"

"That would put us back to investigating Mrs. Pinot—"

Tracey could not finish her sentence before a knock sounded at the door. The two exchanged surprised glances. "Could that be Mr. Matthews?" Tracey said.

"Doubt it," Mittie replied.

Tracey stood and walked into the foyer, observing the figures at the door. Through the curtains, she could see a tall figure standing next to a much smaller figure. "It's two people," Tracey called to Mittie.

"Do you think it could be"—Mittie shuffled to the doorway, peeking into the foyer—"Mr. Berkley and Harriet?"

Tracey frowned. "Likely. After our dispute last night, though, I'm not certain if I want to see *him* again." She paused. "But we do have more important matters at hand."

A knock sounded once more, and a muffled conversation could be heard from the other side. She sighed, then opened the door.

As expected, there stood Mr. Berkley and Harriet, engrossed in conversation.

"...sure that this is the correct address?" Harriet was whispering to Bentam as Tracey caught the last of Harriet's statements.

Bentam stood engrossed in his portable document device. "Yes, Harriet," he responded. "The database shows this to be her residence, and I'm certain that the High Constable is never wrong."

"Never wrong, indeed," Tracey grimly responded, glaring at Bentam. "Hello, you two."

# CHAPTER 21

# In Which the Pieces Take Shape

"HELLO, TRACEY!" Harriet piped. "Did we catch you at a bad time?"

Harriet beamed at Tracey as if she were trying to distract her from Bentam's icy demeanor. The distraction did not work. Tracey glanced toward Bentam before sighing and refocusing her attention on the girl. Harriet still wore her prim dress and shoes, and her hair, rather than the curls from last night, was styled into her usual neat bun.

"Of course not, Harriet. Come in," Tracey said. *Poor thing*, she thought. *She must not have slept last night with her brother missing.* She very well knew the feeling, with her employer and guardian being missing for nearly a week. Tracey had spent the better part of her week sleepless and anxious. Her teas were the only things keeping her going at this point.

She stepped aside to allow the two to walk in.

"I'm sure you must be wondering why we've come here," Bentam finally said, rolling up and tucking his portable document into his pocket.

"Yes," Tracey sharply replied, closing the door with a little more force than necessary. "I thought that you would have found everything you needed by barging in on Mrs. Pinot. Rather careless, don't you think?"

"And you must've found an abundance of information by revisiting what you already have, hm?" he retorted. He cleared his throat. "Anyway," he continued, "we did find some information of interest to you."

"Why don't we go to the sitting room," Tracey said, whisking past the two and reclaiming her seat in the room. "I believe we *all* have new information that everyone would like to hear."

"What happened here?" he asked in bewilderment as they navigated fallen items from the earlier-toppled table.

"Attempted burglary not ten minutes ago."

"I should create a report on this," he muttered, scanning the room and perching on a nearby sofa. "Hello, Mittie."

"Hello, Bentam! How did your constable report go, by the way?" Mittie cheerfully said. "The last time I saw you two, didn't you say you were going to file a missing person's report?"

"We changed our minds," Harriet replied. She sat next to Bentam. "Constables make me a little nervous, so I thought it'd be better if we just continued with our own searching."

"And for the record," Bentam added, "we did *not* barge into Mrs. Pinot's residence last night, as you may assume. We visited her this morning."

"How?" Tracey asked incredulously. "She didn't want to see us again the last time we saw her."

"Correction," Bentam said. "She didn't want to see *you*. I had a better guise for our visit."

"And what was that?" Mittie said.

"I simply went to go over some more paperwork with her. She's been assigned to me for a lawsuit she wanted to reopen. As evidence for old cases goes into Records after a period of time, the responsibility fell to me.

"I've been working on this case with her for a few weeks now, so she wouldn't suspect much of that. In the meantime, Harriet looked around her home under the guise that she was checking all of Mrs. Pinot's fireplaces."

"I still can't believe that worked, to be honest," Harriet said. "I couldn't find any sign of Mr. Porter or Charlie, though— and I searched every corner of that house."

"No hidden rooms?" Tracey asked, thinking back to The Marketplace's hidden entrances.

"Not even that. All I found were some blueprints in Mr. Pinot's old lab."

"Oh? Could they've been blueprints for Mr. Porter's Keeper Book?" Mittie asked, leaning forward.

"No, but they were kind of interesting—that's why I still remember it! It was for some sort of mini self-defense device. I couldn't tell how they worked exactly, but one of the designs looked like the brooch necklace Mrs. Pinot always wears!"

"That adds up," Mittie thoughtfully said. "Mrs. Pinot said her husband gave that brooch to her, so he very well may've made it, too."

"Since we didn't find anything of too much interest at her residence," Bentam continued, "we decided to look more into what exactly keepers do since I couldn't understand why everything about them is so secretive. At the library, I found an interesting fact."

"What was it?" Mittie asked.

"Some keepers are part of a sort of society called the Keeper Embassy. The registration list is public—I even found Mr. Porter to be a member of this said society."

"We did find out earlier today, yes," Tracey said. "Mr. Matthews dropped by our home during the storm."

"Oh?" Bentam said. "Interesting." He frowned, looking down at a book in his hands Tracey noticed for the first time. "What else did you learn, may I ask?"

"Not much," Mittie said with a shrug. "Other than there's an underground marketplace in The Undertown where you can buy combustible paper—my beau is a supplier of it and co-owner of the entire place—and that we got another combustible note that didn't really tell us much other than we need to look for a funhouse, which we thought the funhouse could have been since The Marketplace's nickname is The *Mirrored* Funhouse, but it wasn't—it's literally just a marketplace for illegal goods. Not in that order."

"Wow," Harriet said, slowly blinking.

"I'd say," Tracey agreed.

"I'm going to ignore that matter of the illegal marketplace," Bentam said with a squint. "What did the note say?" he continued.

Tracey frowned. "We didn't get a chance to write it down," she started, "but it said something along the lines of 'I'm disappointed in you, Tracey. Why don't you look at the funhouse?'"

"It said your name this time?"

"Yes."

"Whoever is sending this is getting more aggressive," he muttered. "We need to pick up the pace," he said louder, straightening in his chair.

"Hate to be that person," Mittie said, "but we're at a dead end. Trace an' I were just saying that Mrs. Pinot's home was our last resort, and here you are sayin' they're not there."

"We still have one clue we haven't been able to examine yet, though," Bentam pointed out. "The book."

"Which is still locked," Tracey replied.

"Yes, but I believe this book may be a breakthrough for us." He held out the thick burgundy book. "This is the book I had mentioned about the Keeper Embassy."

He flipped the book open and set it down on the coffee table in front of them. "Now," he said, rifling through the pages, "there's something in this book that caught my interest."

On the open pages was a drawing spanning across the two sheets: a complex drawing of the letter K.

"This is the emblem of the Keeper Embassy," he said. "I had a theory about the book. May I?"

Bentam reached toward the book, waiting for Tracey. With a frown, she reluctantly handed it to him. Twisting and dialing the gears on the cover, he lined up the patterns to create an identical version of the symbol.

"There!" he said, smiling. As he tugged at the lock, his smile faded. "Why isn't it working?" he muttered. "I was certain that was the solution..."

"Was that the plan?" Harriet exclaimed. "If you had told me at the library, I would have told you Charlie already tried that."

Her eyes watered as she mentioned her brother's name. "This is useless," she said, her voice breaking into a sob.

"I-I'm sorry," Bentam said, nervously combing back his hair. "I was certain it would work..."

Tracey looked closer at the drawing. *It certainly matches the book*, she thought, her eyes tracing each K. As she looked around the illustrated K, however, she noticed something different—a thick line bordering the tall left side of the letter.

*What's this?*

Following the line, it branched off, twisting into the intricate patterns. It formed a sideways key.

"I wonder..." she murmured, taking the book from Bentam's hand. She stared closer at the cover's gears.

Almost indistinguishable in the golden metal was a series of tiny rectangles. Using a fingernail, she pressed a rectangle to the immediate left of the K. It sank with a quiet *click*. Tracey's eyes widened. "I think I have it!" she said.

Tracey followed the line of buttons, gently tapping the same pattern as the book's illustration. The outline of the key came into shape. Upon pushing into the last spot, the book softly popped open.

For a moment, the room stilled in hushed silence.

"It actually opened," Mittie quietly said.

"What do we do now?" Harriet asked.

"We look for any reasons why Mr. Porter may have been kidnapped," Tracey said. She hesitated. "Without that book from the library," she quietly said, "I would have never figured out the key to opening the book. Thank you...Bentam."

Bentam's eyebrows shot up. "Glad to help, Ms. Hig..." he stopped. "Tracey."

Mittie and Harriet looked between the two. "Does this mean there's a truce now?" Mittie said.

"Yes," Tracey replied, clearing her throat. "Now," she said, flipping the pages open, "the best place to look would be his last entry."

Tracey scanned through the numerous scribbles of Mr. Porter's handwriting, familiar names of previous clients standing out to her. The torrent of words slowed to a trickle, and at last, she reached the final entry. "Here it is," she said. "It's dated the day before his disappearance." She read the passage aloud:

*I can no longer condone these actions of Mrs. Pinot and allow her to continue down this path. I plan to take this evidence in the morning to the High Constable. This breaks every code of the Keeper Embassy, but I can no longer passively watch.*

"So it *was* Mrs. Pinot?" Harriet asked, her face crestfallen. "It's so unlike her, though!"

"Criminals often can fool those around them," Bentam replied.

"Do you think Mr. Porter wrote any more on what exactly Mrs. Pinot was doing, Trace?" Mittie asked.

"Let me see." Tracey flipped through. "Oh, here's something. It appears there are more documents on those fraudulent performances."

"She must've been trying to hide the fact that she was ruining Jon's reputation by sabotaging him with those fake ones," Mittie said. "Maybe she was blackmailing him, hence why Jon's men are working with her. That could be why you saw them at that theater, Trace."

"That makes sense," Tracey said with a slow nod.

"And you must've seen Jon's men kidnap Mr. Porter, Harriet, because she was using them as well," Bentam added. "She couldn't have done it herself, so she must have used whatever resources she had to help herself."

"Gears, that's positively ruthless!" Harriet cried.

"I'm almost certain that Mrs. Pinot is working with Jon Starr's employees," Tracey said. "She's wealthy enough to own a steam car, and it's plausible that her husband could have had a silencer on theirs. Not to mention I found a handkerchief with the initials of RN abandoned at the shop, which matches Jon's chef Rollo. He has the last name of Nicholson. She could have had Rollo both kidnap Mr. Porter using her silenced steam car and acting as security at her fraudulent performances!"

"That's very plausible," Mittie said thoughtfully.

"Mrs. Pinot doesn't own a steam car," Harriet piped.

"But Jon Starr does, no?" Tracey replied. "Seeing that she doesn't hesitate to use his men, she wouldn't hesitate to use his vehicle either, correct?"

"And along that line," Mittie said, "if she'd use him for all those things, why wouldn't she use Jon's home as a place to hide Mr. Porter and Charlie? It'd certainly keep any suspicion from herself."

Tracey looked at all the evidence in front of them, then slowly stood. "Let's put these away," she said. "I have a safe in my room." She grabbed up the handkerchief, book, ring, glasses, and papers as she led the way.

Tracey paused in the doorway.

"Except these," she said, placing Mr. Porter's glasses in her pocket. "I think it's time we paid Mr. Starr a visit, don't you think?"

# CHAPTER 22

# In Which They Enter the Funhouse

IT WAS VERY MUCH the same plan as Bentam and Harriet had earlier done at Mrs. Pinot's home: Bentam would distract the household with paperwork and documents, and the rest would search his home under the guise that they were searching for the restroom. "Are we ready?" Bentam said to the rest as he approached Jon Starr's door, squinting in the evening sunlight.

"Yes," Mittie said, her eyes determined.

Harriet nodded, her eyes brimming with excitement.

"I surely hope so," Tracey sighed, trying to ignore the knots forming in her stomach. She swallowed and shook the feeling away, focusing on the door.

Bentam nodded and turned the door's gear handle, starting its chain of gears. Soon enough, they produced small clouds of steam and finally ended in a familiar "ting ting."

Almost immediately, the door swung open. A familiar tall and slim man stood in the doorway: Hassan, Jon Starr's butler. His eyes locked with Tracey's and narrowed in suspicion. Tracey's mind flashed back to the previous night at Baldgrass Theatre, where she heard the butler there with Rollo when Charlie was kidnapped. "May I help you?" he evenly said.

"Yes," Bentam said, stepping forward and holding up a small folder. "I'm here to discuss more on the case of Jon's fraudulent performances."

"We weren't expecting you. I'm afraid that he's busy at the moment."

"May we wait inside? It's rather pressing, and I cannot move this case forward with the High Constable until I sort this out with Jon."

"I don't mind you coming in, Mr. Berkley, but may I ask why," Hassan paused to fix a scathing glare on Tracey, "you're bringing guests with you, once again?"

Tracey stifled a nervous gulp and instead steadily held the butler's gaze.

"They're with me on business once again. Unfortunately, I had to walk and work with this group. We're stopping by the High Constable office immediately after this visit."

Hassan stared at each of them, his eyebrows knitting as he deliberated what he should do. Finally, he sighed and stepped to the side. "Come in. I see you've all remembered Jon does not like dirt or dust. Thank you for remaining clean."

"What's that supposed to mean?" Mittie hissed to Tracey, who rolled her eyes.

Tracey barely noticed the grand entryway as they entered Jon's home. She instead thought of their next steps. She hovered back, watching as Hassan ushered Bentam into the sitting room.

"Excuse me," Tracey called out to the butler. He turned around, his eyes squinting in a glare.

"Can I help you?" he frostily said.

"Yes, we've been walking all this time with Bentam," she said, gesturing to herself, Mittie, and Harriet, "and I'm afraid that we need the powder room. Could you direct us to it?"

Hassan hesitated.

"Please, sir?" Harriet said, clasping her hands innocently.

He sighed. "Mr. Berkley, please wait there. I'll get Mr. Starr shortly." He turned back to the group. "Follow me."

As they walked away, Tracey caught Bentam's eye. He held the gaze for a moment, then looked away, bowing his head in a subtle nod. She took a deep breath and followed the butler, willing her steps to push her forward.

Tracey lagged behind as they climbed the grand stairs and entered a spacious hallway. Along the walls were posters of Jon's previous performances, all of which featured his likeness illustrated in the forefront. Doorway after doorway passed them by as they walked, any of them possibly hiding Mr. Porter and Charlie. Tracey anxiously wrung her hands. Were they behind the forest green door? Or maybe perhaps through the arched entryway, where its interior was shrouded in darkness?

"Please keep up," Hassan said, slicing through her thoughts. His eyes pinned Tracey in place. "Is there something of interest to you?"

"N-no," she stammered.

"Then please, keep pace with me."

"Oh, yes, of course," Tracey responded, quickening her pace.

As she approached the others, Harriet discreetly looked back at her and Mittie, the latter of which had lingered to admire the posters. Harriet pointed at a hallway.

*"Hide there,"* Harriet mouthed.

Tracey nodded, then slowed her steps, tapping Mittie's shoulder. *"Over there."*

Mittie glanced from Tracey to the hallway, an incredulous stare on her face.

*"Go, now!"* Tracey silently said, pointing more insistently.

Carefully, they drifted over to the hallway, then darted in. Harriet waved, smiled, and then turned her attention back to Hassan. "Do you think you could tell me more about these posters, sir? I find this all very interesting!" she cheerfully said, running ahead to touch one.

"Miss, I ask you to refrain from touching the posters!" he called out as he darted after her.

"Looks like we're in the clear," Mittie finally said as the two moved out of sight. "Let's go."

As they had earlier planned, the two turned back and descended the stairs, passing briefly by the waiting room to give Bentam a thumbs up, and then into another hallway. "If Bentam remembers properly," Tracey said, scanning the doors, "the basement should be—ouch!"

The sudden exclamation was caused by Mittie, who abruptly jabbed Tracey in the side, vigorously pointing to the door at the end of the hall. The door creaked open, and a large figure began to appear. They exchanged panicked glances, their eyes wide and mouths agape. "Rollo!" Tracey hissed. She grabbed at the door immediately behind them and pulled Mittie in with her, closing the door as quietly and quickly as possible.

They held their breaths as they heard his heavy footsteps click through the hall. The footsteps stopped in front of their door. Tracey held her breath, not even daring to let out the faintest of exhale. Next to her, Mittie was tense, her jaw clenched. They could hear his breathing.

"Hmm," he grunted.

Finally, he walked away, his steps fading in the distance. Tracey exhaled, and Mittie shook herself. "That was too close," Mittie said.

"Yes, that was," Tracey agreed. She quickly located a switch, turned on the lights, and looked around. "Say, Mittie," she said, "doesn't this room look awfully like..."

"A funhouse?" Mittie completed.

The space did indeed look like a funhouse. Its walls were a rather offensive shade of orange and red, and the carpeting was a bright shade of purple. The light fixture was more whimsical than practical: formed in a twisting shape which resembled a ball of yarn with small dots of light within. Mirrors adorned the ceilings, walls, and even the door. It was just as Charlie and Mittie had described to Tracey a few days ago: a room full of disconcerting colors and lights.

"Weird...I thought we were looking for a basement," Mittie said with a frown.

"Look, stairs," Tracey said, pointing.

Blending into the confusing array of colors were the stairs descending into a yellow passageway.

"That's our best chance at a basement, right?"

"So the funhouse was the basement!" Mittie quietly exclaimed. "Will ya look at that?"

Tracey turned off the lights, and they began their careful descent down to where they had earlier seen the stairs, being sure to listen behind for any sounds of steps approaching behind. The stairs opened up to a surprisingly drab hall at the bottom. The steamlights were on.

The hall's walls and floors were plain gray stone, unlike the entrance at the top of the stairs. "It's just a basement..." Tracey said in bewilderment.

"I thought it'd be a bit more than this," Mittie agreed. "Maybe Jon never finished it..."

Tracey wandered down the hall. "It splits here," she said. "We should stick together."

"This place isn't exactly the sort of place I'd want to split up with you, anyways," Mittie nervously chuckled. "Let's go right."

They walked down the hall, only to be met with three more paths. "This is a maze," Tracey said.

"Certainly feels like it." Mittie looked between the three. "You choose this time."

Tracey looked at each of the three paths. They all seemed rather ordinary, nothing out of place. It was hard to discern where any of them led to. "Hm..." She looked closer. "Two of the hallways are far brighter than the third one. We should be avoiding anyone, and we don't know where Jon is either, so I say we take the darker middle hall."

Tracey and Mittie cautiously entered, descending deeper into the labyrinth of Jon's basement. Soon, to their right, was another opening. "That's the same light I saw from earlier!" Tracey whispered, pointing at the opening.

"These halls must lead into each other."

"Let's keep going this way—"

"Hello?" a voice called out.

Tracey and Mittie froze. They stared at each other. *That's not Charlie or Mr. Porter*, Tracey thought, a sinking feeling in her stomach. *"Run?"* Tracey silently said. Mittie looked between the opening and the hall ahead, panic in her eyes.

*"Nowhere to hide!"* Mittie responded.

Footsteps sounded from the adjacent opening. A person's shadow was now visible. "Is anyone there? Hello?"

*"Retreat?"* Tracey asked.

Mittie nodded, and the two began to turn back. Unfortunately, they were unable to as much as take a step before the person exited the opening.

"Hello?" Jon Starr said as he came bursting into the hallway, his back facing them. He spun around, his eyes wide and eyebrows knitted. "Oh!" he said, smiling in relief and holding his chest. "You scared me. For a second, I thought it might've been a burglar."

They awkwardly stood across from him, still in a walking stance.

"Ah," Jon awkwardly started. "Tracey and Mittie, is it?" he finally said.

"Y-yes," Mittie stammered, her face devoid of color.

"We're sorry!" Tracey blurted, stepping forward. "We were looking for the powder room."

Jon stared.

"We got distracted by your performance posters, y'see?" Mittie added. "And by the time we realized it, your butler was already gone with our other friend!"

"Oh?" he slowly said, a frown appearing on his face.

"And we're a little lost. We didn't realize that this was such a maze!" Tracey finished, nervously laughing.

"Well," he said after a moment's hesitation, "it's a good thing I found you, then, isn't it?" he said with a small smile. "This basement is quite literally a maze. I don't think you'd have found your way out of here on your own."

"Oh, we didn't get far."

"Good, good," he replied. He turned around. "Let me escort you two out."

They followed Jon as he continued down the hallway they had started down. "So, to what pleasure do I owe your visit?" he said, his demeanor noticeably more cheerful.

"We were tagging along with Mr. Berkley while he sorted out some documents with you," Mittie said. "We have some business with him after this, like last time."

"Really? Are you sure you didn't tag along so you could see me again?" He laughed.

"Well, maybe." Mittie laughed in return.

"How delightful!" He smiled at the two of them. "It's wonderful to have you visit again, despite the odd way we met just now. Once we get back upstairs, I'll be sure to ask Rollo to make another round of refreshments. I'm glad that I'm not terribly busy today with rehearsals as I was last time. I was simply heartbroken that I didn't have a chance to dine with you!"

"Oh, yes," Tracey said, surreptitiously glancing at the numerous doorways they passed by, "I was rather disappointed myself with how short our last visit was. It's truly a pleasure to meet you again."

Jon warmly smiled, then briefly frowned. "Ah," he murmured. "If only it were under happier circumstances. Bentam is here to discuss more about those fraudulent performances plaguing me, no?"

"He never mentioned what case he's here for, exactly, but I would assume so."

"Oh, bother," he sighed. "Well, I'm sure we'll have more than enough time to eat once that's sorted out."

They walked in more silence. The hall stretched ahead.

"We're taking a different route out," he explained. "This will lead right into the sitting room. I can get Hassan to take you to the powder room again. Terribly sorry for any of these inconveniences."

"Not a problem," Tracey responded, looking at the walls. Gradually, it became more finished. First, the flooring became wood, then the lighting became more ornate, from simple steambulbs to small steam chandeliers. Finally, they reached a section where the walls were wallpapered, and portraits hung on the wall.

"Oh!" Mittie gasped, her eyes lighting up. "Is this you, Jon?"

On the wall hung a portrait of what looked to be the boyish version of Jon Starr. Although his eyes were larger and his figure more childish, the face was unmistakably his. Even then, his eyes had a dreamy, wanderlust look about them. "Ah, yes," he gently said, smiling fondly at the portrait. "I was around seven when that was made."

"You look very much the same," Tracey said.

"I do, don't I?" He stared for a few moments longer before turning and continuing their journey. "You have a good eye, Mittie!" he said as he walked on.

Tracey dropped back to look closer at the portrait. His clothing in the painting was frilly, looking to be of fine lace. *He must've always been wealthy*, Tracey thought with a small audible sigh. A glint in the lights caught her eye: the gold plaque of the portrait's title. She scanned over it.

"Rodger Neal?" she whispered.

"What was that?" Jon called, glancing behind. "Please keep up, Tracey. I don't want you to get lost again!"

"Yes!" Tracey responded, running up to meet them. Her mind raced with her jog, overpassing it at a frenzied, dizzying speed. *Rodger Neal?* she thought. *That makes him out to be RN as well. That could mean—*

"Mittie?" Tracey whispered as she reached Mittie.

"Hm?" she responded. Mittie was lagging behind too, as she was observing yet another painting in the strangely located art gallery.

"I just realized something," Tracey whispered. "Mrs. Pinot wants nothing to do with Jon Starr. Don't they have a feud going on?"

"That's right," Mittie quietly replied, raising an eyebrow.

"And we see that his men are unwaveringly loyal to him. I don't think blackmail would work against either of them."

"Yes, they do seem to be the type to use brute force rather than listening to a threat like blackmailing..."

"Unless Jon told them otherwise."

Rodger Neal, Age 7

Mittie nervously glanced ahead to Jon, who was occupied with searching for the exit.

"Wouldn't it be more likely that Mrs. Pinot would be storing evidence against *his* fraudulent performances?" Tracey said, slowing her steps.

"You mean to say that *Jon* is behind the fraudulent performances, and not Mrs. Pinot?"

"Why else would Mr. Porter be kidnapped and his documents ransacked?" Tracey whispered, her voice urgent. "Don't you think that it'd make more sense that *Jon* would kidnap Mr. Porter? Mr. Porter had the evidence against him, so it makes more sense that Jon would ransack the office in search of it. It's not as likely that Mrs. Pinot would kidnap Mr. Porter only for trying to stop her from blackmailing him.

"If Jon did it, he likely did so to protect his scheme and stop Mrs. Pinot's blackmailing—two birds with one stone. How could he have possibly known that Mr. Porter was going to end the blackmailing himself? It was Mr. Porter's last entry in his journal the day before he disappeared!"

Mittie stopped. "Tracey, you're right." She stared at Jon.

"Now!" Jon cheerfully said, turning back to them with a broad smile. "This is the exit. Keep up, I notice you're lagging again. Am I walking too fast for you?"

"Oh...no, no," Tracey quickly said, raising her voice so that he could hear. The two trotted up to him.

"I'll be more mindful of my pace," Jon said as they reached him. "Now, up these stairs, into the parlor, and we'll be on our way. After you," he graciously said, opening the door with one hand and guiding Tracey through the door with the other on her shoulder.

"Thank you," Tracey mumbled, avoiding eye contact.

Tracey looked to the ground as she carefully planted her steps. At once, she realized something terribly amiss—there were no stairs in front of her. In fact, it appeared to be a cramped, windowless room.

"Ms. Higgenbottom," Jon said, leaning down to speak in her ear quietly. His voice was considerably deeper than Tracey had ever heard before. "I know," he slowly said, "that you know."

Tracey's blood ran cold. Her words stuck in her mouth. "Know what?" she croaked. She turned just in time to see Jon's face. His smile was gone, and his face was fixed in a cold stare.

Tracey felt a shove and heard a door slam behind her.

## CHAPTER 23

# In Which (More) Truths Are Revealed

TRACEY SCRAMBLED TO her feet, regaining her balance from Jon's shove. She scanned her surroundings. Mittie had been separated from her, and it appeared as if she and Jon were in a plain, square room. The room resembled the stone hall that she and Mittie had earlier entered.

She spun around.

Behind her was Jon Starr, blocking the path to the only door out.

Outside the door, Mittie could be heard. "Tracey? Tracey!" she yelled. The door shook as Mittie pulled at the handle. "Jon, let her out!"

"Why did it have to be you, Ms. Higgenbottom?" he said, slowly closing the distance between them. His eyes seemed to burn into Tracey's head.

"B-beg pardon?" Tracey stammered, glancing about the room for any sort of way out, any exit she might've missed.

"When I think back to last night, you were the only one not at my performance. I was quite beside myself."

Mittie continued shaking the door.

"I was there for the first act!" Tracey said. "And I wasn't the only one who missed your second act. Charlie wasn't there either."

"The boy?" he said with a deadpan chuckle, his face barely changing expression. "Was that his name?"

"Was?" Tracey said. She stiffened, the knot in her stomach tightening. "Where is he?"

"How should I know, Ms. Higgenbottom?" Jon looked to the ground, his mouth pursing in thought. "Tell me," he said, meeting her gaze once more, "where were you last night?"

She held his stare, stepping back for each step he took forward.

"I was afraid you weren't going to make this simple for me," he sighed.

The door shook once more.

"Tell me what you did with Charlie," she said, "and I'll speak."

"I'm afraid you're not in a position to negotiate, Tracey." He laughed, a cruel smile spreading across his face. "And again, I haven't the faintest idea of where you can find him. I didn't kidnap him."

"Who said he was kidnapped?"

Jon paused, leveling a stare at Tracey. "I meant to say: *It's not as if* I kidnapped him," he evenly said.

Tracey wilted under his gaze. "A strange slip of the tongue, don't you think?" she said.

He continued staring.

"Okay. Let's assume that's what you meant—it wasn't 'as if you kidnapped Charlie,'" Tracey mockingly echoed. "Then who's to say it wasn't someone connected to you? Like, say, it was your chef? That clears you. But Charlie's missing, and someone must have done it."

Jon's smile slowly dropped. "And what brings you to the conclusion that it could have been my chef?" he asked.

"Because..." Tracey trailed off, unsettled by a new silence. The door had stopped moving.

"Rollo must've finally arrived down here," Jon dismissively said, casting a glance behind.

"Mittie—"

"Your friend," he interrupted, "is fine. I rather like her, actually," he thoughtfully said, pensively staring into the distance. "You, on the other hand," he said, glaring at Tracey, "have too many loose ends, too many secrets...it's messy."

"What?"

"I hate messy things, Tracey. I'm sure you already know that. Mr. Porter was a mess in my plans. And now you."

Tracey paused. *So he admits it.*

"You know, don't you?" he continued. "About the performances, of how they were mine? That's where you were last night. To see if I'd show up at Baldgrass Theatre."

"No, actually." Tracey broke eye contact, taking a deep breath to calm her nerves. "We were there for Mrs. Pinot."

"Ha, so you *were* there! That wasn't too hard to say, now was it?"

Tracey pursed her lips, her eyes narrowing.

"What's more, I'm glad to see my plan to frame Mrs. Pinot almost worked!" Jon smiled and clapped his hands. Just as quickly, however, his smile disappeared. "And yet, here we are."

He walked closer. Tracey distanced herself once again, only to find herself running into the wall. She slowly exhaled, willing herself to continue maintaining her eye contact.

"I was to leave on the morrow, Tracey," he said, his stare falling into a glare. "If you had kept quiet, we wouldn't be in this situation," he spat. "We were to leave the country, away from Mrs. Pinot's threats. It was all going so well...until the first mess." Jon's face darkened.

"And would this mess be...Mr. Porter?" Tracey slowly said, discreetly scanning the gap between herself and Jon.

"Yes. Mr. Porter."

"You kidnapped Mr. Porter simply because he had Mrs. Pinot's documents on your double performances—"

"Nothing would convince him," he interrupted. "I-I didn't mean to..." His voice faltered.

Jon's face grew pale. For a moment, it almost looked to Tracey he was afraid. *No*, she thought, *it's something else...remorse? Anger?* She couldn't place his emotion. Within the second, however, his face snapped back to the glare.

"Then came the boy, showing up backstage while we were counting the ticket profits."

"So you do know something about Charlie!"

Jon grew quiet once more. "Perhaps," he finally said.

"Your butler and chef were there. They took Charlie, correct?"

"Tut tut," Jon sounded in disapproval, tilting his head with a small frown. "My butler and chef happen to have names: Hassan and Rollo. Now look at this," he continued. "It comes once more. Yet another mess." He twitched. "And it's you, this time."

He reached for his breast pocket, then jerked his hand away.

"It's up to me," he said, "once again, to"—he scowled—"clean...this mess."

Tracey looked at the door behind Jon. He had advanced close enough that he was a considerable distance from the exit. *If I can make a run for it, I don't think he'll be able to catch me so quickly.* She bit her lip. *But is that door locked?*

"Tracey," Jon said, disrupting her train of thought. "I'm curious—how did you figure out about me? I'm quite certain I took all the evidence from the office."

"Is this some kind of joke?" she snapped. "Why did you keep sending those combustible notes that taunted me every step of the way? You should have been more careful than that if you didn't want to be found."

"Notes?" Jon blinked and frowned.

"The...the notes?" Tracey repeated, this time with less certainty. "The ones that were supposed to frame Mrs. Pinot. That was your plan, was it not?" *They were pointing at Mrs. Pinot...were they not?*

Jon stared. "Why would I..."

Frustration welled up in Tracey. "Why should I believe a word you say?" she burst. "You're an actor! Of course, you can just be pretending during every second of this conversation." She glanced at the door once more. *If I time this correctly...*

"I'm being genuine." His face twisted in bewilderment. "I don't understand what you mean?"

"You must be having fun with me, aren't you?" Tracey sniffed.

"Yes," he said, his face breaking into a smile. "This *is* rather fun. I haven't had this sort of fun in a *very* long time. But, no," he added with a serious expression. "Why would I ever send you clues?"

"I don't know, because you're a madman?" she said, keeping her face stoic against her racing heart.

"Strange you should use that word—madman," he said with a laugh, his mouth twitching into a small smile. "You said it yourself: I'm an actor. I must be acting convincingly." The smile dropped. "Unlike you."

Tracey discreetly pointed her feet to the exit.

"I can see your fear, Ms. Higgenbottom," he said. He made as if to step forward, changed his mind, and shifted on his feet instead. "Tell me," he said, his eyes wide and threatening. "Why. Are. You. Here?"

Tracey swallowed. "You know why. You...you said it yourself," she said, venturing to echo him. "We had reason to believe that Mr. Porter is here."

Jon did not react.

"Y-you see, we had hoped that..." Tracey trailed off. Her skin crawled under his gaze.

The silence was almost deafening.

"Hoped?" he quietly chuckled. "Hope is for cowards."

*Good, he's monologue-ing. Maybe I can make a move now.*

Tracey inched to the side, trying to position herself into a running stance. He resumed his advance, walking closer. *No! Too close!*

"There is only hardship, Tracey. You know it. I know it." With each sentence, he took one step closer to her.

Tracey shuffled more. "Please, Jon. I have no interest in whatever you're doing with those performances. I just want to know where Mr. Porter is. Tell me where he is, or let me *peacefully* leave and search for him myself."

Jon smirked and closed their distance. He was almost directly in front of her. Tracey clenched her jaw in disgust. *His breath stinks!*

"Not another step!" she hissed.

"Oh?" he stopped. "You mean like this?" he stepped again.

"Stop that!"

"Or what? Try me."

Tracey discreetly held her breath.

He chuckled. "I'm surprised you'd think I wouldn't notice you trying to distance yourself from me. Where are you running to?"

He reached for his breast pocket once more, this time grabbing hold of the red brooch pinned to his pocket. *The brooch!* she remembered, thinking back to Mittie's earlier excitement at seeing it.

"Oh, you recognize my brooch?" Jon smiled, fondly looking at it in his hands. "Mr. Pinot made this for me a decade ago."

"*Mr.* Pinot?" she said, momentarily distracted. *He knew Mrs. Pinot for so long?*

"Yes, Mrs. Pinot's late husband. He was a good man. Pity he died." Jon's eyes flicked up and met Tracey's once more. "Did you know Mrs. Pinot blames me for his death? How was I to know he'd die while making my steam car's silencer? He was the one who insisted on making it!"

"Is that how no one heard you when you kidnapped Mr. Porter?" Tracey ventured, eyeing the exit once more.

"You're testing me, Ms. Higgenbottom," he growled with an edge to his voice. "I never said I *knew* where Mr. Porter is." He stared out into the distance. "As for that steam car silencer... What more could I do but take my car back, show my appreciation for his efforts, and use it?" he continued, a small laugh escaping from him.

Tracey bent her knees, posing to run. *If I could just reach for that door...*

"Ah ah," he chuckled, firmly placing a hand on Tracey's shoulder. Tracey flinched, shrugging off the hand and stepping to the side. "Tracey, don't you think that you're a bit *too* knowledgeable to just go walking around Mondon after our little tête-à-tête?"

"Oh, no, no!" Tracey said in an exaggerated fashion. "I hardly can even remember what we were speaking of!"

Jon's smile dropped once more. "You truly are a terrible actor, Ms. Higgenbottom." He held out the red brooch to her. "Oh, well, I'm sure you won't need those skills—if you can call them that—where you're going."

"What are you doing? What is this?" Tracey stammered, scooting out of his reach.

"You'll just sleep for a few minutes, no worries."

"Everything you've been saying has been worrisome," she retorted. *And I'm not staying around for that!*

Tracey broke into a run and dashed to the door. Her hand closed on the handle, and she desperately wiggled it. *Locked from the inside, too?*

"Do you take me for a fool, Tracey?" Jon laughed, his voice alarmingly close behind her. *How did he get here so fast?*

Tracey deeply sighed and turned around, staring at the ground.

"This is really a fascinating device, Tracey," he said, holding up the brooch and looking at it with an admiring gaze. "Think of it like an off switch. For your brain. It's a shame. I wonder what other sort of inventions Mr. Pinot would have made had he survived."

*He must have the key on himself somewhere*, she thought, her clasped hands trembling. She bit her lips. *But how can I figure out where it is?*

"Do you know that Mrs. Pinot has one similar?" Jon continued. "The gear brooch," he clarified. "She must keep hers for self-defense."

*Right, the blueprints!* Tracey thought, her mind flashing back to Harriet's earlier findings.

"And now, Tracey..." he said, his eyes flicking to her.

Tracey darted toward him, dodging his hands, and pushing him backward. "Oof!" he grunted, falling to the floor in a heap.

"Thank you for the key," she said with a smirk.

A bluff.

But it was enough – Jon's hands flew to his left pocket.

*There it is!*

Tracey swooped and bumped into his shoulder, causing him to flail and throw his arms out for balance. In the same motion, she reached and plucked the key from his pocket. *I've got it!*

Pivoting, Tracey dashed back to the door. Much to her relief, it fit! Tracey unlocked and swung the door open. *I'm glad I still remember how to pick a pocket.*

Before she could take her hand off the knob, however, Tracey felt a hand yanking her other arm back. The door slammed shut. *No, no, no!*

"You're a tricky one, aren't you?" Jon said, a wild look in his eyes. His grip tightened on her arm.

"Ow!" she exclaimed, trying to wiggle out of the surprisingly strong hold. It was no use.

"Did I mention how much I hate messes?" he said, his grin ripping away to reveal a furious glower. "Look at my clothes, Tracey! Do you see how *dirty* these floors are?" He shook her arm with each sentence. "Don't you think that you've done enough?"

"Let go," she weakly protested through clenched teeth. There was no more plan. She had run out of all options. Tracey felt helpless, at the mercy of this madman. *How did it come to this?* she thought in despair.

"This was a lovely chat, don't you think?" he growled. Jon placed the device on the back of her head. "It's really a shame I have to leave you like this, Ms. Higgenbottom," he sighed.

He paused.

"No, considering how *you* just tried to leave me, I suppose I'm doing you a favor, am I not? Let's go, shall we?"

"Wait!"

Tracey hardly had the words out before he flicked the device to life. She felt its little gears as they whirred and spun. "This should only take a few seconds," he said, a pleasant smile once more on his face.

"What should onl—ack!" A sharp, shrill sound blasted from the device and rang in Tracey's head.

She did not remember the fall.

CHAPTER 24

# In Which Tracey Higgenbottom Hits Rock Bottom

THE FIRST THING Tracey felt was her throbbing head. "Oh," she groaned as she slowly regained her senses. "What happened?" she muttered.

Her eyes fluttered open. The ceiling above was plastered and simple, adorned with a plain crown molding. The surrounding walls were bare, painted a bland shade of cream. She moved her head to the side with great difficulty, each shift causing a jolt of pain in her head and neck. Tracey squinted against the garish lighting of the steamlights, her ears ringing. The flooring was ordinary, polished wood, and she lay on a rug.

Other than the rug, the room was empty. Tracey blankly stared at the wall. Her mind confusedly wandered over the past few events. *Powder room...funhouse...basement?* she groggily thought. *Oh, right. Basement. Mittie and I...and...Jon? Jon.* Tracey's arms twitched, and she moved them from beside herself with great difficulty. She rubbed her face. "My head..." she said.

She tried, to no avail, to roll over. Every muscle screamed. "Ouch," she muttered. Tracey shut her eyes against the lights. *Let's see...* she thought. *Jon...we were walking in the basement. Mittie and me. And then...a room? We were separated...Jon and I...we...talked...* She sighed again. *Something with his brooch? The red brooch.* "Oh," she said.

Snippets of memories came flooding back. Their conversation (although the contents of the conversation were hopelessly muddled), her near escape, Jon's device. Tracey frowned. There was something else that she remembered. *A staircase? It was dark.* "What in the world happened to me?"

Tracey remained on the floor, staring at the walls as she waited to regain some energy. "Where's Mittie?" she slowly said. "Or Jon, for that matter."

She stared at the wall.

"Where's anybody?"

Tracey attempted once more to move—this time, much to her relief, discovering she could move her limbs with slightly more ease. Tracey forced herself into a sitting position. The room dizzily swam around her. She groaned. Tracey buried her head into her lap. "I need to find Mittie," she muttered.

After what felt to be a few minutes, Tracey slowly raised her head. The room had stopped swimming and was now at a gentle tilt, moving from side to side like a seesaw. *Am I on a boat?*

"Let's see if I can stand," she said.

Carefully, Tracey positioned herself into a squat, then laboriously rose to a stand. The room's tilt intensified, and she stumbled backward, barely catching herself. Something odd suddenly stood out to Tracey. She stared at each wall. "Where are all the windows?" she said, trudging to a nearby wall and leaning against it. She glanced around once more. "I must be in a cabin under deck," Tracey said with a frown. "How did we get onto a ship so quickly? Maybe some fresh air would be good."

Tracey followed the wall, leaning heavily against it to combat the swaying floors. "Wait," she said, slowing to a stop. "Where's the door?"

Scanning the room in front of her, then rolling around to face behind herself, Tracey could find no door. Only the plain, cream walls. "That can't be right..."

Tracey circled the room again, to no avail. No doors were to be seen, and Tracey was quickly growing tired. "I think I need to...sit here," she said, sliding down the wall into a crouch, taking deep breaths. *If I weren't so groggy, I'd be able to figure out what's going on*, she thought in frustration. She leaned her head against the wall, staring at the ceiling.

"What if the door were hidden?" Tracey muttered, laughing to herself. "I'm looking for a door that's invisible! Which means...it's impossible!"

She smiled, then lowered her head. "Impossible..."

Tracey fell into silence, listlessly staring at the floor.

"I wonder where Mr. Porter is?" she said. "Oh, yes. Charlie, too. Where are they?"

She frowned, trying to piece together her jumbled memories. "Maybe I'm...where they are..." She looked at the walls again. "But I have to...get out of here first? Ugh." Tracey vigorously rubbed and patted her face, trying to knock the heavy drowsiness away. "Focus, Tracey!"

She took a deep breath, then exhaled.

"This is just another puzzle...clue. It's not like I haven't done any of those before. It's been my entire week so far! Let's check for a trapdoor."

Scooting to the center of the room, she tugged at the rug. Nothing but pristine floors.

"Oh," she said with a frown as she patted the ground.

Solid.

"What about the walls, then?" Scooting back to the walls, Tracey carefully examined each wall. "Perhaps if I can find a groove..."

She rose to her feet, steadying herself against the sway.

Tracey whipped out a hairpin, putting its tip against the wall and continuing her rounds about the room, feeling for any sort of bump in the wall.

The pin's narrow head fell into a groove. "What do we have here?" she said, pausing. Sliding the pin up and down, she found it fit snugly inside, making what seemed to be the side of a door. "Aha!" she yelled with a grin. She winced. *I should talk a little quieter. My head still hurts*, she thought as she dug deeper into the wall. The groove deepened to reveal embedded door hinges.

"Good, good," she muttered, moving farther down the wall. The tip snagged into another groove, and she repeated the steps, this time revealing the door's striking plate. *Maybe if I wedge this pin in...* There was a small, audible click. *It's not locked!* "Jon must've assumed I wouldn't be able to find the door," she chuckled. "Now, let's pry this open..."

She dug her thumbnail into the groove, forcefully wedging the door away from the wall. The door slowly creaked inward before fully swinging open. The force of its swing threw Tracey off balance, causing her to take a stumbling seat on the ground. Dazedly, she looked into the hall.

It was a dark, short hall, and it appeared that the room in which she had woken was at the end of it. On the opposite end was an intersecting hallway, modestly wallpapered with drab green flowers. "That wasn't too impossible," she said, returning her hairpin to her bun and scrambling back to her feet. The floor's swaying intensified. Tracey stumbled forward into the doorway. "Right. The deck," she grimly said, beginning her shaky steps into the hallway.

After she took a quick listen to the area, Tracey determined there was no one in the immediate vicinity. Leaning on the walls, Tracey slowly walked through the hall and rounded the corner into the adjacent hall.

It was an ordinary hall. Plain, as she had seen from the room, with worn, brown wainscoting and sad green wallpaper. The hall had several alcoves on it, each branching off elsewhere. Despite its drab decor, it made up for it in its bright lighting— twice as bright as the room she had just left.

"Ow," she groaned, squinting her eyes against the brighter lighting.

From one of the alcoves, she heard a muffled, shuffling noise. Tracey froze. "Oh, no," she whispered.

Much to her confusion, however, there was the absence of footsteps. *Only shuffling?* Slowly, Tracey peeked. It was a dark hall, similar to the one her room was off of, with a solitary door at the end of the hall. Nobody was in the hallway. She crept to the door, her fingers brushing against the wallpaper and her eyes adjusting to the darker lighting. "Good," she muttered as she felt the headache subside.

Tracey reached the door. Cautiously, she leaned her ear against it. "Singing?" she whispered, listening closer.

Inside, she could hear a voice singing:

*Get a gear for me lady,*

*And a gear for me baby,*

*And a gear for me...no, wait, that's not the right words.*

"Charlie?" Tracey quietly said, her eyes widening. She stopped herself from wildly swinging the door open. "Wait," she said to herself. "Let's be careful, Tracey."

Slowly, Tracey turned the knob and opened the door by a crack.

There in the middle of an equally empty room was a small figure, their back to the door as they were lounging on the floor, singing along to their song. It was unmistakably Charlie. "Charlie!" Tracey said, beginning to rush into the room. She stopped herself, steadying against the tilting floors.

"Tracey?" Charlie replied, scrambling to his feet and spinning around to face her. "Gears! Am I glad to see you! I knew you'd find me!" He stared agape at the open door. "Ya mean t' say there was a door here this whole time? I thought I'd have to climb the ceiling or somethin'!"

"I was in a room like this myself just now. I've just gotten myself out," she shakily replied, leaning against the doorknob. "I'm sorry, Charlie—this should have never happened to you in the first place."

"No need to apologi..." Charlie paused, peering closer at Tracey. "Are you all right, Trace? You don't look too good."

"No, no, I'm fine," Tracey said with a small wave. "Just a little seasick, I think."

Charlie stared. "Seasick?" he slowly repeated.

"Yes, you haven't noticed how much these floors are tilting?"

He looked at the ground. "Gears, Trace...uh, maybe I haven't noticed anything yet?"

"You must have your sea legs, then," Tracey said with an airy laugh.

"Right..." Charlie replied.

"So," Tracey said, turning back to the hallway's walls. "What's happened to you since last night?"

"They just blindfolded me and took me to this room," Charlie said with a shrug, following Tracey's slow walk. "Wasn't too bad. I mean, they gave me food an' all, so I can't complain. I didn't think you all would find me so quickly!" Charlie laughed. He paused, noticing a lack of reaction from Tracey. "Really, Trace, are you sure you're oka—"

"We opened the book earlier today," Tracey said.

"Really?" he said, his eyes brightening. "Gears, I wish I saw that!"

"You will once we make it out of here," she replied, briefly pausing to accommodate for another sway in the floor.

"So, um," Charlie paused beside Tracey, staring hard at her. "Uh, what d'ya find out in the book?" he finally said.

"Oh, that Mrs. Pinot was the reason for Mr. Porter's kidnapping."

"Really?"

"Except that it wasn't Mrs. Pinot," she continued. "It was Jon." Tracey stopped to rest her head against the cool cloth of the wallpaper.

"Tracey—" Charlie began to protest.

"I'm fine!" she snapped, straightening herself.

"Sorry," he quickly said, raising his hands in surrender. "So," he started again, looking away. "Do you mean Jon was the one who did all those fake performances?"

Tracey nodded, swallowing back a wave of nausea. "We must be sailing through a storm," she muttered, watching as the hall tilted more drastically. She glanced ahead, seeing the alcove from where from which she had originally exited. "We need to continue past there. Do you mind if I lean on you since you have such good balance in here?"

"Sure," Charlie said with a slow blink, surprised. He took her arm. "I'm so small, though. I'm not sure how much help I'll be to you," he added, looking up to Tracey.

"It's fine," she distractedly replied as she looked down the hallway as they passed it. "That's where I was," she said, pointing to the open doorway.

"How did *you* end up in a room? Did Rollo get you, too?"

Tracey shook her head. "It was Jon, I think," she said. "Thank you, Charlie," she said as they reached another patch of wall. Tracey stepped away from the boy and leaned against the wall, closing her eyes.

"Gears, Tracey, I'm no doctor, but I think you should at least sit—"

"We can sit," Tracey retorted, "when we find Mr. Porter and the deck!" *I can't stop now,* she thought, gritting her teeth in determination. *Not when we're so close!*

Tracey made as if to take another step but instead stumbled as the floors tilted again. "Come on, Tracey!" Charlie said as he grabbed her arm, exasperated. "You might be too...uh...seasick or whatever, so can ya just take a moment to catch your breath, at least?"

"Charlie, if you were taken here, and I was taken here, I'm positive Mr. Porter is here too! I've got to find him—"

"What good is findin' Mr. Porter if you're half-alive by the time you reach him?" he exclaimed. "I dunno, Trace, but I doubt that you'd be good enough to rescue anyone like this! Look, you're sweating!"

"It's the seasickness, Charlie," Tracey replied, flaring her nose. The floor swayed once more.

"Well, even if it is, then sit down 'til you're used to the ocean!" he replied. "Gears, I wish Harrie were here. She'd be able to convince ya easier." He frowned. "Is she all right, by the way?"

"Yes," Tracey slowly said, struggling to focus her eyes. "She's with Bentam at Jon's home."

"Oh, good," he sighed. "I'm glad she's with someone safe." Charlie guided Tracey to sit on the floor. "C'mon, Trace. Let's just chat a bit, ya?"

"Okay. Okay, fine. You're right," Tracey responded, sitting next to Charlie. She leaned her head on the wall and closed her eyes against the pounding in her head. "Let's chat."

The two caught each other up to speed with what happened in the past hours they've been separated: Tracey with all their traveling and meetings, and Charlie with how he spent his time in general dullness, filling his time with singing and superficial games. After a while, the two fell silent. "Are ya feelin' any better, Trace?" Charlie asked, carefully watching Tracey's reaction.

Tracey looked at the ground. "No," she admitted. She glanced at Charlie, a determined glint hardening her gaze. "But I am ready to keep going now."

"Are you..." Charlie started to say. Upon seeing Tracey's determined stare, however, he sighed in defeat and stood. "All right, all right." He offered a hand to Tracey.

"Thank you," Tracey said, rising to her feet and leaning on Charlie's arm. *How much time has passed?* she thought as they continued down the hall. *I hope everyone is doing all right.*

They reached another identical, short hallway.

"Let's check here," she said.

They turned down the hallway. Rather than a solitary door at the end, however, they found an assortment of doors. "Should we check them all?" Charlie nervously said. "I dunno if any of 'em will pop up, ya know?"

Tracey nodded. "I'm surprised we haven't heard anyone come in here yet..."

"Maybe they're busy?" he suggested.

"Or..."

Farther down the main hall, a door creaked open.

"Or," Tracey started again, dropping her voice to a whisper, "maybe we spoke too soon. Let's try one of these doors."

Charlie quickly walked over to a door—or, rather, walked as quickly as Tracey's sluggish pace allowed—and tried a handle. "Locked!" he hissed.

Footsteps sounded, and an unseen person cleared their throat. "They're getting closer, Charlie!" Tracey urgently whispered. "Don't worry about me, just hurry!"

"But—"

"Go on!"

Obediently, Charlie pulled Tracey along, pulling at each knob. Tracey stumbled. "Trace?" he said in alarm.

"Don't worry about it!" she hissed.

The footsteps grew louder, slowing down as they approached their hall. "I can't believe him," a voice muttered. "Why would Jon put her in *here*, out of all places? It's as if he *wants* us to get caught."

The two exchanged terrified glances. "The butler!" Tracey whispered.

Charlie pulled Tracey along and made one last attempt at opening a door. To their relief, the door opened. They rushed in. Charlie quietly shut the door. They listened as the footsteps passed their hall and went on to where they had just been imprisoned.

There was a brief moment of silence, then a loud groan.

"Of course, they'd escape!" Hassan yelled. The footsteps turned into stomps as they grew louder, then past them. It briefly paused once more. They heard muffled talking, then silence. The running became quieter yet. Finally, a distant door slammed shut with a loud thud.

The two let out a breath. "They're probably going to be searching down this boat for us now," Tracey sighed, settling into a sitting position against the wall.

"I'm just glad we got into this room!" Charlie said, looking around. "I didn't think we'd be able to hide in time."

The room was cluttered with furniture and boxes of all shapes and sizes. Everything was covered in various-sized sheets. Charlie sneezed. "It's dusty in here!" he sniffed.

"Mhm," Tracey agreed, closing her eyes against another room tilt. "This is quite a storm, don't you think?"

Charlie stared at Tracey. "You're really not joking, are ya?"

"What do you mean?" Tracey asked, opening her eyes to look at him. She was surprised by the scrutinizing stare Charlie returned to her, unlike his typical carefree smiles.

"We're not on a boat," he said.

"Don't be silly," Tracey said, waving a hand.

"Trace, don't you think that something might be wrong? I'm kinda worried..."

"Well, don't be," she said, mustering a small smile. "We're going to get out of here, Charlie. We just need to find Mr. Porter, get off this boat, then rejoin everyone else."

"We're not on a boat," he repeated.

"And what makes you think that?"

"Well, for starters, the ground's not even moving! You've just been stumblin' around this whole time," Charlie said.

"Really?" she asked incredulously.

"And second," Charlie continued, "I may have been blindfolded, but I was awake the whole time. Rollo made me walk the whole way to my room. We didn't go anywhere near the ocean, or any water, for that matter!"

"I—" Tracey paused. "I need a moment," she finally sighed.

"You need a doctor, that's what you need," he grumbled, stalking to a covered chair in the corner of the room.

Tracey stared at the swaying floor in front of her. "He can't be right," she muttered.

"Huh?" Charlie said.

"Nothing."

Behind her came a faint sound. *"Hello?"*

"Lovely. I'm hearing voices now, too?" she grumbled. She struggled to her feet, shaking her head. "Let's go. We still have a few doors to check in this hall—"

*"Hello? Hello, there!"*

Tracey stared at the wall.

"What is it?" Charlie said, peering closely at her.

"I think you might be right," she said, slowly backing away. "I'm hearing voices over there."

Charlie jumped from his seat and dashed to her side, putting his ear on the wall.

His eyebrows furrowed.

"You're not wrong!" he whispered. "I hear something, too! Someone calling for help."

"Let me hear," Tracey said, leaning against the wall.

*"Hello?"* A man's voice could be faintly heard. The wall lightly thumped with what Tracey could only assume to be someone hitting it. *"Hello, can anybody hear me? I'm trapped in here! Hello?"*

"Hello?" Tracey responded, her heart pounding.

*"Hello? Can you help me?"*

"Y-yes, just a moment!" Tracey turned to Charlie. "Charlie, I think they're next door!"

"But there's no door there," Charlie said with a shrug. "This is the last door on this side of the hallway."

"Then there must be another hall," Tracey said. "Come on." She turned back to the wall. "We're coming!"

*"Oh, thank goodness. I hope the constables are with you!"*

"About that..." she muttered, turning away.

The two ventured out into the hall and back into the main hallway, following the walls (and occasionally halting for Tracey) before reaching another small hall. "This is the last one," Charlie said, looking ahead at an oak door at the end of the main hallway, a dreary brown against the dismal green walls.

"And there's only one door!" Tracey triumphantly said, scrambling to the door and turning the knob. It didn't move. "Of course, it's locked," she muttered, loudly sighing. "Let me check something," she said, leaning closer to the door. "Mr. Porter?" Tracey quietly called.

*"Tracey? Is that you?"*

"It is!" she said. Tracey grinned, turning to Charlie.

"Is it Mr. Porter?" he said, an edge of excitement in his voice.

"Yes," she replied, her heart racing. *We did it! We found him!* Her eyes watered. After four days of searching, she finally found success—they found Charlie again, and now Mr. Porter!

"Gears!" Charlie ran up to the door. "I can't wait to meet 'im!"

"After we unlock this door."

With trembling hands, Tracey pulled her hairpin out again, attempting to place the tip in the keyhole. Unfortunately, as her eyes still struggled to focus, she missed the door several times, instead jabbing at the surrounding wood. Charlie watched a few attempts before politely taking the hairpin from Tracey's hand.

"I can pick it, Trace," he said with a sympathetic smile.

Tracey hesitated for a moment before sighing and stepping to the side, resigned. She leaned against the wall and watched as Charlie made quick work of the lock. "There we go!" he happily said, pulling the pin out and handing it back to Tracey.

"I see your picking skills are still sharp," Tracey said with amusement as she placed the pin back into her hair.

"It's only been yesterday since I needed it last," he replied with a shrug. "I'll leave ya to open the door," he added. "Since you've been searching for 'im all this time," Charlie said bashfully, with flushing cheeks, "I thought it'd be fitting that you're the first one he sees."

"We've all been searching for him, Charlie. I wouldn't have gotten this far without your help. You can open the door."

*"It doesn't matter who opens the door, really!"* Mr. Porter called from inside.

"All right, I'll do it," Charlie said, swinging the door open.

Charlie and Tracey stepped inside, looking around the brightly lit room. There were modest arrangements inside: a bed, a small steam lamp, and a few books. And there, sitting on a chair by a wall, was Mr. Porter.

# CHAPTER 25

# In Which They Navigate the Labyrinth

MR. PORTER SAT in a chair at the far end of the room. His round face beamed with joy, and he still sported the vest and suit pants Tracey had last seen him in. Joy flooded Tracey's heart—she didn't know whether to scream, jump, cry, hug him, or all of the above. Instead, she did none and stood rooted in the doorway, beaming at him.

Charlie ventured into the room. "Mr. Porter, is it?" he said.

Mr. Porter tipped his head. "It is!" he chortled. "And to whom do I have the pleasure of speaking?"

"Charlie, sir!" he replied, his carefree grin returning.

"Mr. Porter!" Tracey said, her voice breaking.

"Tracey. I must've given you quite a scare, my dear," Mr. Porter gravely said.

"Oh," she said, making her way across the room and giving him a quick hug, "just a little."

"As much as I'd love to hug you back," he said with a smile, "I'm afraid that my hands are a little tied up. To this wall, in fact."

Mr. Porter raised his hands to show it was connected by a series of complicated knots that led to a metal anchor on the wall.

"They tied me enough to walk around the room, but not enough to reach the door. I've tried gnawing at this rope, with no changes—it must be woven with metal or something," he said, shaking his head. "And every hour, one of the men comes in here to make sure I haven't untied the rope. The closest I'd gotten to escaping, they decided to redo the rope with twice as many knots. Very infuriating!"

"Well, the butler just left, so we should be safe for at least another hour," Tracey said.

"I'm good at knots. Let me see if I can get ya out of there!" Charlie cheerfully said. He immediately started un-knotting, working his way from the wall toward Mr. Porter's hands.

"Thank you, my boy!" he said with a smile. He looked up at Tracey. "Where did you find a resourceful lad like him from?"

"She saved me from vigilantes!" Charlie said.

"Haven't you been busy?" Mr. Porter said as Charlie finished un-knotting. He shook his hands out. "Much better. Thank you, again!"

Charlie nodded before shyly retreating to Tracey's side.

"Now," he continued. "Where're the constables? I'm sure they'll need some statements from me," Mr. Porter said as he dusted himself off.

Tracey and Charlie stared.

"What? Why are you two so silent?" he squinted. "If I could see you two any better, I'd say you look like you're hiding something."

"We're not hiding anything, Mr. Porter," Tracey sighed. Out of her pocket, she pulled Mr. Porter's glasses. "Here," she said, handing them to him.

"Why, thank you!" Mr. Porter said as he donned the glasses. He paused upon putting them on. "Are you quite all right, Tracey? You don't look well."

"No," Tracey said, pushing back her annoyance.

"Well, take my arm!" he said. "We'll ask the constables to send for a doctor."

"About that..." Tracey said, taking Mr. Porter's offered arm. They exited the room and entered the small hallway/alcove. "There are no constables."

"They wouldn't listen to Tracey!" Charlie supplied.

Mr. Porter stopped. "What?" he said in dismay. "Then how in the world did you get in here?"

Tracey frowned.

"I got in here because I was kidnapped," Charlie stated. "Trace and I were try'na look for you somewhere else, and I got caught. They put me in another room here. Tracey found me, though."

"You've put yourselves in danger?" Mr. Porter said in horror. He glared at Tracey. "How many times have I had to tell you to stay out of trouble?"

"We did what was necessary," Tracey plainly replied. "Besides," she added, "we have a records keeper with us."

"And what is a records keeper going to protect you from? They only work with constables. They're not an *actual* constable." Mr. Porter frowned at Tracey's silence. "How did you get in here?"

Tracey, in the meantime, was unaware of Mr. Porter's questions, for she still struggled with the adverse effects of Jon's device. She swayed in place, noticing that the ringing in her ears had returned and that the tilting floors did not still—in fact, they were sloping even more drastically. Tracey briefly closed her eyes.

"Tracey?" Mr. Porter said more urgently, shaking his arm.

"What?" Tracey replied, her eyes flying open. "I'm sorry... I was just thinking of how we're going to get out of here..."

"I was asking: How did you get in here in the first place? Perhaps you can retrace your steps?"

Tracey frowned, piecing together fragments of her memories. "I don't remember," she finally said.

"If it helps, I was led here blindfolded," Charlie offered, casting a concerned glance at Tracey. "I remember I walked up a flight of stairs before goin' into a hallway." He peeked past them, looking out to the main hall. "That one fits the bill!"

Charlie squeezed past them and crept into the hallway.

"It's clear!" he said, beckoning to them.

"I heard the butler enter and exit from somewhere up here..." Tracey said as she and Mr. Porter joined Charlie.

"That would be from that door," Charlie replied, pointing to the lone door at the end of the hallway. "There are no other doors in this direction, and I'm certain that's where he'dve come from." He approached the door. "Let me check!"

"Be careful!" Mr. Porter said, making as if to step after him but pausing in consideration of Tracey.

Charlie nodded, then turned to the door. Slowly, he pulled it open. He peered into the gap. "It's kinda dark," he started, "and I can't see very much in here."

"Is there anyone in there?" Mr. Porter responded.

"Not that I can see."

Mr. Porter glanced at Tracey before joining Charlie.

"Let's go," he said.

Charlie swung the door open farther, then scrambled back. "Gears!" he exclaimed.

"What is it?" Mr. Porter quickly responded.

"There's no floor!"

"It must be the staircase, then. We're in the right spot."

"Oh, you're right," Charlie said, squinting. "I'll lead!" he said as he entered. Tracey and Mr. Porter followed, Mr. Porter pausing to ensure the door had fully closed back.

Tracey looked around as they descended the stairs. For a brief moment, a vague memory flashed through her mind. "I remember this place," she slowly said. She frowned. *But, how?*

"Do you?" Charlie responded, looking around.

"We must be on the right track then," Mr. Porter said with a small smile.

*I don't remember being here with Mittie, so—*

The memories rushed back: She had woken up there; she felt much more alert at that point. There was Jon.

Standing.

She was sitting.

Or leaned over, perhaps?

Where was Mittie? Jon stood at the door.

The same door she, Charlie, and Mr. Porter had just entered.

Jon noticed her.

He saw she had woken up.

He reaches for the brooch again and...

That was it. Tracey could remember no further. She bit her lips. "I...I think Jon carried me here," she said.

"Who?" Mr. Porter said, his eyes widening as he whipped his head to her.

"What's this?" Charlie said in dismay.

"What?" Tracey said, distracted by the boy. "What's wrong?"

"What sort of stairs lead to a wall?"

The stairs had indeed ended, its final tread stopping directly in a solid stone wall.

"That can't be right," she said. She reached out and touched the wall. "There has to be some way to open it."

"There must be a button somewhere," Mr. Porter said, placing a hand against the wall.

"We could always just kick it," Charlie said with a shrug.

"Charlie, I don't think that kicking it will solve anything." Tracey said.

Charlie kicked the wall. The wall smoothly slid open.

"See?" he said, a grin on his face. Tracey shook her head, forcing back a chuckle.

They stepped out into the newly opened passageway. "Huh, we really aren't on a boat," Tracey said.

"You don't say," Charlie replied, casting a wry glance at Tracey.

"In fact, I remember this place," Tracey said, looking around. "Mittie and I were here!"

"Where is this?" Mr. Porter replied. "And who is Mittie?"

"We're in the basement," she groaned. "This isn't good. No, no, no, Jon could be anywhere down here!"

Mr. Porter frowned, looking between Tracey and Charlie. "I hoped I had misheard you earlier, but apparently not," he finally said. "Jon as in Jon Starr? Is that whose house we're in?"

"Yes," Tracey said.

"Then he's more foolish than I thought," he said, rolling his eyes. "Why in the world would he think taking me to his own home would be a good idea? He's practically incriminating himself here."

"Jon strikes me as the overconfident type," Tracey said, scanning the hallway. "He relies too much on his power and wealth."

"I agree," he replied. "At any rate, we need to get out of here. I say the best route will be to the outdoors."

"But the others are still upstairs!" Tracey exclaimed. "We have to help them, too!"

"We can do what should have been done in the first place: get the constables here. That's how we'll help them," he curtly replied. "Now, Tracey, can you tell me where you and this Mittie were in this basement? Perhaps we'll trace our way back."

Tracey shook her head. She frowned.

A picture of Jon's face flashed in her mind.

"He had said...this was a maze," she slowly said. "Oh. We were down there." Tracey shakily pointed to one end of the hallway.

They followed Tracey's direction, pausing to look down each side of the expansive halls.

"This way," she said, following the path she and Mittie had earlier taken.

The group tensely walked, listening for the sounds of any others that may have been roaming the basement.

"I only know the way into the main level of the house," Tracey said with a small sigh as they approached a split in the hallway.

"No worries," Mr. Porter replied. "I've got a plan."

"Really?" Charlie said, raising his eyebrows. "You've only just got here!"

Mr. Porter licked a finger, then held it in the air. After a few moments, steered Tracey in another direction. "We'll go this way."

"What was that for?" Charlie piped, trotting after them.

"I'm exhausting all options," he explained.

Charlie froze. "D'ya hear that?" he whispered.

"What?" Mr. Porter said, listening closer.

Tracey heard nothing other than the ringing in her ears.

"No, you're right, I can hear something," Mr. Porter said, his voice dropping to a hush.

"Let's get closer!" Charlie said, scampering toward the noise.

"Charlie, wait!" Mr. Porter said, pulling Tracey along.

They stopped close to a corner in the hall as shadowy figures came into view. Tracey picked up on the last part of a woman speaking.

"—can't believe he'd think that was ever a good idea," the woman sighed.

"I'm still furious with 'im," replied a voice that Tracey recognized to be Rollo's. She noticed Mr. Porter flinch at the sound of the chef's voice.

"I know that one," Mr. Porter whispered, leaning down to Tracey's ear. "He's dangerous."

Tracey nodded. *And I recognize that woman's voice, too...*

"Have a speak with him, eh?" Rollo continued. "I'm sure you can get through to 'im, you being his girl and all."

"Yeah, yeah, I'll see what I can do," the woman replied. "Have you checked outside for those two yet?"

"They're searching for us!" Charlie quietly hissed. Mr. Porter grimly nodded.

"Yeah," Rollo growled. "No sign o' them."

"It's fine," the woman said. "We still have the upper hand. That man is still locked up, isn't he?"

"That's right."

"They don't know I'm out yet," Mr. Porter said, his face lighting up.

"Good," Rollo said. "Let me find Jon." Brisk footsteps and the swish of skits sounded. Tracey held her breath.

The woman briefly came into view before disappearing into an adjacent doorway. She was soon followed by Rollo. Tracey noted the woman's hands were full of carpet bags.

*I know who she is!* Tracey's mind flashed back to a previous day when a gruff woman had handed them a pamphlet for the fraudulent performance. "Was that Ms. Halpin?" she said, careful to keep her voice low.

"Who?" Charlie and Mr. Porter whispered.

"Elizaveta," she said, knitting her eyebrows. "The one Bentam was chasing."

"Oh, that lady full o' coal dust?" Charlie said in surprise. "She did look like 'er! Gears, would'a never made the connection."

"She sounds different now," Tracey whispered back. "She's using a different, fancier accent."

"This is nice and all," Mr. Porter interjected, "but let's keep going, hm? Before they come back." He took a few cautious paces forward, peeking around the corner. "I felt a draft this way." His eyes lit. "Ah! Look!"

Charlie peeked from behind Mr. Porter. "Gears!" he exclaimed. "A door with a window!"

"Charlie!" Tracey hissed. "Keep your voice down!"

"Did you hear something?" Elizaveta's voice distantly echoed.

"Hurry, hurry!" Mr. Porter said, trotting with Tracey and reaching the door. He pulled at the handle. "Why would this be locked?" he said in exasperation.

"Did you try pushing the door?" Tracey dryly replied.

The sounds of swishing skirts and stomping feet could be heard, its noise growing steadily louder. Mr. Porter pushed the door, to no avail.

"Why must everything in this place be locked?" Tracey groaned. *And why is it night?* she thought in alarm. *We arrived at the house in the evening! How long was I out for?*

"Hey! You three!"

Tracey glanced back to see Rollo and Elizaveta in the distance, sprinting into a run toward them.

"Let me try something," Tracey said, taking her arm from Mr. Porter's and lunging forward.

Bracing herself against the sudden dizziness, she leaned on the door handle, pulling the door to the side. The door slid open. "Go, go!" she said, gritting her teeth and struggling to focus her gaze.

"And leave without you?" Mr. Porter responded, linking his arm with hers again and breaking into a run. "Charlie, are you keeping pace?"

"Right behind ya!" Charlie yelled, keeping pace with Mr. Porter. "It's a little dark, though!"

"Don't worry about that, just keep close!"

The yells faded into the distance as they made space between themselves and Jon Starr's home. "No," Tracey finally gasped, her knees giving way. "I can't take another step." Despite their stopping, Tracey still felt as if the ground itself was spinning below her.

"Tracey!" Mr. Porter exclaimed, trying—to no avail—to lift her to her feet.

"No. Leave me here," she said, loosening her grip on Mr. Porter's arm and plopping ungracefully onto the ground. "I...I can't."

"Trace!" Charlie exclaimed, trying to pull her hand. "C'mon, we finally made it out! We just gotta get some constables and everything'll be fine, right?"

Charlie's voice was muffled, blending with the incessant ringing flooding her ears. "I can stay here," she mumbled.

"Where are we, anyway?" Charlie said.

The place in which the three had run was a garden of some sort. Tall hedges surrounded them, and not too far away a serene fountain gurgled away. The ground was a hard cobblestone, much to Tracey's discomfort. The serene moonlight revealed they were near another building, its purpose indistinguishable in the dark lighting. Its facade matched the brick exterior of the house they had just escaped. They were undoubtedly still on Jon Starr's property.

"It sounds like those two are looking for us in the streets," Mr. Porter said. "I'm going to get help—"

"N-no," Tracey said, squinting to see Mr. Porter. "It's too dangerous."

"We need help, Tracey," he firmly replied. "Charlie, can you make sure she doesn't sleep?"

"What?" Charlie said, confused. "Why would she sleep for?"

"It's important. Trust me."

"All right," Charlie said with a glance at Tracey, who found herself lying on the ground after an unsuccessful attempt to lean into the bushes. "I'll try."

"I will be back," Mr. Porter said, looking hard at Tracey. "All right?"

"Okay..." Tracey slowly said.

With that, Mr. Porter departed. For a while, Charlie and Tracey stayed in silence. Charlie cast a few concerned looks to Tracey, but otherwise quietly observed his surroundings.

"Charlie?" she finally said.

"Yeah, Trace?"

"Are you afraid?"

Charlie thoughtfully looked at the sky above. "A little, I suppose. But you're here, so I trust it'll all turn out fine."

"I hope it will," she said, staring at the spinning ground and listening to the ringing noise. Her eyes grew heavy.

She jolted in surprise as she felt a small hand enter her own. Looking over, she found Charlie looking back.

"I'm glad I'm here with ya, Trace," he said with a small smile.

Tracey smiled in return. "Me, too."

In the distance came the slow click of what could only be shoe heels striking against stone.

"Trace, it's coming this way!" Charlie urgently said, looking around. "We need t' hide. What about over there?"

"Where?" Tracey said, struggling to sit up. "I...I don't think I can, Charlie." She blinked, trying to focus her vision.

The footsteps grew louder.

"They're almost here!" Charlie said, looking back. "C'mon Trace, I can help you up!"

"Charlie," Tracey protested, struggling to stand.

"Well, hello there," a person said as the footsteps slowed to a stop.

# CHAPTER 26

# In Which We Encounter Figures

TRACEY FINALLY MANAGED to rise to her feet, swaying as she regained her balance. Beside her, Charlie began to shrink back but then straightened himself and defiantly glared at the person. Tracey looked in defeat at the figure, unable to distinguish anything other than their dark, shadowy figure.

"What good timing!" the voice Tracey recognized to be Jon's said. "I was worried we'd have to delay and search for you. Hiding next to the garage may not have been the wisest choice."

"Stay away from us," Tracey demanded.

"And if I don't?"

The figure stepped forward. Tracey quietly sighed, watching in despair as Jon Starr stepped forward into the pale moonlight. The light cast garish shadows over his face. His piercing blue eyes were even more striking in the nighttime. "Tracey," he said with his usual pleasant smile. "Would you care to explain why you're out here? At this hour?"

Without breaking eye contact, Tracey wrapped a protective arm around Charlie's shoulder. *How can you smile as if nothing happened?* she thought in disgust.

"Back to silence again," he sniffed. Jon glanced at Charlie. "Charlie, was it?"

Charlie shuffled closer to Tracey. "It's okay," she whispered, giving Charlie a reassuring pat. *We just have to wait until Mr. Porter comes back with help.*

"Tell me, how did you get out? I'm rather surprised, Tracey. I didn't expect for you to be able to move, let alone break out both of my guests so quickly."

"They were not guests, they were prisoners," Tracey quietly replied.

"And so she speaks!" he said with a broad smile. "Now, did you have to run much? You must've been very fast to evade Rollo and Elizaveta."

"We had a head start," Charlie piped, glaring at Jon.

"Did you," he said in a disinterested fashion. He pulled out a pocket watch and cranked a dial on the side, causing it to whir to life and emit small puffs of steam. The face of the clock softly illuminated. "Well," he said, closing the watch and stuffing it back into his pocket, "this may be a bit out of the plan, but they should be back soon."

"They?" Tracey echoed.

"Why, Rollo and Elizaveta, of course," he replied, raising an eyebrow. "Why else did you think they didn't catch you?"

"I thought we lost 'em!" Charlie exclaimed.

Jon laughed, paused, then blinked. "No," he said. "As I speak, Rollo is paying another visit to Mrs. Pinot, and Elizaveta is closing down my house."

"Where are the rest?" Tracey demanded. "What did you do to Mittie?"

"Oh, Mittie is fine," he nonchalantly said. "They've been blissfully unaware of all of this for the past few hours or so in the sitting room. I've given Bentam enough paperwork to last him a week. They're not involved. For now."

"For now?"

"Well," he continued, "Elizaveta should have finished sending off our staff and will rejoin us momentarily with the others. In the meantime, I've sent Rollo to look for a special device of Mr. Pinot's. It's the last thing we need before we can leave."

Jon paced away, wandering to the nearby water fountain. "It's called a memory altercation device," he said, staring at the rippling water. "Mr. Pinot had grand plans for it—help amnesia patients, wake people from comas! But alas," he sighed, shaking his head.

"That device," he continued, "is the key to letting all of you out of here—safely." He looked first at Tracey, then Charlie. "It's very simple. Wipe your memories of ever meeting me, and I leave the country. Continue on tour."

Tracey's grip tightened on Charlie. *Mr. Porter must've reached the constables by now. If I can stall him...*

"Of course, I'm not sure of what sort of learning curve that device will have," Jon continued. "But I'm sure we'll figure it out, won't we?"

Tracey shivered, the faint ringing in her ears feeling more like warning bells by the second. *At least he's monologue-ing again,* Tracey thought. *Enough time for me to come up with a plan!*

"In the meantime," Jon said, carefully perching on the edge of the fountain, "I notice that Mr. Porter is absent." Jon pulled his gaze from the water to look at Tracey. "Which means he's gone for help, correct?"

Tracey raised her chin but remained silent. Her heart pounded. *Think, Tracey, think! I've got to find a way to get Charlie out of here.*

"Hm," he sounded, turning away with a frown. "We might not be able to wait for Rollo here, after all. Yet another mess in my plans," he muttered, his voice barely intelligible. Jon fell into a brief moment of silence, transfixed by the rippling water.

*Now's our chance!* Tracey thought, looking down at Charlie.

301

"Not thinking of any trickery, are we?" Jon abruptly said, glancing over to them. "I hardly think that you're in any condition to challenge me, Tracey."

"I wouldn't be so certain of that," Tracey growled in return.

Jon leveled a glare, then looked once more at the house. "They're taking too long," he said, quickly standing. "We don't have time, assuming Mr. Porter has already reached the constables. 'Liza will know where to find us."

"What?"

"Come along," he said, gesturing for them to follow. "To the garage."

"Why should we?" Charlie defensively said.

"Because of this?" he said, touching the red brooch attached to his breast pocket. "I'm sure this should be convincing enough for you."

"Why would a tiny piece of gem ever scare me?" Charlie scoffed.

"Charlie, listen to what he says," Tracey evenly said, patting Charlie's shoulder. *I can't run in this state*, she grimly thought.

"Why?" Charlie exclaimed.

"Why do you think Ms. Higgenbottom is so disoriented? Unless you didn't notice?" Jon sniffed. "I suggest you listen to your friend."

Jon marched past Charlie and Tracey, leading the way to the garage. He whipped out his pocket watch once more and lit the face. "We're running out of time," he muttered. "Follow along," he said, watching the two. Charlie lingered behind.

"Charlie?" Tracey said. "Come on!"

He looked between Tracey and Jon, distrust in his eyes. "I dunno, Trace..." he said.

"Just do as he says," she evenly said. *"Play along!"* she mouthed, staring hard at Charlie.

He paused, staring up at Tracey. "If you say so, Trace," he hesitantly conceded, catching up to Tracey.

"I'm glad to see you agree," Jon said with a smile. "Come along."

Tracey and Charlie shared a look and continued the trek to the nearby garage. Jon busied himself in unlocking the door. *Good, he's distracted. Now, if we're fast enough, we can hide in one of these paths—*

Tracey's train of thought was interrupted by the sound of the door unlocking.

"Come in," he said, holding it open and looking back at them.

Tracey stifled a sigh and followed Charlie into the garage. Her eyes adjusted to the lighting of the space.

Moonlight streamed in from a solitary window. Save for the prominent steam car in the center and a pile of boxes in the corner, the room was largely empty. She cast a glance at Jon, surveying his stance. He was preoccupied with locking the door. Charlie stood a distance away, halfway between the steam car and herself. *We could use the window to escape*, she thought, measuring the distance between them, Jon, and the window, *if I could run*. Tracey quietly sighed.

Charlie looked between Tracey and the window, evidently thinking the same as her. Eyeing Jon, he pointed to the window, then to himself.

No longer locking the door, Jon remained by it, hunched over his pocket watch. "Where are they?" he muttered.

*Good, he's still distracted*, Tracey thought. Slowly, she raised a hand and pointed at the window. Holding Charlie's gaze, she nodded. *I'll have to trust he can reach safety.*

Immediately, Charlie edged toward the window, reaching for the lock. "Are you certain you want to do that?" Jon said, without raising his eyes from the pocket watch.

"Do what?" Charlie innocently said, lowering his hands from the window.

"You may be able to run," he said, flipping the watch shut and tucking it away, "but I doubt your friend here can."

Jon deftly pulled a chain, sending a series of gears into motion, which rolled a large garage door open. He tapped at the red brooch.

"I fear to see what the effect of using this a third time would be on Tracey."

"Third?" Tracey echoed. *I only remember once...unless that stair memory was the second time?* She briefly closed her eyes. *My memory is so foggy. I can't think straight.*

Jon smiled. "Charlie, do come over. We cannot drive without you."

"Drive?" Charlie said in dismay.

"They're late, which tells me that your other friends may have already hindered that part of our plans," Jon said, his smile plastered on his face. "We have no choice but to reconvene at our meeting place."

"And where would that be?" Tracey said, backing away from him.

"You'll find out soon enough," he said, stepping behind Tracey and ushering the two toward the steam car.

Tracey hesitated, staring at the machine. "I...I don't like steam cars..." she haltingly said.

Jon blinked. "Well, what of it? Come along now."

She clenched her jaw, remaining frozen in place. "No," she said, her eyes locked on the car.

Unwanted memories crept at the edge of her mind: scalding steam. She, a young girl.

The screams.

The heat at her back and blasting horns.

The sounds getting louder, and—*No!* Tracey squeezed her eyes shut. *I've been doing so well in forgetting those memories! Why now? Not now!*

Tracey bunched her shaking hands into a fist, taking deep, heaving breaths. Her neck prickled with sweat. Or was it steam? She couldn't tell the difference.

"What's the matter with you?" Jon impatiently said. "Let's go!"

"All of you," a voice said from behind the steam car. "Stop."

# CHAPTER 27

# In Which Reputations Are Threatened

TRACEY'S EYES flew open.

From the depths of the shadows came a figure of tall stature—a woman. Her hair was pulled tight into a severe bun. A gear brooch around her neck glimmered in the moonlight. Her sleeves billowed, softly glowing in the night lighting. Tracey recognized the sharp eyes. "Mrs. Pinot?" Tracey slowly said.

"It is!" Charlie said. "What's she doing here?"

"Why are you in my garage?" Jon said, pushing past Tracey and Charlie and throwing his hands up in exasperation. "Is everyone out to trespass my home tonight?"

"I'm here for good reason," Mrs. Pinot said, stepping toward the group. "I heard your men are trespassing my own home as I speak, no?"

Jon stiffened. The two exchanged intense glares.

"You were looking for this, correct?" Mrs. Pinot held up a small, thin object in her hand. It looked like a miniature metal bar with small grooves on the sides and top. A strange comb of sorts—if a comb had teeth on three of its sides and were wide squares, that is. "Your men must be half-done tearing my home apart for it."

Jon's face twisted into a perplexed frown. "Is that..." he started.

"Yes. The memory alteration device." She lowered it and looked at it closer, cradling it in her hands. "Horace never finished designing this one," she said, her voice taking on a soft tone. "It's very dangerous. Of course, Jon, I'm sure you wouldn't let that stop you, would you?"

"Whatever are you talking about—"

"I heard you talking about using the device again," Mrs. Pinot frostily said, gesturing to Tracey. "Her current state is your doing, no?"

Charlie shuffled closer to Tracey, defensively hugging her arm. She forced a smile at the boy.

"I merely used the device," Jon flippantly said, glancing at her. "I'm sure you know the adverse effects it sometimes has."

"There are no effects," Mrs. Pinot replied, her voice clipped. "Unless you abuse its use. I made it alongside Horace. *I know.*"

*She made it?* Tracey thought with a blink, looking at Mrs. Pinot's gear brooch. *I thought she said it was a gift...*

"You know that it's dangerous to use on a person more than once," Mrs. Pinot continued. "That was only meant to be used *once* for self-defense! That's why Horace gave it to you—to help protect yourself with that status of yours!" Her voice wavered, and she cleared her throat. "And yet," she continued, quieter, "I hear you threatening to use it for a *third* time? That could *kill* her, Jon—"

"I'm not a killer, Mrs. Pinot," Jon interrupted. His face switched from anger to a strained smile. "I'm rather hurt you think of me that way."

"You were a killer the day you left Horace behind," she retorted, her voice breaking.

The air hung heavy. *We best escape while they're still distracted*, Tracey thought. She glanced down at Charlie and waited for him to return her gaze. Once he made eye contact, she pointedly looked at the fountain outside of the garage, then back. Charlie nodded—the silent exchange was a success.

In the distance, Tracey noticed flashing lights. *The constables!*

"What is it that you want, Corsetta?" Jon finally replied, his voice taking on a serious tone Tracey vaguely remembered to have heard before. For the first time, Jon Starr appeared to have dropped all pretense and instead acted as his true self—Rodger

Neal. He looked angry, tired, and, for the smallest of moments, vulnerable.

"That is for you to discover shortly," Mrs. Pinot responded.

"Her name is *Corsetta*?" Charlie said in bewilderment. Tracey jabbed at him, casting a warning glance.

"Charlie," Mrs. Pinot said, taking notice of them. "How do you always manage to find yourself in the worst scrapes? Come here."

Charlie froze, staring at Tracey with panicked eyes. She nodded and loosened her grip on his shoulder, watching as he took a few steps forward. Her eyes flitted to the distance. The flashing lights were brighter. *We may not have to run after all.*

"Take another step, and you'll force my hand," Jon said in a warning tone, intercepting Charlie's path.

Charlie froze.

Any previous weakness was gone—Jon Starr was back with his airs.

"Jon," Mrs. Pinot said, stepping forward, "let them come with me. I'll make sure that your precious reputation is not marred."

"And why would you help me?" he spat, his face flushing red. "You've always hated me. Aren't you the same person who blackmailed me? So much so that I make *less* money with two performances than I had with just one! Why should you care what I do with my own time? Why is *my* reputation such a concern for you? *Why do you care so much?*"

Mrs. Pinot paused, a bitter smile growing on her face. "What does reputation mean to you?" she finally said.

Jon squinted, taken aback. "What?"

"Does reputation mean respect from your adoring fans? A free pass in life? More money?"

He stared.

"Now, tell me. What does a *ruined* reputation mean to you?" Mrs. Pinot paused. "To have the scorn of everyone around you?" she asked. "To be ostracized? To lose everything to your name?"

Tracey eyed Jon. *He's too close for us to run.*

"When Horace was killed—"

Jon flinched.

"—he left me behind. With nothing but the tattered remains of his reputation," Mrs. Pinot said. "I'm sure you can imagine what they said. 'The mad inventor is dead! He had what was coming to him.' 'His poor wife, he must've wasted all their money on those contraptions.' 'What if she had something to do with his death?' 'She was rather a strange person, don't you think?'"

With each quote, Mrs. Pinot's voice rose and quickened, until it grew to almost a frenzy.

"When Horace died," she continued, "I lost everything. I lost my life as I knew it: I lost the love of my life, my friends, and my reputation. You couldn't begin to fathom how lonesome it is, Jon. And it's all your fault..."

She finally stopped, gasping for air and blinking away tears.

Charlie slowly shuffled backward, closer to Tracey. Unfortunately, it drew the attention of Jon, who gave each of them a warning stare. Tracey stifled a sigh.

"So, how could I simply watch you climb the ranks?" Mrs. Pinot said. "The more my status sank, the more *yours* rose. I was swallowed into oblivion, and you rose into the spotlight! You had to be stopped. I couldn't stand by and watch. That's why I care so much about your reputation, Mr. Starr," she spat. "I want to see you experience the same darkness that I've been trapped in all these years."

"So, you had no plan of helping me by taking them," Jon said, raising an eyebrow.

"Of course not!"

"Clearly, your plan wouldn't work," Jon scoffed, curling his nose in scorn. "Even if you succeeded here in Mondon, I'd simply leave and continue elsewhere."

"I feel like we've walked in on a conversation that we shouldn't have," Charlie whispered to Tracey. She nodded. The lights in the distance suddenly cut off. *They must be close. They're probably trying not to be seen.*

Much to her horror, however, she noticed Jon was watching in the same direction.

He had seen the lights.

"Constables?" he muttered. He turned to Tracey and Charlie. "Move, you two. Into the car."

"What? No!" Tracey protested.

"Wait," Mrs. Pinot said. "Do not take them!"

"No, no," he said, glancing into the distance again. "Into the car."

Farther up what Tracey presumed to be the driveway, the quiet rolling of wheels could be heard. *They're here*, Tracey thought in relief.

Without warning, Jon strode up to Tracey and grabbed her arm, yanking her along as he walked to the steam car. "I said," he growled, "into the car."

"W-wait!" Tracey said, struggling to keep pace.

"Tracey!" Charlie exclaimed, the force of the yank rending her from his arms.

*If I can delay him for just one more minute!*

"My patience is wearing *very* thin, Ms. Higgenbottom," Jon said, his eyes flashing with anger.

"What do you think you're doing?" Mrs. Pinot snapped, trying to block Jon's path.

Without a word, Jon steered around her, coming to a stop at a passenger door. He let go of Tracey's arm and swung it open. "Sit," he said, pointing to the chair.

*Just pretend it's a carriage, Tracey,* she told herself, as she forced her heavy feet to move forward. *A normal, not-steam carriage.*

Tracey sat in the car, perching on the edge of her seat. Her heart pounded. The one thing that Tracey so vehemently hated—steam cars—was exactly the place she found herself trapped in. *I can't breathe,* she thought, struggling to rouse herself out of the drowning, frenzied feeling of panic. She scanned her surroundings. *I need to stall him long enough for the constables to arrive...*

Jon opened the back door and ushered Charlie in. The memories threatened once again to return. Tracey closed her eyes, frozen in place. *I can't do it!* she thought. *I can't think straight in here!*

"We'll see you around, Corsetta," Jon said with a smirk, taking a seat next to Tracey in the driver's seat and grabbing a lighter from underneath it. "We'll be out of your hair soon."

"Don't start the car," Mrs. Pinot said, running up to the passenger side. "Not with them with you!"

Jon flicked the lighter to life. He stuck the flame into a port next to the steering wheel.

Mrs. Pinot slowly backed away from the car, eyes darting between Tracey and Charlie. Tracey bounced her knee, taking in sharp breaths as she struggled to calm herself. *It's too much!* Her head swam and throbbed, her hands trembled, and a new feeling of nausea grew in her stomach.

"And now," Jon said, pumping a lever on the other side of the steering wheel, "we leave."

The steam car's engine whirred to life, and its countless gears cranked and clacked as the dashboard gradually built up a soft glow. Tracey tensely watched as steam seeped through the exhaust pipes. From behind, she could hear Charlie quietly shuffle so that he sat directly behind her. *How am I supposed to protect Charlie in this state?* She lowered her head. *I can't lose him again!*

"This vehicle is state of the art," Jon said as the gear's clacking increased in speed. "You won't find another steam car on the market that can turn water to steam in such short order."

Tracey glanced out the window.

Mrs. Pinot stood to the side, a strange expression on her face. *Why does she look so afraid?*

Jon continued to pump the lever. His face twisted into a frown.

"Is something wrong?" Tracey said.

Jon pumped the lever quicker. The small puffs of steam in the back of the car grew into larger plumes of smoke, and the car began to shudder. "Why isn't the car moving?" he muttered, his eyes darting between the dashboard and steam.

"I hope you remember what you did to Horace, Jon," Mrs. Pinot said, her voice barely audible over the growing din of the steam car's engine. She raised her chin and glared.

Jon paused, slowly lifting his hand from the lever. Despite his action, the engine roared all the louder. He stared at Mrs. Pinot. "What did you do to the car?" he yelled over the noise.

"I used to build alongside Horace," she icily said. "I can destroy your car just as easily as he could build it up."

The car shook all the more. Charlie threw open his door, hopped out, and opened Tracey's door. He pulled her out with him. "I know trouble when I see it," he said, "C'mon, Trace!"

Tracey scrambled to her feet, regaining her balance and holding her head. "Come on, keep going!" Charlie urged, pushing them until they were distanced from the car.

"And just where do you think you two are going?" Jon said, scooting into the passenger seat.

Before he could slide out of the steam car, however, steam poured into the car's main cabin, engulfing him in white clouds.

"Argh!" he screamed, knocking against the seatback. Jon threw up his arms to cover his face from the steam as it flooded around him. Tracey froze, transfixed. For a moment, she was back to being a young girl, caught in the scalding steam of a malfunctioning steam car. How she had wished for someone to help her instead of watching from the sidelines. How so many turned a blind eye.

"That was meant for when you and your little fugitive group fled the country," Mrs. Pinot spat, raising her head defiantly. "I suppose earlier than later is better than no result."

"No!" Tracey cried, her own voice startling herself out of her stupor. Without thinking, she darted forward, reaching for Jon's shoulder. Gritting against the heat of the steam, she yanked his arm, causing him to tumble out of the car. He knocked Tracey down with the force of his fall. Tracey lay stunted on the ground, the world wildly spinning, before she forced herself to her feet and limped away from Jon, swaying as she moved.

"You could've gotten killed, Trace!" Charlie exclaimed, rushing to her side and grabbing an arm.

"I...I couldn't just watch that happen," Tracey said, catching her breath. "He could have gotten killed, too!"

"You should have left him!" Mrs. Pinot snarled. "He needed to get the same taste as my poor Horace had in his final moments."

"You'd never understand what happened," Jon said, his eyes blank and shocked. His voice quavered as he spoke; his facade was broken once again.

Moving to a sitting position, he stared at Tracey. "Why did you..." he started. "No, thank..." He shook his head. "Who am I kidding?" he muttered, shakily rising to his feet and glaring at Mrs. Pinot.

His hair and clothes were disheveled, and his face and arms were red from the steam. The car continued pumping out steam, causing the garage to fill with fog. "Look at me. I'm a mess," he quietly said, his nose flaring. "Look at this mess you've made, Corsetta."

"You deserved every second of it," Mrs. Pinot growled in return.

"H-ha!" he laughed, raising an unsteady hand to flatten his hair back. Without warning, he lunged forward, grabbing at Mrs. Pinot's sleeve. "I deserved every second of it?" he wildly said. "Do you think this mess was deserved? The moment you got involved, it's been nothing but *messes*!"

"No!" Charlie cried, dropping Tracey's arm and rushing to Mrs. Pinot's side.

"Stop!" Tracey said.

"Get off of 'er!" Charlie cried, pulling at Jon's coattail.

"You should have stayed in the car," Mrs. Pinot wretchedly said, struggling to push Jon away.

*Maybe I should have just left him in the car*, Tracey thought, watching the chaotic scenario with a twinge of regret.

"Tracey!" a familiar voice said from behind. "You should have stayed in one place, as I had asked!"

Tracey turned around. "Mr. Porter!" she said with a sigh of relief.

Beside Mr. Porter were two constables.

They rushed past Tracey into the foggy garage. "Stop this behavior this instance!" one of the constables yelled. Through the fog, Tracey could see a constable struggle to separate Jon from Mrs. Pinot. The other constable took Charlie away from the tangle and guided him to Tracey.

"Please stay out of harm's way, young man," he said. "We've got this under control now."

"Come on, Charlie," Tracey said, reaching for Charlie and hobbling out into the night air. She took deep breaths of the fresher, steam-free air.

"I thought I told you not to move!" Mr. Porter said, taking Tracey's free arm.

"Circumstances called for otherwise," she replied, glancing at her stinging hands.

"Mr. Jon Starr, you are under arrest!" a constable yelled from inside the garage, pulling a now-cuffed Jon Starr in tow with him.

"For what reason?" Jon said, his voice near a snarl. He looked even more disheveled than before.

"For three cases of kidnapping and twenty counts of fraud. One for each of 'em performances," the officer said. "And one case of assault."

"The assault, I can understand, but can't that get cleared up without arrest?" Jon said, looking at the two officers in confusion. "And you have no proof for those other charges."

"Terribly sorry, sir. Just following my job. We can talk more in the office."

In the distance, Tracey noticed three other figures being loaded into the police steam truck: one woman and two men.

"Why are they going?" Jon exclaimed, noticing their departure.

"There's a link to the case with an Elizaveta Halpin, Rollo Nicholson, and Hassan Hamdi. Not to mention you."

Now, Jon Starr was silent. He deflated, looking rather small as all of his fight melted away. "What?" was all Jon could choke out, his jaw slack.

"I suppose this is satisfactory as well," Mrs. Pinot said with a small smirk, emerging from the hazy air of the garage, her dress and prim bun as disheveled as Jon's clothing.

"'Fraid you're under arrest too, miss," the constable escorting her apologetically said as he handcuffed Mrs. Pinot.

"What?" she exclaimed.

"We just got a warrant in for you with a blackmailing charge," he said, pulling out a portable document similar to Bentam's. He turned a series of dials along the top of the tube, then unrolled it to show a warrant. "We were s'posed to stop by your home after Mr. Starr's residence, but I guess not anymore," he said with a shrug. "Saves us time, I s'pose. Not to mention this new assault charge."

Jon grimly chuckled.

"Let me ride in a different carriage from him," she said.

The constable shook his head. "We've only the one car," he solemnly said. "Come along, you two."

The two constables walked away, each with a bickering individual. As Tracey stared at the retreating figures, the pounding in her head returned. "Well..." she said, struggling to find her words.

"Tracey!" a loud voice yelled from the distance. Tracey heard the sound of several pounding feet approaching them. In the forefront of the group was Mittie, her face plastered in a grin. She immediately rushed to Tracey, squeezing her in a tight hug. "I thought you were dead!" she exclaimed.

"I..." she dazedly said, "I suppose I'm not..."

"Charlie!" Harriet said, running up to him and wrapping him in an equally tight hug. "Oh, thank goodness. I was so afraid!"

"It's all right, Harrie! Trace got everythin' under control," he replied with a nonchalant grin, playfully pushing his sister aside.

"Not without Mr. Porter's help," Tracey said, flashing a grateful smile to him. "And all of yours." She swayed as Mittie let go.

Mittie frowned. "Now that I'm gettin' a good look at you," she said, giving her an appraising look, "you don't look too good, Trace."

"As everyone has told me," she sighed.

"You know, I saw when Jon was takin' you out of the room. I was certain you were a goner!" Mittie said, watching as Jon was rather ungracefully pushed into the constable's carriage.

"You...saw me?"

"Sure! Rollo nearly caught me, but I was hidin' in a broom closet right by the room. Couldn't find ya before Jon caught me, though."

"He caught you?" Tracey replied in dismay.

"Yep. Took me back to everyone else in the parlor," Mittie said with a point to Bentam and Harriet. "Say, how did you get Charlie and Mr. Porter? Did you break them out yourself?"

"Oh, well—"

"Tracey," Mr. Porter gently said. "The doctor's in his carriage out front. Why don't you discuss this later?"

"Of course," Tracey agreed, nodding. "Oh, yes. Mr. Porter, this is Mittie."

"So this is Mittie?" he said in surprise. "It's a pleasure to meet you! Of course," he said as the group began their walk to the front of Jon Starr's residence, "I wish it were under less dire circumstances."

"No worries. I'm glad you're safe, Mr. Porter," Mittie said with a friendly tip of her head before walking ahead to the rest of the group. "I'll let you two catch up!" she called.

Bentam, who had thus far remained hovering behind the others, lingered to walk beside Tracey and Mr. Porter. He looked at her with a frown.

"Are you going to say that I look terrible as well, Bentam?" Tracey dryly said, stifling a sigh.

"No," he replied, "but, for the record, you do, yes."

"Of course."

Bentam looked ahead. "I was going to ask if you could describe what happened?"

"Oh," she sighed. "I can tell you later. You need it for your records, I presume?"

"Correct," he said with a slight nod. Bentam cleared his throat and cast a side-eye to her. "Also," he awkwardly added, "I'm...glad that you're at least alive."

Mr. Porter eyed Bentam. "I don't believe I've gotten a chance to meet you?" he said, furrowing his eyebrows.

"Ah—" Bentam started. He stopped, then bowed his head. "Mr. Bentam Berkley, records keeper at the High Constable," he quickly said. Just as quickly, he cleared his throat and sped his pace. "I'll check on Charlie," he muttered, hurrying forward to Charlie, who was walking in the lead with Harriet.

"So that was the record keeper crazy enough to leave his desk to help you. He seems respectable," Mr. Porter said with an approving nod.

"Oh, I'm glad it's over," Tracey sighed, leaning into Mr. Porter's arm.

Mr. Porter and Tracey walked in silence the rest of the way.

CHAPTER 28

# In Which (All) Truths Are Revealed

"GOOD MORNING!" Mr. Porter cheerfully said as he pushed open the door to Porter Keeper Shoppe, sending the bell ringing. "Has the motor-mail sent in today's news yet, Tracey?"

"Not yet," Tracey replied from the ground. She had spent the better part of her morning sorting through the aftermath of Mr. Porter's kidnapping and now found herself sitting comfortably on the wooden floors, surrounded by paperwork. "But then again," she added, "I've been so focused on refiling these papers, I might've not heard it."

"You've been gone for two weeks and already you're back at it, aren't you?" he chuckled.

"Tomorrow will be the first time the business opens to the public since everything that happened, Mr. Porter. We can't accept customers in a space that looks like this!" Tracey said. "It looks exactly as I had found it three weeks ago! Did you even touch anything while I was out sick?"

"And back with the chastising, too," Mr. Porter said, raising an eyebrow. "Glad to see you're up and going again, Tracey."

She smiled. "I'm just glad to get rid of all those bandages," she said, touching her hair.

"As well as I," he said, setting his bag on his desk. "I can't thank you enough for finding me."

"Think nothing of it!" Tracey sighed as she once more surveyed the mess of the room. "I wonder...if Jon were simply searching for one document, why would he leave the office in such a mess? This is going to take ages to clean!"

"Hmm," Mr. Porter hummed. "Likely to stage a burglary, I suppose," he said with a shrug. Mr. Porter checked the motor-mail, found it to be empty, and returned once more to his desk.

"A poorly staged burglary," Tracey sniffed. "Who leaves windows and doors open in the middle of the night? And with all the lights on? It's as if he *wanted* to get caught."

"Who knows what was on his mind? He's a hard fellow to read." Mr. Porter began sorting the documents strewn across his desk. "He had been visiting the shop after hours rather frequently before he...abducted me. I had suspected that he knew I had Mrs. Pinot's evidence, but I never thought he'd be so desperate to keep me silent!" Mr. Porter paused as he separated the pages into stacks. "I was supposed to have turned in Mrs. Pinot's evidence to the High Constable when he stopped the night before—him and that chef you've called Rollo. Can't say I remember too much from it," he said, squinting. "He used some sort of red gear device on me."

"I know it well," she grimly replied. "And...done!" Tracey triumphantly said as she sorted the last sheet of paper, stood, and snatched a couple of stacks of paper. She walked over to the filing cabinet. "Did he ever find any of the evidence? I can hardly tell what's what in this chaos," she said, placing the stacks into their respective folders. "Other than Mrs. Pinot's bank statement, I mean."

"Thankfully not," he said. "Wait," he said, his eyes narrowing. "How did you know about the bank statement? I never—"

The door jingled as it slammed open. "I'm sorry, we're not open today," she started, both surprised by the interruption and grateful for it.

"Worry not, Ms. Higgenbottom. It is I, Mr. William Matthews!" boomed the familiar, loud voice of the banker.

"Mr. Matthews!" she said, quickly closing the drawers and straightening to greet him. "What brings you here?"

"Remington over here told me he'd be in the shop today," he said. The small man stepped inside and slammed the door shut behind himself.

"I thought you'd drop by later," Mr. Porter said, giving him a friendly wave. "How've you been, old pal?"

"Fine, fine. I needed to come and see for myself if you were fine," he said, twiddling his mustache. "Too many inconsistencies these past few weeks! Firstly, you sent me a letter via...motor-mail." Mr. Matthews shuddered.

"I'd never do that, William."

"Secondly," Mr. Matthews continued, dramatically holding two fingers in the air. "Ms. Higgenbottom was very suspicious when she visited me!"

"You did what now?" Mr. Porter said, looking at Tracey.

"I can explain later," Tracey quickly said, busying herself with filing the papers.

"And thirdly," Mr. Matthews continued, his voice close to shaking the room with its volume, "she had your Keeper Book!"

"I never told you we did," Tracey retorted.

"Ah, but you never denied *not* having it!"

"To the contrary!" Mr. Porter said with a jovial smile. "I always keep my book safely locked away in my desk. As you can see here..." he paused, looking closer at his desk. "There are scratches on here. Did someone break the lock to my drawers?"

"Oh!" Tracey said, briefly pausing. "Yes, Charlie opened one of them with a letter opener."

"Did he?"

"No worries, Mr. Porter. We've returned the book since."

"So you *did* have the book?" Mr. Matthews roared. "I *knew* you looked suspicious! I may not be good at being a sleuth, as you are, Ms. Higgenbottom, but the way you've evaded my answers was downright suspect!"

"I'd rather that Tracey found my book than you, William," Mr. Porter said with a twinkle in his eye. "You'd have opened it in a heartbeat."

"Of course I would have! I know you have your chess strategies in that book!" he exclaimed. "That was my one opportunity to get your book—ruined!"

"And those strategies," Mr. Porter said, opening the drawer and inspecting the book in his hands, "are for you to never learn! How else will I keep my two-year winning streak? Now, Tracey," he said, turning to her, "you couldn't open it, could you?"

"Well..." Tracey said. She moved on to returning books to their shelves.

"Tracey?" Mr. Porter prodded, a warning tone in his voice.

"We might've..." she said. "But we wouldn't have found you otherwise!"

"Is that so?" he said. Mr. Porter sighed, pinching the bridge of his nose. "I don't think you understand the gravity of opening a Keeper Book, Tracey," he said. "How did you figure it out?"

"Bentam found a book at the library that had a similar picture. Why?"

"Why would they make it so easy?" he muttered. "Did you get any strange contact after opening the book?"

"After opening it? No," she said. Tracey slowly set down a book. "But before—there was someone who broke into my home trying to open your book. I thought it might've been Jon or Mr. Matthews since he had just left—"

"I assure you, it was not me!" Mr. Matthews bellowed. "I was at my desk precisely one hour after my lunch break!"

"Yes, I figured it couldn't have been you. And Jon seemed preoccupied with fleeing the country when we found him. Although he could have sent his staff..."

"No, I have an idea of who it was," Mr. Porter said, a frown on his face. "I'll have to have a word with them," he mumbled. "Actually," he said louder, "William, do you think you can send through correspondence for me? On your way back? I might not be able to today, seeing as we have to clean up the shop still, and this is rather urgent."

"Of course!" Mr. Matthews said. Tracey winced at the volume of his exclamation.

Mr. Porter scrawled on a sheet of paper. "Here you go."

"Chess game, tomorrow evening?" Mr. Matthews said, taking the paper.

"Of course!" Mr. Porter said, his smile strained.

"All right, see you then!" he replied, stomping out of the shop and slamming the door shut, rattling the windows in the process. Mr. Matthews sent one last jovial wave before wandering away into the streets of Mondon.

Mr. Porter visibly relaxed as he watched Mr. Matthews disappear from view. "That shouldn't be an issue anymore," he said with a reassuring smile. "Don't worry about having opened the book. Please make sure that you don't do that again, however. Do you understand, Tracey?"

"I'll try not to," she said, raising her eyebrows.

The two fell into uncomfortable silence, only interrupted by the occasional sounds of shuffling papers, opening drawers, and sliding furniture. "Tracey," Mr. Porter started, looking up from his neat stacks of paper, "I know you've already given statements to the High Constable, but I am curious...how exactly did you locate me? I'm sure that one document from William and the handkerchief couldn't be the only clues you were working from."

"There was more..." Tracey haltingly said. She paused. "I couldn't tell the constables, you see," she continued, "because I'm positive it'd have gotten us all in trouble."

"What was it?"

"I received a series of combustible notes. Two here, and one at my home."

The frown on Mr. Porter's face deepened. His eyebrows knit. "What did they consist of?" he asked, his voice low.

"Just clues on how to find you. I thought it might've been Jon since the notes were so threatening—a sort of strange cat-and-mouse, you know? But I'm not too certain about that anymore."

"I doubt he'd ever have the knowledge of where to source that sort of stuff, anyway."

"I don't know about that," Tracey said with a shrug. "Mittie and I found out about The Marketplace fairly easily."

"Just how much trouble have you gotten yourself into, Tracey?" Mr. Porter said in exasperation.

"None! In fact, Mr. Matthews told us of it!"

"Did he? I'll have to have a word with him." He picked up a stack of paper and placed it into a drawer, closing the door a little more vigorously than necessary.

"Say," Tracey said, slowly turning around to face Mr. Porter. "Would you say Mr. Matthews knew about The Marketplace because of this 'Keeper Embassy,' by any chance?"

"I can't answer that, Tracey," he responded.

"For a keeper of secrets, you certainly have your own fair share of them," she dryly said, placing the last book onto the shelf. "I'm really starting to wonder about this whole Keeper Embassy," she muttered, pushing an armchair beside the bookshelf.

"The less you know, the better."

Behind her, the motor-mail whirred to life.

"And there's today's news," Tracey said, relieved for the change of subject. She snatched the large newspaper and unfurled it. "Will you look at that title! 'Double-Acting: Jon Starr To Be Tried in Court for Fraudulent Performances.' Now that's something."

She smirked as she scanned through the paper.

"Can you believe that he's pleading insanity?" she said, glancing at Mr. Porter.

"I wouldn't be surprised if he gets off with only a fine," Mr. Porter replied, curiously leaning closer to get a better glimpse of the paper.

"Yes, it says that he created the double performances to double his profits. That was a terribly complicated scheme for extra money..."

"I'd say," Mr. Porter agreed. "Far too messy. He'll lose it all with the court fines alone. Is there any mention of me?"

"Hm," Tracey murmured as she scanned through the papers. "Yes. 'Mr. Jon Starr is also charged on two counts of kidnapping, one victim being a Mr. Remington Porter.' That's all."

"Well, I suppose that protects the business," he thoughtfully said. Mr. Porter took the last stack of papers on his desk and walked over to the filing cabinet, distributing the sheets into folders. "What about Mrs. Pinot?" he said. "I would think she'd be mentioned."

Tracey scanned the article. "Nothing on her. But," she said, "it looks like Shrimp Reginald has been shut down due to...cutting corners on recipes? 'Shrimp Reginald falls under steam due to recent complaints about watery juices, flavorless dishes, and lackluster appetizers.'" She frowned. "That is the last thing I'd have thought they'd be shut down for."

"I'm sure they'll be back, one form or another," Mr. Porter said. "Let me see the newspaper," he said. He took the extended sheet. "There may be an article on her somewhere else."

Tracey took a broom and swept the now-cleared flooring. The door's bell rang. "Sorry, we're not taking any customers at this moment," Tracey said.

"It's a good thing I'm not a customer, then!" a familiar voice said. There in the doorway was Mittie, wearing the same attire as she had when they first met.

"Mittie!" Tracey said, placing the broom aside and jogging to meet her. "I should really look at who's entering."

"It's fine," Mittie said. "Reminds me of the first time we met!"

"It's good to see you again, Mittie!" Mr. Porter happily said, walking up to shake her hand. "I have to thank you once again for helping my dear Tracey."

"It was of no issue," Mittie graciously replied, tipping her head. "I came by to say goodbye, actually."

"I thought you'd left already," Tracey said. "It's been two weeks, and I didn't hear much from you while I was recovering at home."

"No," she replied. "There was a delay in some goods' arrival here in Mondon, so I stuck around. Sorry for not keeping in touch, Trace. The goods had me stuck in the customs office for the past week, and my remaining free time was spent repairing some burnt bridges with this fellow over here." Mittie pointed outside to where Tracey could see a tall man sheepishly standing to the side, just outside of the view of her and Mr. Porter.

"Why," Mr. Porter said in surprise, "is that Reginald?"

"Y-yes," Reggie said, ducking his head into the shop. He took a few uncertain steps forward.

"I didn't know you knew each other?" Tracey said, looking between the two.

"I was surprised myself when Reggie told me so," Mittie agreed.

"I've delivered goods for Mr. Porter a few times," Reggie awkwardly replied. "Keepers, remember? I also needed to...apologize to you, Ms. Higgenbottom."

334

"Whatever for?" Tracey said in bewilderment.

"I gave you and Mittie quite a hard time back at Shrimp Reginald, so sorry about that. I'll try my best to make it up to you some other time."

"Apology accepted," she replied. "I'm sure we gave you quite a fright showing up in your marketplace!"

"Oh...yes, rather." He nervously smiled.

"I heard Shrimp Reginald has been shut down," Mr. Porter said. "Have you figured out how you'll be reopening?"

"Oh, Louise has been saying we need to open a gear repair shop," Reggie said with a shrug. "She's better with mechanics than waiting tables, anyhow."

"I hope we're not interrupting anything?" a voice said from the doorway.

The four of them turned to see two constables standing in the doorway. "Can I help you?" Mr. Porter said.

"Yes, sir, we're here following up on a break-in report?" a constable said, holding up a sheet of paper. "We were here a couple o' weeks ago to take some steam photos, and we're now here t' open investigation. Ms. Higgenbottom, was it?"

"Yes? It's been over three weeks, actually," Tracey slowly said. "And how did you get in here without ringing a bell?"

"Fortunately for you," he continued, ignoring the latter comment, "we've got a lead on the break-in."

"Oh?"

"Yes, this one's a serial robber, and he was on your side of town the night of the incident."

"Oh. That's great and all," Tracey said, glancing over to see Mr. Porter's baffled face, "but we were able to resolve the matter."

"Really now?" the constable responded, his jaw slack.

"I told you," the other constable muttered, "'alf these break-ins turn out t' be false cases!"

"S-sorry for the inconvenience," the constable stammered. "We'll make a report of that once we get back. C'mon."

"I told you we were too late!" the other constable said as the two of them lumbered from the shop. After a few moments, Mr. Porter wandered back to his desk, resuming his search in the newspaper. Reggie hesitantly closed the door and wandered around the office, gathering stray sheets of paper strewn on chairs and tabletops.

"Well, then," Tracey finally said, at a loss for words.

"Right, well then," Mittie laughed. "I'm glad you didn't leave Mr. Porter's case to them. They would have probably come next week to start searchin'!"

"They would have been too late," Tracey sighed, a jolt of fear in her chest. She was afraid of what might have been, but ultimately grateful for what came to be.

"Here's something on Mrs. Pinot," Mr. Porter said, shaking the newspaper to straighten it. "It's not much. 'Late Inventor's Widow Arrested on Charges of Blackmailing: Mrs. Corsetta Pinot has been arrested on charges of blackmailing. No further evidence has been released.'"

"I'm kinda sorry for her," Mittie said. "From what you told me, Trace, she sounds like she's really hurtin' after Mr. Pinot's accident."

"Jon seemed like he was too," Tracey replied, thinking back to the way he momentarily broke down.

"Nope!" Mittie firmly said. "We're not speaking about he-who-must-not-be-spoken-of here."

"Not a fan?"

"Absolutely not. Not anymore." Mittie sighed. "Trace, I saw him carrying you like a sack of potatoes! I really thought he had killed you. There's no coming back after a stunt like that, even if it was....he-who-must-not-be-spoken-of."

The door rang once more.

"It seems as if there's a party we haven't been invited to," Bentam said from the doorway, Harriet and Charlie in tow.

"Welcome! Hello, children. Bentam," Mr. Porter said before burying himself once more into the newspaper.

Reggie gave a small wave from his station in the back of the shop, and Mittie warmly smiled.

"What brings you here?" Tracey said, turning to face Bentam.

"Not even a hello, I see," he sniffed. "Charlie has been asking to see you and Mr. Porter," he said.

"Actually, *I* did," Harriet volunteered. "I was asking Bentam last night—during our teatime—if we could pay you a visit!"

"You have teatimes now? And at night?" Mittie said in surprise. "Isn't it dangerous for you and Charlie to be walking in The Undertown at night?"

"Oh, we don't have to worry about that anymore!"

"Really?" Tracey said, raising an eyebrow.

"Yup, my bread thievin' days are over!" Charlie proudly said.

"I'm going to ignore that you've just admitted to stealing bread," Bentam said, loudly clearing his throat.

"Did you adopt them?" Mittie said, grinning.

"Moreso, offer them more accommodating quarters. To which they agreed. And I've legally documented their change of address." With each sentence, Bentam's face flushed a deeper shade of red.

"What of your home in The Undertown, Harriet?" Tracey asked.

"Oh, it's still in my name, so I plan on fixin' it up when I'm grown," Harriet confidently replied. "So Bentam," she added, casting a coy glance at him. "Were you going to ask Trace—"

"On a change of subject," Bentam quickly said, ushering Harriet and Charlie toward the door, "I see that you're fine. I suppose we'll see you around—"

"Hold that thought," Mr. Porter said, glancing from the newspaper. "I found some side articles on the others that were working with Jon Starr. 'Partners in Crime—How Jon Starr Fooled Us All: Among his associates of Hassan Hamdi and Rollo Nicholson, Jon Starr reportedly had another ace up his sleeve: his belle Elizaveta Halpin. Our reporters have been able to find that Miss Halpin is registered as an actress under the Dnalgne Acting Board. The two have reportedly been courting for many years, keeping their relationship under wraps with the help of their acting skills and from the aforementioned associates.'"

"So, Rollo and Hassan were helping Jon and Elizaveta to hide their relationship," Tracey said, slowly nodding her head, "which allowed for her to openly advertise for his double performances. That solves why we saw her everywhere we went!"

"Does it?" Harriet asked.

"We saw her in front of Mrs. Pinot's home, undoubtedly to cast suspicion on Mrs. Pinot. By keeping near her home, then fleeing when found, Elizaveta gave the appearance as if Mrs. Pinot was directly involved in the pamphlet distribution," Tracey said. "She was also at the bank—likely to make sure that we received that evidence against Mrs. Pinot...or she might've wanted to take it from us. I suppose we'll never find that part out, though."

"U-um, Tracey, is it?" Reggie said from beside the motor-mail. "I hate to interrupt all this, but I noticed that there's a letter here for you."

"It's no worries, Reggie. I must've missed it being so focused on the newspaper coming in," she said, blinking in surprise. "Thank you." Tracey took the large cream envelope from him and observed the outside.

"It's not another combustible note, is it?" Charlie groaned. "Bentam, let's go. I don't want to get arrested!"

"Arrested?" Reggie exclaimed in alarm.

"Don't worry, it's bigger than the combustible envelopes," Tracey laughed. "Besides, this one has a return address. A combustible note wouldn't have that."

"There's no name on it...except for a return address to the other side of the country."

"Ooh, Strattengear?" Mittie gasped, leaning over Tracey's shoulders. "That's from where I'm from! I didn't know you had friends over there, Trace!"

"Just one," Tracey said. "I suppose two—if you're from there," she added with a small smile.

Mittie returned her smile. "I suppose we *are* friends now, huh?" she said with a friendly bump on the shoulder.

Tracey ripped open the envelope and scanned its contents. "Oh, it's Meredith!" she said, her smile growing. "She wants me to visit her by the sea!"

For a moment, Tracey closed her eyes, thinking of the pleasant countryside of Dnalgne, and imagining the pleasant breezes and quiet atmosphere. *I've never seen outside of this city—I wonder how different the world will seem?*

She then noticed the equally quiet atmosphere of Porter Keeper Shoppe.

Tracey raised her eyes to find all looking at her.

"I-I'll read it later," she stammered, stuffing the letter into her pocket. "I suppose you all must be very busy and are on your way out?"

"Sure!" Mittie said with a shrug. "C'mon, Reggie. You said you wanted to take me somewhere before I left?"

"Right," Reggie said, hurrying to hold the door open for Mittie. "I'll see you around! Lovely meeting you properly," he said, pushing the door open.

"Before you go," Bentam said, stepping forward. "Would you like to join us at *Bon Norriture* this evening at seven o'clock? I...I was going to ask Tracey and Mr. Porter, so I suppose you may want to come as well?"

"I heard it's nearly impossible to get a reservation there!" Mittie said in surprise. "How d'ya manage to get so many seats?"

"Friend of the owner," he said, with a small wave. "She's reserved the entire second floor for me."

"What d'ya think, Reggie?"

"We'll be glad to go," Reggie said, smiling. "Thank you!"

"I would be happy to go as well," Mr. Porter added. "What say you, Tracey?" he added, glancing at her with a twinkle in his eye.

"Of course!" Tracey said, blinking in surprise. *Why is he looking at me like that?*

"Then it's settled," Reggie said. "See you all at seven!"

Tracey and Mr. Porter waved as everyone shuffled out of the shop. Bentam lingered behind, leaving Harriet and Charlie waiting outside. "Of course, Tracey," he hesitantly added, "if you're not fond of the menu, I could always plan for somewhere else."

"Why should you worry about me?" she said, taking up the broom and resuming her sweep.

"Ah," Bentam started. He froze. "Of course. Good day," he mumbled, nodding his head and bumbling out of the shop. The door's bell jingled in his wake.

"Interesting fellow," Mr. Porter said, raising an eyebrow, his eyes darting between Bentam's retreating figure and Tracey's face, the hint of a smile on his lips.

"I'd say," Tracey replied, grabbing the dustpan. "There," she said as she tossed the contents into the bin.

Tracey surveyed the space. Mr. Porter had taken to his usual seat behind his desk and had already begun to undergo his morning routine—sorting through appointments while his cup of tea steeped in the corner. *Business as usual*, she thought with a smile. Walking to her own desk, Tracey Higgenbottom opened her notebooks and began another morning at Porter Keeper Shoppe.

# Acknowledgments

WHERE TO EVEN START? This book was originally written as a way for me and my sister to pass the long days in lockdown. It was an old story I had shelved years ago, and I had revived it to fill that time with entertainment. So, I'd like to thank Heather for being the best live audience, critic, inspiration, and cheerleader. If it wasn't for her, I would have returned this book to the shelf again!

I'd like to thank my parents for tolerating my long hours locked away as I crafted this story. Their enthusiasm for the whole process of publishing this book has been invaluable to me.

To the countless friends (in-person and online): Thank you for rooting me on as I completed this story.

Thank you to the early readers of this work, back when the only form available of this book was online as a web novel. Your countless comments, likes, and reviews cheered this author's heart.

In that same vein, thank you to the following Kickstarter backers: Kristen Altmann, Stefanie Chu, Michael Gilmore, Katherine McRea, Amanda Balter, 'Will It Work' Dansicker, Moe Fosse, Samantha Newberry, Tegan O'Connell, Audrey, Jennifer Cory, Richard Novak, Emma Hill, S Rodgers, Jorge y Heather, David Bock, Jennifer Corry, Christy S, Tracy Popey, Jess Instone, Anne LaMont, Alexandra Corrsin, Nery, Eileen Coxe, Florentina, SerendipityKimberly, and Nathan Covington (to name a few!). This story would not have been possible without your support!

Thank you to my editor, Taylor Morris, for your insightful notes and edits. Your feedback has been invaluable for helping to polish this story into a gem!

And finally, thank you to my teachers throughout the years, helping me to cultivate a love of reading and books. To my middle school librarian, Mrs. Warren (who believed that I would one day put a book in her library): Here it is!

# About Hailey

HAILEY MORRISON is a middle grade/young adult author and illustrator, with her debut work *A Curious Case of Plagium* (or *Plagium* for short) being her first foray into combining both her art and storytelling skills. The book has since garnered attention, winning the 2022 Wattys award hosted by storytelling platform Wattpad in the Mystery/Thriller category. In addition, Plagium won a grand prize for its story to be considered for an animated adaptation for one year. Hailey lives in the Atlanta, GA, area where (besides clacking away behind a keyboard) she can be found hiking, gardening, sewing, building, volunteering, or painting—a Renaissance woman, indeed!

*You can find her lurking on Threads and Instagram:*
*@haileymorrisonwrites*

www.ingramcontent.com/pod-product-compliance
Lightning Source LLC
Chambersburg PA
CBHW021455110726
47899CB00001BA/171